Praise for Award-Winning Author Hank Phillippi Ryan

On the Charlotte McNally Series

"*Prime Time* is current, clever, and chock-full of cliffhangers. Readers are in for a treat."

—Mary Jane Clark, *New York Times* bestselling author

"*Face Time* is a gripping, fast-paced thriller with an important story line and an engaging and unusual heroine. As Charlie McNally wrestles with aging, ratings, her mother, and her lover's little girl, she gives us a vivid behind-the-scenes look at television news; we meet a cast of characters whom we hope to see again."

—Sara Paretsky, *New York Times* bestselling author

"Sassy, fast-paced, and appealing. This is first-class entertainment."

—Sue Grafton, *New York Times* bestselling author, on *Air Time*

"Hank Phillippi Ryan knows the television business entirely; she understands plotting; and she writes beautifully. No wonder I loved *Drive Time*. Anyone would."

—Robert B. Parker, *New York Times* bestselling author

On the Jane Ryland Series

"*The Other Woman* does everything a great suspense novel should. . . . Ryan raises the bar sky-high—I knew she was good, but I had no idea she was this good."

—Lee Child, *New York Times* bestselling author

"Whip-smart writing and a dizzying pace make *The Wrong Girl* a thrilling, one-night read!"

—Tess Gerritsen, *New York Times* bestselling author

"Smart, well-paced . . . Ryan, a Mary Higgins Clark Award winner, cleverly ties the plot together, offers surprising but believable plot twists, and skillfully characterizes the supporting cast. . . . Just the right amount of romance."

—*Publishers Weekly* on *Truth Be Told*

"Award-winner Ryan is a master of her craft. . . . This is exceptional suspense written in Ryan's inimitable style."

—*RT Book Reviews* (Top Pick!) on *What You See*

Books by Hank Phillippi Ryan

The Jane Ryland Series

The Other Woman

The Wrong Girl

Truth Be Told

What You See

Say No More

The Charlotte McNally Series

Prime Time

Face Time

Air Time

Drive Time

PRIME TIME

Hank Phillippi Ryan

A TOM DOHERTY ASSOCIATES BOOK | NEW YORK

PRIME TIME

A Forge Book
Published by Tom Doherty Associates, LLC
175 Fifth Avenue
New York, NY 10010

www.tor-forge.com

The Library of Congress Cataloging-in-Publication Data is available upon request.

ISBN 978-0-7653-8474-4 (hardcover)
ISBN 978-0-7653-8475-1 (trade paperback)
ISBN 978-0-7653-8476-8 (e-book)

Our books may be purchased in bulk for promotional, educational, or business use. Please contact your local bookseller or the Macmillan Corporate and Premium Sales Department at 1-800-221-7945, extension 5442, or by e-mail at MacmillanSpecialMarkets@macmillan.com.

Originally published by MIRA Books

First Tor Edition: February 2016

Printed in the United States of America

0 9 8 7 6 5 4 3 2 1

Dear Reader,

Has an e-mail ever changed your life? I remember the very moment one did for me. It was in 2005, and I was hard at work at my desk in the newsroom. I clicked open an e-mail spam by mistake—and was baffled by what it said.

I can't reveal much more about that, because it'll give away the secret of the plot. But that very instant—and I get goosebumps telling you—was the moment I thought of my first novel of suspense, *Prime Time*.

That night, I went home and said to my husband: "I've got it! I've got the plot of the mystery I've wanted to write ever since I was a little girl."

And I typed: Chapter 1.

I've been a journalist for more than forty years now. In my high-stress, high-stakes job as a TV investigative reporter, I've wired myself with hidden cameras, chased down criminals, gone undercover and in disguise—covered hostage situations and murders, arsons, explosions, riots, and bombings. I've had people confess to murder, and convicted criminals insist they were innocent. Our stories have changed laws and changed lives, and won thirty-three Emmys. Still, I always think my best story is yet to come.

Because that's what it's all about: telling a great story.

But *Prime Time* was my very first step into the world of *fictional* storytelling. To use my imagination and storytelling skills to create new worlds, and new characters. To solve fictional crimes and track down fictional bad guys. What a challenge!

When I got halfway through writing *Prime Time*, I realized

how difficult it was to write a suspenseful page-turner. So I did what we all do if we are lucky—I called my mom. I told her: "I love this book, and I think readers will, too. But wow, I'm not quite sure I know how to finish it."

And she paused, and then said, "Well, honey, you will if you want to."

You will if you want to! And I did want to. When I finished writing it, I called my husband into the room, and said "Sweetheart, watch this." And I typed: THE END. And then I burst into tears.

I shouldn't have cried, of course. Because it wasn't the end at all. It was the beginning.

That book became *Prime Time,* the book you are about to read. *Prime Time* went on to win the coveted Agatha Award for Best First Novel.

And it's now the first in my series of suspense novels starring reporter Charlotte McNally. I am so pleased, now, that in these brand-new editions, I get to share her with you—her adventures, her passion, her determination, her humor, and her joy.

With much affection,

Hank Phillippi Ryan

PRIME TIME

CHAPTER ONE

Between the hot flashes, the hangover and all the spam on my computer, there's no way I'll get anything done before eight o'clock this morning. I came in early to get ahead, and already I'm behind.

I take a restorative sip of my murky-but-effective vending machine coffee, and start my one-finger delete. Away go the online offers for cheap vacations, low refinancing rates and medicine from Canada. Adios to international driver's licenses and work-at-home moneymaking schemes.

At least I'm not the only one here. Downstairs in the newsroom, overcaffeinated producers working the graveyard shift click intently through the wires, scanning their computers to find stories for the noon newscast. The sleek new anchorwoman, Ellen Cavenagh, doesn't have to be in her chair for the local news update until 8:24, so the "new face of Channel 3," as the promos brand her, is probably in her dressing room perfecting the shimmer level of her lip gloss.

Ellen's essentially a supermodel with reading skills, and I applaud anyone who can come out so cover girl so early in the morning. But as the station's investigative reporter, I spend most of my time tracking down sources and digging through documents. As a result, I don't always have to look TV-acceptable.

Good thing. At forty-six, it's possible my "hot flashes" owe more to the station's eccentric heating system than to a sudden dive in hormones. But facing reality, facing the camera takes a lot more time than it did twenty years ago. And considerably more makeup. Still, as long as they're not calling me "the old face of Channel 3," I figure I'm in the clear.

Today I'm planning total off-the-air mode. My usually high-maintenance hair is twisted up with a pencil and I'm on a hell-or-high-water mission—come up with a blockbuster story so Channel 3 will win the November ratings contest and I can keep my job.

I was initiated into ratings worship my first day at the station. Back then I was very eighties in my high-necked blouse and cameo brooch. Big eyebrows. Big shoulders. Big dreams.

"Here's a course they don't teach you in J-school," my news director said, gesturing me into his office. "Bottom Line 101: TV News Is Not All About Journalism—It's All About Money." Then he clicked open a computer spreadsheet, revealing a screen filled with tiny numbers.

"These are 'the overnights,'" he intoned.

I remember thinking: *Who's staying overnight?* Luckily, he continued before I could actually ask such a naively newbie question.

"The overnight numbers arrive electronically every morning," he went on. "They show us how many viewers watched each newscast the day before. It's a contest. Whichever TV station gets the highest viewership ratings gets to charge the highest rates to advertisers."

He nodded, narrowing his eyes, and pointed to me.

"You win—especially the all-important November ratings—and you're in the money," he pronounced. "You lose, you're a goner."

As it turned out, he's the one who's gone, but I'm still frontlining in the ratings wars. And that's why every fall for the past twenty or so years, I've had to dig up a big story, a heavy hitter, one that'll get a ratings home run. Score, and my job is safe for another year. Strike out, and I could be shipped away from Boston and sent to cover the news in some small-market backwater. So far, I haven't had to call my agent or a moving company.

But now, because the arrival of my new boss has unfortunately coincided with the arrival of my contract expiration date, I've got to come up with a bigger story than ever.

If I don't, news director Kevin O'Bannon may be tempted to hire some half-my-age Cyndi from Cincinnati for half my salary. Everyone at Channel 3 will get one of those transparent "Charlotte McNally has decided to leave Boston to pursue other opportunities" e-mails.

They say you're only as good as your last story. Fine. My last story was a three-part series on State House bid-rigging that gave a few slimily corrupt politicians a new job making license plates. November ratings? Bring 'em on.

"Charlie—hey, Charlie. You here?"

I look up from my spam deleting. Someone's crashing open the heavy glass double doors that lead into the Channel 3 Investigative Unit. And they're looking for me.

My brain starts to buzz. Maybe there's breaking news. Maybe I'm the only on-air type here. Face time is always good. More likely, though, whoever it is probably wants me to go interview the latest lottery winner or something equally predictable. Dog falls in well. Tree falls on house. Ratings-grabbers, I suppose, but not what I call journalism.

I briefly contemplate hiding under my desk, but a quick assessment tells me that won't work—my collection of backup shoes occupies all the available space. Besides, my news Spidey-sense is pinging into high. I remember when Mom caught me reading the last chapter of my Nancy Drew first. She was bewildered, but as nine-year-old me explained, *I hafta know what happens.* All these years later, I'm still incurably curious. And now, maybe "what's happened" is actually something newsworthy.

"Yup, in here," I call out. If it's the saving-the-dog-in-the-well gig, I'll just say no. Let 'em fire me. I touch my wooden desk to defuse the jinx. Didn't really mean that.

Teddy Sheehan, his shirttails out and khaki pants already splattered with coffee stains, arrives in my doorway with a look on his face I instantly recognize: producer emergency. He bats his plastic water bottle against his leg, making a little pocking sound that punctuates his obvious agitation.

"I can't find Ellen," he says, inspecting my tiny office as if she might be lurking there. "She's supposed to be on the anchor desk for the next newsbreak, but she's nowhere. It's crazy. If I can't find her—"

I know where this is headed. A jolt of news adrenaline erases my ill-advised third-glass-of-white-wine hangover. "No problem," I assure him. "Let's go."

The instant the network commercial ends, someone has to read the script from the teleprompter. This morning, it appears that someone is going to be me.

We racket down the stairs to the newsroom. Four minutes till airtime.

Teddy stops suddenly, and turns to stare at me, pointing at my do-it-yourself up-do. "The folks at home are not going to buy the pencil-in-the-hair look," he says. His panicked expression reappears. "It's early, but nobody's that sleepy. Can you do anything to . . . ?"

My eyes go wide, picturing myself. He's right. Not only is my hair a big *Glamour* "don't," I have on zero lipstick. This is supposed to be the morning news, not night of the living dead. And now it's three minutes to airtime.

Ten years ago, Teddy would have said, "Don't worry, Charlie, you're the best-looking investigative reporter in town. Just get your little blond self into that anchor desk and let the camera love you."

Today he says, "Never mind."

Teddy careens into his desk chair and types out the new production info for the control room as he dictates the same instructions out loud to me. "We'll run the opening animation graphics, then go straight to videotape. You just voice-over the pictures, then hand it off to weather—it's Becca this morning. Just read. We'll never see you on camera."

He glances at the digital clock ticking relentlessly over the anchor desk, and goes pale. "It's less than a minute to air. Do it!"

I dash to the desk and plug my earpiece into its black box so I can hear the director in the control room. As I clip the microphone onto the sweater tied around my shoulders, I pray the video actually rolls, so our million or so viewers don't wake up to the alarming vision of Charlie McNally without mascara or lipstick.

I settle in the chair, all plugged in. Just one thing missing. A big thing.

"Where's the script?" I yell.

The camera operator points to me. "On the air in—thirty seconds," he says calmly.

"No script!" someone calls out from under the stairs.

That's a very bad sign. Under the stairs is where the . . .

"Yo, Charlie, printer's broken," I hear someone yell back to me. "Just read the prompter."

I should have hidden under my desk. The prompter had better work or I am going to kill someone.

"Fifteen seconds!"

My heart sinks. This is what I get for coming in early. All I wanted to do was get a head start on my story. Now, instead, I'm going to be humiliated in front of millions of—

"In five, four . . ."

The teleprompter flashes into life. The floor director gives me a quick finger point. Showtime.

"Good morning, this is Charlie McNally in the newsroom."

I've never seen the script that's rolling by in front of me before, I'm just reading it cold. But after twenty-some years in the business, my brain can read a line or two ahead of my mouth.

"Topping the news this morning, investigators searching for the cause of a fire overnight in Allston. Witnesses say the apartment was being used as an off-campus dormitory for Morrison College."

Hmm. There's a possible story, the reporter track of my brain muses. Wonder if that's legal, stashing students in some apartment and calling it a dorm. Wonder if we could sneak a hidden camera inside.

I keep reading.

"Big traffic problems on the Expressway this morning. Commuters stalled for up to half an hour, as a truck filled with twenty-pound bags of ice skids and rolls over . . ."

Is there a story here, too? Wonder if the driver was drinking? Had the truck been inspected?

I keep reading.

"Finally this morning, police are asking for your help in finding a Lexington man reported as missing earlier this week. His wife released this picture of forty-one-year-old Bradley Foreman. You see it now on your screen—"

I glance at the monitor, confirming. Good job, control-room guys.

"He's described as around six feet tall, brown hair and eyes, medium build."

That's helpful. Medium everything. Must be a slow news day if this is a story.

I keep reading.

"His wife says she last saw Foreman when he left for work Thursday morning, but his colleagues at Aztratek Pharmaceuticals say he never arrived at their Boxford office complex."

The minute my mouth says *Aztratek*, some part of my brain goes into alert mode. It shoots me a definite wakeup message, but there's no time to listen.

I keep reading.

"If you see this man, police say, please call Lexington police."

I change my voice to perky and check the monitor for the weather map. It's there.

"Now, the weather. Channel 3 meteorologist Rebecca Holcomb has all the weather info you need. Becca?" I see the camera shot switch to Becca. I'm done.

"Thanks, Charlie," the director's voice buzzes into my ear. "You're clear."

I yank out my earpiece and unclip the microphone. Teddy's right behind me, way less freaked than five minutes ago.

"That was perfect, Charlie," he says. "You're the best."

"La-di-da." I give a dismissive little wave. "All in a day's work."

I rummage under the anchor desk to retrieve the shoes I kicked off, and Teddy turns to go back to his workstation. Because of me, he's not going to get nailed for missing the local newsbreak. He lives to produce another day. But I'm suddenly wondering if my tomorrows are numbered.

I stay in the anchor chair, chin in my hands, staring at the now-opaque camera lens. Not good. What I thought could be a career-enhancing chunk of face time didn't show my face at all. They actually had to roll video to make sure no one would see me. Not good. Without a moment's hesitation, Teddy erased me. Made me invisible. Brenda Starr's just as photogenic today as she was thirty years ago, but this ain't the comics. My flesh-and-blood future is beginning to scare me, much more than reading the news, cold, with no makeup.

Since I'm married to my job, what happens when the camera doesn't love me anymore? Will a career divorce leave me a media old maid?

A T-shirted assistant director, coiling his headphone cord, walks up, surprised I'm still at the desk. "We're done, right?" he asks.

I nod, but I'm smiling a smile I don't feel. What's more, I've just thought of something else not good.

"Hey, Teddy," I call. I put my shoes back on, pulling up one elastic strap over my heel as I hop across the newsroom floor toward his desk. "Hey, Ted!"

He turns around, quizzical.

"Ellen," I say, regaining my balance. "Where's Ellen?"

Teddy scratches his head and looks off into the distance. "Dead," he mutters.

I know this is just TV-producer frustration. He's not really expecting the worst. But "missing your slot" is a massive newsroom mistake, almost as unforgivable as getting scooped. If Ellen's not dead, her excuse had better be good.

Back in my office, my once-hot coffee is now barely warm. I risk a chalky sip and stare at my computer screen.

I know I should focus on finding my big story. Check out those off-campus dorms or the uninspected trucks. And I've got to remember to run those ideas by my producer, Franklin, when he comes in. But my mind just won't let go of the missing "medium" guy from the pharmaceutical company. Some part of my brain alerted on that Aztratek name like a K-9 dog at a crime scene, and my instinct says that's not something to ignore.

Tapping my fingers on the desk, I delve into my memory bank. Where have I heard of Aztratek? And it was—Brandon? Bradley? Foreman? How am I supposed to figure this out? Or how am I supposed to figure out if there is anything to figure out?

What if this is the biggest story ever, and I'm missing it? I need . . .

Makeup. If I look better, I'll think better. I take my little mirror from the wall and prop it on my computer keys so it leans against the monitor.

Brown eye shadow. More black mascara than Mom would think necessary. A little bronzing blush where my cheekbones ought to be, and then my trademark red lipstick. I went through a phase of Vixen, moved through Rage and now I'm loving Inferno. Seems as if even the makeup marketing honchos are capturing my sudden free fall into old age. Which comes first, the wrinkles or the lipstick name? If my next favorite is Reincarnation I'm really going to worry.

One last glance in the mirror. Great. Now I still look like a tired person, just a tired person wearing makeup.

I park the way-too-unsympathetic mirror on the floor and click open my e-mail again. I've got to go back to basics. What investigative reporting is all about. Not how you look, but how you look for answers. Relentless inquiry, focus on details, The Quest. I sit up straighter as I type my way through my fancy e-mail search system, my caffeine-fueled brain charging toward the light. I remember. His name is Bradley Foreman. Nothing can stop me now.

A tiny hourglass flips over and over on the screen. Any second now, all will be revealed.

No matches found.

My shoulders slump. No Bradley Foreman has ever e-mailed

me. The next search informs me I've never gotten an e-mail that mentions a company called Aztratek Pharmaceuticals.

But I've got Google. And I'm feeling lucky.

The cursor beckons. I type "Aztratek."

According to the screen, my search takes 1.7 seconds.

"Do you mean Aztratech?"

Google is so patronizing.

What I meant was, whatever the company the missing Bradley Foreman worked for. Works for, I correct myself, choosing the more optimistic words. I click on yes.

Aztratech Pharmaceuticals. It pops up instantly. Images opening and closing, sleek logos, hip graphics. It looks legit, but I have no idea what any of it means. I click on "About us."

Aztratech Pharmaceuticals, 336 Progress Drive, Boxford, Massachusetts. I smile. That's the one.

And—do I smell coffee?

"Hey, Charlotte—heard you on the newsbreak! What the hell is up with that?"

Franklin, predictably immaculate in a pressed pink Polo knit shirt, tortoiseshell sunglasses hanging over the top button, puts a steaming latte on my desk. "Room service," he says. "Triple venti non-fat. Thought you might be needing it."

Franklin is the only one, except for my mother, who calls me Charlotte. With his rural deep-South drawl it comes out like *Shaw-lit.* I still smile every time I hear it.

Franklin Brooks Parrish, age fifteen years younger than I am, is the latest in a longish line of investigative producers who've shared my office. I'm embarrassed to admit he's one of the few of color the station has hired. Louisiana State undergrad, a culture-shocking jump to Columbia Journalism School, then first TV job at some little station in Charleston, another in Albany, then CNN

Investigates, then here to Boston. All part of the market-climbing odyssey necessary for TV success.

He doesn't know I know he's already putting together résumé tapes. I also know he'll leave me when network bigwigs offer New York. TV relationships—don't ask, don't tell, don't get attached. And I'm very comfortable with temporary. Still, I'll miss Franklin when he goes.

"Hey, Franko, thanks so much for the replacement coffee. How do you already know just what I need?"

"No prob," Franklin replies. Master of multitasking, he's already opening his e-mail, checking his phone messages and clicking on our office TV. He's a computer wizard, so organized he arranges his books by the Dewey decimal system. Give Franklin the half-full/half-empty test—he'll find out who the glass belongs to, what's in it and whether it's contaminated, illegal or the product of some political corruption. He's also as much a goal-oriented perfectionist as I am.

I fill him in on the missing Ellen, as well as the missing Bradley Foreman. "So, bottom line," I finish. "After all that, I've accomplished zero. Except, listen. Have you ever heard of a company called Aztratech?"

Before Franklin can answer, I look up as the glass doors to the investigative unit swing open again. This time no one's running, so that's good. Then the shadow of doom falls across my desk. That's bad.

Overpermed, makeup challenged and clipboard in hand to signal how important she is, it may be that assistant news director Angela Nevins doesn't hate just me. It may be she hates everyone. But she's at *my* door.

"Charlie, Franklin, good morning. Great job on the newsbreak, Charlie. Thanks for bailing us out."

Angela has apparently read in one of her management manuals that it's productive to begin potentially contentious conversations by using some sort of a compliment. Softens up the peons for what's to come.

I don't dare glance at Franklin because one of us is sure to roll our eyes and make the other laugh. Plus I can never forget that even though on paper Angela's my boss, she's at least five years younger than I am. Maybe six. That she's allowed to tell me what to do is unrelenting torture.

"And what made it even better you were here," she goes on, attempting some replication of a smile, "is that since Ellen is out of the picture now—"

Franklin sees an opening and pounces. "Yeah, Angela . . . what happened to Ellen, anyway?"

Angela's smile disappears. "We're looking into it," she says. "I'm sure it's—"

Franklin interrupts, wrinkling his forehead in concern. "Is she . . . ?"

Angela turns her back as if Franklin doesn't exist and picks up where she left off with me. "Since Ellen is out of the picture now," she continues, "we need you to handle an interview we've arranged with the wife."

Am I supposed to know what she's talking about?

"What wife?" I say out loud.

I get one of those "I can't believe you reporters are so dense" looks.

"The accident victim's wife." Angela looks down at her clipboard, taps on it with her pencil. "Bradley Foreman? Aztratech? He's dead. Car accident. Apparently went off the road in Thursday's rain. His wife told the assignment desk she'd talk. But we've got to move quickly, before some lawyer shows up and orders her to keep quiet. So, Charlie, you're the only reporter here at the station. If we wait for the next one to arrive, we may lose the story."

This is simply unfair. She's assigning me vulture patrol. I loathe vulture patrol. I paid my on-the-street dues for years, trying to convince the brokenhearted and miserable there was some noble reason they should go on camera. I'm supposed to be done with all that now. But because I'm here early, I'm the only reporter who's available. And as a result, I'm the one who's nailed.

Course they don't teach in J-school: The Early Bird Gets the Work.

I look at Franklin in defeat. He's already looked up the Foremans' address in Lexington, and hands me directions with a sympathetic smile.

"I'll check into that Aztra company," he says. "No problem. Have fun, y'all."

"Fine," I say. I shift into all-business-brusque-reporter mode, knowing Angela will relish her power play even more if she thinks she's upset me. "Who's my photog?" I ask. "And where do I meet him?"

Angela tilts her head, narrowing her eyes at me. "You can fix your hair in the car, I suppose. Not that it'll matter—we don't need you on camera anyway. We'll just hand off your interview to the morning reporter. Oh, and your cameraman's Walt," she adds. "He's already waiting for you."

I see Franklin smothering a smile.

"Let us know what you get," she goes on. "We'll certainly want the interview on the noon news." She flutters her fingers and turns away. "Ciao, newsies."

My brain bursts into flames.

The noon news? I'm supposed to drive all the way to Lexington with a passive-aggressive lunk of a photographer who has the social skills of a petulant teenager, do a compassionate, thoughtful interview with a grieving widow, and then get back to the station in time to get something coherent, relevant and interesting on the noon news?

Fine. I can do that.

But news flash: at this rate I'm never going to find my big November story. TV news is the real reality TV. If this is the year I blow it, it's also the year I'll get voted off the island.

CHAPTER TWO

"So where to, Charlie? You got directions?"

I clamber into Walt's pale green Crown Vic news car, and struggle to find a spot to stash my briefcase and leftover latte among his screeching and flashing collection of two-way radios and squawky police scanners. He even calls it—with a straight face—the Walt-mobile.

Before I can even click on my seat belt, Walt peels out of the station's driveway, scattering gravel and a pack of flabbergasted camera-toting tourists.

"Move it!" he yells out his window. "So whose life you making miserable today, Charlie?" he growls.

"Funny," I reply, finally managing to adjust my seat belt. "And anyway, in this case, she's already miserable. You know the car accident victim this morning? His wife's going to talk. Surprising, don't you think? I wouldn't give a TV interview if my husband just died. Anyway, she lives up in Lexington." I hold up the paper Franklin gave me. "Directions say . . ."

Walt drives a little faster, apparently to emphasize his disdain. "I already know how to get there. Lexington, huh? Big dough."

Walt descends into his own cheerless world, punching the

buttons to change stations on the radio as he growls obscenities at any offending drivers, which seems to be all of them.

I tune it all out. I can feel myself scowling, and it's not from the noise. It's barely nine-thirty in the morning and already two people so much as told me I'm past my prime. They can't—or don't want to?—put my face on TV. I suppose I can ignore Angela's haughty assessment as another tactic to drive me crazy. But Teddy? That's troubling. He's the sweetest of guys, hardworking, reliable. It wasn't personal for him, just practical. Video's out of focus. Audio level's too hot. Charlie's—too old. I stare out the window, resting my forehead on the chilly glass.

It's not like turning forty-six was a surprise. You're forty-five, then you're forty-six. And okay, soon, forty-seven. Through a fortuitous combination of good genes, good makeup, and reluctant but diligent exercise, I don't really look my age. Whatever that looks like. I don't kid myself, local television news is as much about glamour as getting the journalistic goods, and I've certainly started my plastic surgery savings account. For someday.

But meantime, I've carved out my investigative niche so I no longer have to battle the unpredictable video pitfalls street reporters can't possibly avoid. You have to stand in front of the fire if you're talking about the fire, even if the lighting is better on the other side of the burning building. Even if the wind is blowing your hair into your lip gloss and spray from the hoses is melting your mascara into Goth-girl grotesque. I've happily bequeathed that kind of news to the twentysomethings.

I flip down my visor and do a quick reality check in the mirror. It appears my new and way-too-expensive miracle skin stuff isn't working yet, since my dark circles are still browner than my eyes. But other than that, am I that bad? I squint to get a better look, but that's difficult because with my contacts in, I can't see close up. If

I put on my reading glasses so I can, then I won't see how I really look because I'll be wearing my reading glasses.

A twinge of conscience hits. Mrs. Foreman certainly won't care how I look. I snap the visor back up. Her husband is dead. I need to care about her reality. I'm a journalist. I love my job. I look fine.

Walt settles on some venom-spewing talk radio show and pushes the volume to "harassment." I recognize this as his power play to make sure there's no possibility of conversation, and also to make sure I know who's in charge. And I do know who's in charge. I turn down the volume.

It would be so satisfying to dump the rest of my latte on his head. But that, no doubt, is some kind of union grievance, and would probably result in him getting some kind of benefits and me fired.

Outside the car, it's far more peaceful. New England in October. Even on my way to the interview from hell, I get distracted by the sun spackling through the just-turned trees, the early red of the maples lining the winding streets of the well-kept neighborhood. It's a school day, so bikes of all sizes lean against garage doors, blow-up wading pools twinkle in the front yards even as their season wanes, an occasional porch dog, left behind by his kids, lifts his head inquiringly as the noise of our Crown Vic interrupts his nap.

"There it is, number 2519," I finally say and point out the yellow clapboard two-story house. I can't help thinking it now has a tragedy connected to it. And the family—I don't even know if there are kids inside—will forever mark its history based on today. Before the accident. After the accident.

Course they don't teach in J-school: Bottom-Feeding 101—Knocking on the door of a grieving family.

We crunch up the gravel walkway, Walt with his camera at his side, a crimson leaf or two fluttering down in front of us. I've been through this moment so many times, intruding on some stranger's grief to fill twenty seconds on a few newscasts, and it never gets easier.

Audrey Hepburn answers the door. Obviously, not really Audrey Hepburn, but she's a remarkable clone—elegant bones, flawless complexion, luminous eyes, pixie hair, even a little black sweater and narrow black pants. Mrs. Foreman looks pampered and classily understated. Tiny diamond studs. Delicate gold necklace. I glance at her left hand. Someone's college education sparkles on her ring finger.

"Charlie McNally," she says. Her voice is gentle, and seems weary. "They told me you were coming. I'm Melanie Foreman." She offers a tentative smile. "Melanie. Come in."

We step through the door into a tasteful and immaculate buttery-yellow entry hall. Bandbox white moldings, indirect lighting, a well-worn Oriental covering the high-gloss hardwood floor. I sneak an assessing squint at the intricate designs. The rug's almost threadbare in places, but it's real.

Melanie closes the door behind us and turns inquiringly. "And this is?"

"Walt. Petrucelli." He gives her a nod. "Sorry for your loss."

Well, point for Walt. That's civilized.

"Set up in the living room?" he asks, hefting his equipment. Melanie gestures to the next room, and we follow her in. Walt quickly puts up his lights and clanks open his tripod. Even he must feel how uncomfortable this is. I get out my notebook, dig for a pencil, try to check my hair in a way that's not incredibly rude.

Melanie, however, seems off in her own world. She sits quietly, her alarmingly thin body scrunched all the way into one corner of the oversize cream-and-chocolate couch. She smoothes the fringes of a throw pillow, staring at her hands. I think I recognize the pillow's plaid as Ralph Lauren, and it's his latest.

Then I notice the lumpily cushioned couch, the mismatched tables, and an outdated flame-stitch wing chair, all going a little shabby around the edges. Wonder if they have money problems? Or perhaps they're simply comfortable with themselves.

Except there's no more "they," I remember, as Melanie finally looks up.

"Oh, sorry," she says with a wan smile. "What is it you'd like to ask me?"

Actually, I'd like to ask why she's agreeing to do an interview with the grief-sucking creature called TV news. But I won't.

"Thanks for letting us talk with you, Melanie," I begin. I'm using my sympathetic voice. Today, it's genuine. Has she faced his closet full of clothes? His toothbrush? Closed the book he was reading? She can't possibly have grasped, yet, how sinkingly alone she's about to be. "What is it you'd like people to know about your husband?"

Melanie replaces the pillow against the back of the couch. A tawny little terrier-looking dog pads across the rug to curl up at her feet.

"My husband—Brad—is—was . . ." Suddenly she looks as if she's going to lose it. Over my shoulder, I hear the motorized zoom of Walt's camera lens. He's going in for a close-up because he thinks she's going to cry. Welcome to TV news.

"Are you okay?" I ask this as slowly as possible. I know this is difficult for her, but if she's going to dissolve into anguish, I've got to make sure we get the shot on tape. Vulture patrol. "Mrs. Foreman?"

"No, I'm fine." Melanie blinks and curls the pillow back into her lap. She sighs and starts again. "Brad was an honest, reliable person who just wanted everyone to play by the same rules." She smiles for a moment. "You remember Jimmy Stewart? In the *Mr. Smith Goes to Washington* movie?"

I nod. "Of course."

I hear the zoom motor pull back. Walt's decided she's not going to cry.

"That's exactly who he was like," she continues. "Principled, devoted. Would you like to see a picture of Brad? Of both of us?"

My inner reporter is salivating. We already have the photograph of him we used on the air when he was missing, but I'll score big news points if we can get another one now. Especially if it's both of them. Vulture patrol.

"Of course," I say sincerely. "Whatever you like."

She picks up a black-and-white photo, framed in etched sterling silver. It's obviously from their wedding, and so unconventional it's almost out of focus. It looks as if a gust of wind caught the new couple off guard, Melanie holding down the skirt of what could be a gauzy Vera Wang, Brad in a sleekly Italian-looking suit.

"It's the one we sent to the newspaper," Melanie explains as she shows it to me. "Wedding announcement."

I look at the picture more closely. Brad even looks Jimmy Stew-arty, in a lanky, almost gawky kind of way. He's gazing lovingly at Melanie, but her eyes look confidently into the camera. Seeing the happiness on their faces makes this whole thing even more tragic, if that's possible.

"Hold the photo steady, ma'am, can you?" Walt rolls off a quick shot, then turns the camera back to Melanie. She's still staring at the photo.

"So?" I look at her encouragingly. I can't let her lose concentration. More than twenty minutes here and we'll blow our deadline. "He worked at Aztratech?"

"Yes. And he was happy there." She replaces the silver frame on a glass end table, wincing as it clatters down. "He worked at headquarters ever since we moved East a few years ago. My parents were here. They left us this house, in fact . . ."

Aha. Not their house.

". . . and so it was perfect when Aztratech started up. It was very bare bones at the beginning, sometimes Brad didn't get paid. . . ."

Another aha. Money problems.

"And he wasn't a pharmaceutical researcher, he was in accounting. Budget forecasting, that kind of thing. He was always interested in numbers. . . . He was top of his class at Princeton, did you know?"

And just as she seems to be comfortable again, I hear the ping of an arriving text. Of course.

I glance down. *Suicide?* it says. *Angela says ask.*

Now there's a charming suggestion. Angela's telling me I'm supposed to sit in this little waif of a widow's living room and casually throw out a couple of questions about whether her oh-so-recently deceased and beloved husband may have killed himself on purpose in a gruesome crash of twisted metal. I work for local news. That's exactly what I have to do.

"Sorry, Melanie," I say. "Forgive me. Anyway, anything else you'd like to add?" Here I go. I glance at my notebook, as if I have a list of questions. "You said your husband was happy at work. But otherwise, any worries or concerns you'd noticed? About, um, money, maybe?"

I cringe at myself. Subtle, kiddo. She is so going to throw me out of here.

She doesn't.

"No, not that I know of," she says slowly. "When he left that morning, it was like any other morning for him. Everything was—as usual."

But I notice her fists are clenching and now Melanie is looking at the photo again. The little dog looks up at her, nuzzles her leg, and she gives her an absent pat.

"Charlie . . . may I ask you something?"

"Of course."

"Must we have the camera on?"

With that one question, I'm tossed overboard into the murky waters of J-school ethics class. TV news is all about getting the story on tape. If we turn the camera off and she says something newsworthy, I'm sunk. But if I tell Melanie no, we can't turn the camera off, she probably won't tell me whatever it is she wants to tell me. And I'm really curious.

"No problem." I take the plunge. "Walt, we're done."

Walt clicks off the lights, and starts wrapping cords and twisting down light stands. He doesn't care what happens with Melanie; he's figuring in ten minutes we're outta here. He can dump me off at the station and go back to chasing fires. I register a flutter of envy. To him, this is just nine to five plus overtime. If I lose a story—well, the dominoes may start to fall. On me.

"Why didn't you answer my husband's e-mail?" Melanie asks. She doesn't look angry. It's almost as if she's—hurt. "He sent it the day before he disappeared."

My brain brakes into a stall, crashing my words together.

"Why didn't I . . . answer . . . what? Your husband sent me an e-mail?" My conscience pangs into guilty and my worry level shoots into the red zone. Could I have missed his letter? "I don't remember seeing it," I insist, trying to sound reassuring. I'm all too aware the black hole of my voluminous e-mail could have sucked the letter into oblivion. Or our constantly crashing system simply ate it. "You're sure—?"

"I'm sure, Charlie, very sure. In fact, I thought it was why you came this morning. To ask about it."

I'm confused. Off balance. Bradley Foreman is dead. And his wife thinks I ignored him.

What's making my search for equilibrium tougher, I'm feeling sympathy instead of objectivity. I could say goodbye and thanks so much for the interview, leave and never see Melanie Foreman again. And that's what I should do. TV reporting is like SWAT team duty. Get in, do your stuff, get out. Get too involved in someone's life and—never fails—you get into trouble. Like I said, I'm very comfortable with temporary.

But my heart breaks for this newly minted widow. She chose to stay home, be with her husband, probably wanted to start a family. Thought it was the right decision. Then the universe crushed her. Alone at thirtysomething. Been there, done that.

At least I have a job. She has nothing left. No friends are here to comfort her. There are no flowers. No family.

"Do you know why he e-mailed?" I ask. "What he wanted to tell me? Or since I'm the investigative reporter, maybe he wanted me to—investigate something?"

Her life must feel so chaotic now. Maybe I can help her feel some closure.

Melanie pushes up the sleeves of her thin black cashmere sweater, turns her watch around once, then again.

"I just don't know, Charlie, I really don't." Melanie shrugs, looks at the floor, then back at me. "Could you have—deleted his e-mail? Without reading it, maybe?"

I desperately try to come up with some comforting response, but Melanie interrupts my escalating distress.

"Oh well," she says, almost whispering. "It doesn't matter."

So much for helping. Melanie thinks I've dissed her husband, never bothered to answer his e-mail, and it appears she's somehow blaming me for what happened. Although how could not answering an e-mail cause a car accident? I mentally stamp my foot. And then, suddenly, I'm saved.

The terrier starts barking and bounds to the front door. We head for the entryway, and through the window, Melanie and I can see two big white vans, emblazoned with the logos of Channel

6 and Channel 13. Photographers, reporters, cameras and microphones disgorge into Melanie's driveway. Doors slam, gravel crunches and soon a media parade is marching up the front walk.

Melanie, her face evolving from surprise to panic, actually takes a step or two backward. She puts one hand over her mouth and the other on the banister of the stairway to the second floor. She's like a fair maiden, trapped in a castle that's come under siege.

I realize I can be her knight in shining armor and win the joust for my team at the same time.

"You know, Melanie," I say, hoping I'm successfully hiding my ulterior motives, "you don't really have to talk with these people. Just go upstairs, and don't answer the door. I'll check for that e-mail as soon as I get back to the station and then I'll call you."

She looks relieved. She looks grateful. She heads up the stairs.

"By the way," I call after her, "what's his e-mail address?" *Was* his address, I don't say.

As the doorbell starts to ring, Melanie turns on the stairway to look at me again. "B4@mmpr.net," she says. "Call me if you find his e-mail."

I'm baffled. "Before?"

"Like the letter *B*, then the number *4*. B4." She turns and begins to climb the stairs. "Like Bradley Foreman," she says over her shoulder. And she's gone.

With that, this day potentially gets more rewarding. I grab my notebook and write down Foreman's e-mail address before I forget it. Walt arrives in the entryway with his gear and I quickly give him the lowdown. Then there's a barrage of knocking and the doorbell rings again. This is going to be a pleasure.

I try not to look superior as I open Melanie's front door. These crews have certainly figured out Channel 3 is here—Walt's porcupine-antennaed Crown Vic out front is a dead giveaway. And they're also thinking if Melanie talked to whomever is already inside, she'll certainly give interviews to every other station. But I am now going to get the delightful opportunity to disappoint them.

Course they don't teach in J-school: The Art of the Scoop.

"Hello, all," I say. Straight-faced, pleasant, not at all smirky. "Mrs. Foreman says she's not interested in any interviews. And she asks if you could please not disturb her."

"Are you crazy?"

"Did she talk to you?"

"What did she say?"

They're a buzzing pack of angry journalists, deprived of their prey.

"I'm only telling you what she told me," I call out. I'm on a beeline to the car. "Sorry, gang." And I hop into the Waltmobile.

My photographer finally bestows a smile. "Cool." Walt nods and hands me the videocassette he just shot. "Very cool."

The force of several g's hits as Walt floors it, and we are headed back to the station. On time and with an exclusive interview. What's more, if Melanie's correct, there's some very intriguing e-mail buried somewhere in my computer.

CHAPTER THREE

Angela Nevins greets me at the newsroom door. She's still carrying her management-prop clipboard, which she points at me like a weapon.

"Charlie," she says. "Word from the police—Bradley Foreman's death was a suicide."

"Suicide?" I slowly place my videocassette on the assignment-desk counter. "Oh, Angela," I reply, frowning. "I really don't think so. You know I got your text, and I did ask, and . . ." I look up, ready to pursue my case, but it doesn't matter.

Angela is still chittering. "And as a result, we're dropping the story. You know we never cover suicides. Putting them on TV might encourage people to do it. So—sorry, Charlie." She gives a simpery smile, as if no one's ever used the tuna line on me before. "But thanks for being a team player."

I can't let this go. She's wrong.

"But, Angela, I was with his widow," I persist. "I specifically asked her about suicide, as much as I could without sounding completely insensitive, and I'm telling you. It just wasn't—he just didn't." I pause. "Is there a note or something? A police report?"

"No report I've heard of, and no note, either." Angela looks at the clipboard and reacts as if it's giving her some important instructions to get away from me as fast as she can.

But I have one more question. "Why would she call the assignment desk and ask to be interviewed, if she thought it might be suicide?" This never made sense to me, anyway.

"Charlie, you've got it backward," she says, her tone suggesting she's talking to the slow class. "The desk called *her: We* asked *her* for the interview. I mean after all, her husband had been missing for days, we were helping by broadcasting his picture and we told her we wanted an interview after he was found." She shrugs. "I guess she figured she still had to do it—even though he was found, uh, dead."

Only local news has the guts to guilt a grieving widow into doing an on-camera interview. And I just love it that no one bothered to fill me in on that little tidbit before I showed up at her door.

"Whatever," Angela continues. "Police think it's suicide, and that's what we have to accept. Period. The end."

She starts to walk away, then turns back to me. Big smile. "But let's do set up a time to chat about your stories for November, all right? We're eager to hear what you've come up with." With that, she heads toward her office.

Apparently I'm dismissed.

Making an Oscar-worthy effort to appear calm, I carefully and quietly reclaim the tape of Melanie's interview and trudge to our office.

"Franklin." I slam the tape and notebook on my desk, and throw my bag onto the extra chair. "Never mind about looking up Brad's classmates. Listen to this. Listen. To. This."

I'm probably setting a new land-speed record for talking as I replay the morning's chaos. Franklin actually turns away from his computer to listen, muttering supportively and sympathetically in exactly the right places.

I wind down a little as I get to the end. And now, morning utterly wasted, I collapse into my chair.

"You're a full-blown Prozac candidate," Franklin says. "They're just trying to do what they think is right down there, Charlotte. It's not about you, you know?" He takes a tissue from a box in his drawer and rubs an invisible scuff off one loafer. "Plus, admit it. You're like—" he looks up at me "—an approval addict. You know? Sometimes—"

"I'm not addicted to approval," I interrupt, dismissing his assessment. "I'm addicted to success. You know how it works at this place. If you're not hearing *yes*, you're hearing *no.* And *no* is bad. Soon it means *no job.*"

And already today, I remember for the millionth time, they've decided not to put my face on TV. Twice. Maybe I'm some sort of chronological time bomb. Programmed to disappear. A twenty-first–century Cheshire Cat. Soon all that'll be left here is my smile—on videotape.

Franklin gestures at the awards-ceremony photos I've tacked on the wall. "Twenty Emmys. You have twenty Emmys," he says. "You're at the top. You're Channel 3's golden girl."

"I didn't win last year," I remind him. I glance at the photos. I'm wreathed in smiles, arms around an array of Franklin's predecessors, all of us holding golden statues. I see Sweet Baby James's face, too. Someday I'm gonna Photoshop that man right out of the shot, I think wryly, just the way I did out of my life. "And face it, Franklin, I'm pushing the demos. If they only want eighteen- to forty-nine-year-olds watching, why would they want someone older than that on the air? Do the math," I instruct, my voice bleak. "It's just a matter of time before it adds up to goodbye, Charlie."

"Like I said. Prozac, girl. And something good will come out of this morning, you just don't know what yet." Franklin the philosopher. This is what he always says. "Besides, I think I might be on the track of a possible story."

Franklin pauses for a moment, waiting to see if I'm paying attention. And I am. If Franklin's got a lead, a good story trumps sullen.

"Aztratech," he goes on. "Pharmaceutical company. Very fast track. I also uncovered a bunch of industry newsletters warning pharma companies in general about the latest attack on their bottom line—whistle-blowing employees."

I deflate. I hope Franklin doesn't think *that's* new.

"Any employee can blow the whistle on their company," I interrupt. "We did a big exposé about it, couple of years before you got here. They can rat them out for ripping off the government. If it turns out the company was doing something illegal in a federal contract—overcharging or cheating or something—the whistleblower gets part of the money the feds recover. And that can be incredibly lucrative." I shrug. "But sorry, Franko. Not new."

"Yeah, but listen," Franklin persists. "I found one of those whistle-blower lawsuits has just been filed against Aztratech. The name of the whistle-blower is secret, apparently because the financial stakes are so enormous. Not to mention dangerous to the whistle-blower." He leans forward intently. "So, do you think—"

If I were in a cartoon, a big lightbulb would appear right over my head.

"What I think is—you'd better go buy a new suit for the Emmys, kiddo." I jump out of my chair and sit down again, clamping both my hands on the top of my head. The pencil in my hair falls out and clatters onto the floor. "Listen, Franklin. A peculiar thing happened at Melanie's. She insisted her husband had sent me an e-mail. The day before he went missing, she said. And she was wondering why I never answered him."

"Sent you an e-mail? Did she say what it was about?" Franklin rubs his chin, considering. "It's freaky that he writes you, then dies in a car accident."

"No kidding. Creepy. And no, Melanie said she didn't know what it was about. But I will bet you ten million dollars he was writing to tell me he was either the whistle-blower in that lawsuit you found, or wanted to spill the facts of the case. Or something like that."

Franklin and I always bet ten million dollars. Sometimes one or the other of us is up or down a hundred million or so, but eventually it always evens out.

"And that means," I continue, "somewhere in Bradley Foreman's files, or in his computer or in his notes, there could be some amazing documents. Maybe—the proof his company is somehow ripping off the government." I pause, nodding. "Here's an idea. Since Melanie says Brad wrote to me, let's see if she'll let us take a look around."

Franklin shakes his head. "No way."

"Way," I insist. "This could be a major-league story. I think he did send that e-mail, maybe I even read it. I didn't find it again because I was looking under *Aztrat-e-k*, spelled wrong. And then I searched for his name, but maybe he didn't put his name in the letter."

Big finish. "So I'll be happy to wager his e-mail is right now waiting right here in my little computer, and I'm going to be able to find it in about two seconds. Brad Foreman's the whistle-blower, and we have our story." I sit back in my chair in triumph. Yes. I love to be right.

The ping of a text interrupts my find-Brad's-message mission. *Meet me at the usual place*, the message says. *Big G!*

Big Gossip. My best friend Maysie has such a flair for the dramatic. She's the only woman working upstairs at Channel 3's all-sports radio station, so she's pretty much turned the ladies' restroom into her private sanctuary. It's also our usual place to chat and trade info, sort of a secret clubhouse for grown-ups.

"Back in a second," I tell Franklin. I sprint up to the fourth floor, and open the door marked W. Maysie's sprawled in the black canvas director's chair she's appropriated for her hideout, her shoeless feet perched on the counter under the mirror, the sports pages balanced on her outstretched legs. Her ponytailed hair, still naturally dark brown, is tucked under a Celtics cap, and as usual, she's not wearing a stitch of makeup. Radio is so easy.

"Hey, Brenda." She welcomes me with a wave, then refolds her paper and gestures me to the guest seat on the counter. She knows I'm uncomfortable with the "Brenda Starr" nickname, since I'm hardly as glamorous and definitely not a comic book journalist. But she thinks it's hilarious. And she means well. "Heard you on the newsbreak. How'd that happen?"

I spin out the mystery of the vanishing anchorwoman and describe how secretive Angela was. "And Teddy said something like, 'She'd better be dead,'" I report. "Maybe there's more to this. Maybe heads are going to roll."

But Maysie only laughs. "That was a trick question," she says, eyes twinkling. "I actually have the total scoop."

"Tell all," I demand. Ellen's apparently not dead. And there's nothing like someone else's life chaos to put things into perspective.

"Let's just say . . ." Maysie pauses. "The 'new face of Channel 3' will be facing a judge instead of a camera. She has now learned, in a most unpleasant way, that trying to con the drugstore pharmacist with someone else's prescription for OxyContin is frowned on by law enforcement. And that the cops don't care if you have a newscast coming up."

"She's in . . . ?" I can't believe this.

"The tank," Maysie finishes. "Angela's gone to bail her out. Think I should drop a dime to the gossip girls at the newspaper?"

I know she won't. Maysie and I have been friends ever since we bonded over junk food years ago in the station's basement cafeteria. A surprise blizzard trapped everyone in the building—and a flurry of weatherman-blaming reporters descended to battle for whatever carbs or sugar remained in the station's battered and unreliable snack machines. I caught Maysie kicking at the metal casing of the one with the potato chips, and together we tipped and rattled until two bags of barbecue flavor emerged.

Her real name is Margaret Isobel DeRosiers Green, but on the radio she's Maysie Green, sports reporter extraordinaire. She can hold her own in any locker room, and amazingly for the news biz, doesn't possess a backstabbing bone in her body. She doesn't care if the glass is half-full or half-empty—she looks forward to the fun of drinking the rest of it, and then the fun of filling it up again. And I get to be the older sister she never had.

"Anyway," Maysie says, swinging her legs down from the counter. "Thanksgiving in the works—the in-laws descending from Long Island." She does the Maysie eye-roll. "Should be quite a scene. We're expecting you as usual."

Maysie's a twenty-first–century chick with a 1950s home life—two brainy kids, a devoted husband, big house in the suburbs. Everything I used to wish for. Lately, I've realized I'm fine on my own. Probably fine. I know I've totally missed the baby boat, which upset me for a few years, but now . . . Well, that's just the way it is. I've accepted that my only babies will be those little gold Emmy awards lined up on my study shelf.

Course they don't teach in J-School: Future Shock—The Choice of Fame or Family.

"I'm there, naturally," I respond. "Thanks for adopting me. Again."

"Will it be just you?" Maysie looks at me, eyebrows raised questioningly. "Any love life pending? Someone you're hiding from me? Maybe a hot prospect we can lure for a turkey dinner, impress him with your loving circle of friends?"

"'Fraid not." I shake my head. "Last year's gravy episode with Software Boy was quite enough, don't you think?"

Maysie's shepherded me through two long-ago engagements I called off as well as my recent dead-end relationships with a judge and a corporate headhunter—all of whom grew too needy of attention, too demanding of my time and too jealous of my celebrity. She's tirelessly curious about Sweet Baby James, my first (and only) husband, and constantly prods me to Google the latest on my ex. She's hoping that somehow there's still a happy ending in my future. To her, that means a husband, no matter how often I assure her I'm over it. Probably over it.

"Whatever," Maysie allows. "You know we love you." She stands up, brushing off her trademark black jeans. "How're you doing on your ratings stories?"

I give her a thumbs-up, nodding eagerly. "Got a good lead, actually," I begin. Then I stop, superstitious. "I'll explain when we get it nailed down."

"You're nuts, Brenda," Maysie replies. "I predict your usual Emmy. You live for this journalism stuff."

I turn to the lighted mirror on the wall, suddenly serious. "You know, Mays, Brenda Starr is a fictional character—that's why she looks the same after thirty years. I—don't. Maybe solid journalism isn't enough anymore." I turn to face her, frowning. "And, is it hot in here? Do you—"

"What happened to Miss Forty-six And Not Fighting It?" Maysie interrupts. "Maybe you just need a little more caffeine this morning. Or maybe . . ." she narrows her eyes ". . . you need to get laid," she whispers.

"I had a date," I retort. "Last, um, two weeks ago. With that real-estate guy. You remember." A date that ended, mercifully, about 9:00 p.m., after an extensive monologue about cost per square foot. But Maysie doesn't need to know that.

"Did you—*do* it? Did you even kiss him?" she asks. She waves a hand, preventing me from answering. "Of course not. You probably made him watch *Frontline* with you. I'm just warning, girlfriend, you're going to get out of practice." Maysie's phone interrupts, tinkling a perverse version of "Take Me Out to the Ball Game." She hits Mute without missing a beat. "Anyway, remember we're sneaking the kids off to Disney today for the break between baseball and football—leaving right after my afternoon show. I'll send postcards, as usual. And maybe you can 'practice' while I'm gone." She does a suggestive little shoulder shimmy. "You're still hot as hell, Murphy Brown, if you'd just let yourself go for it."

I give her a quick hug, deciding not to mention that the award-winningly tough Murphy Brown, though not a bad journalism role model, is also a fictional sitcom character. "All I'm 'going for,' Mays, is my next story. And now, I've got to hunt for a mysterious e-mail," I say. "Have a great trip—I'll be missing you. You know you're the only one I can talk to."

"Oh, honey," Maysie says as she adjusts her cap and gathers her tote bag, "don't be a drama queen. We'll only be gone two weeks. What could happen?"

CHAPTER FOUR

Franklin and Melanie, shoulders almost touching, are standing at an old-fashioned dark walnut desk. I hear the rustle of papers as the two of them, engrossed, pull out file folders and pamphlets and page through them. I still can't believe Melanie let us come back to her Lexington home, but the e-mail from her husband I found referred to "paperwork" that he wanted to "share." Even though, as Melanie explained, Brad's will specified no funeral, it seemed like a decree from the grave, impossible to ignore. I wonder if Melanie is feeling that, too.

"This is the box Brad brought home from the office," Melanie explains. "I suppose—" she sighs, glancing at me "—this is what he wanted you to see."

I'm sitting on one end of a chestnut leather couch, ready to check through the files I pulled to examine. "The e-mail I found didn't specify," I reply, shaking my head. "It just said he worked at Aztratech, and wanted to talk to me. It didn't even include his name. He just told me to reply by e-mail. I'm so sorry, Melanie," I add. "His letter wasn't terribly revealing."

Brad Foreman's office, shadowy and masculine, looks as if it's on hold, waiting for him to come back. Franklin and I are invaders, strangers now prying though private documents Brad apparently meant to hide here.

This is all for the good, I attempt to reassure myself. Melanie suspects Brad was on the trail of . . . something. Now the three of us are going to continue his quest, and if we're lucky (as we often are), we'll dig up the journalistic treasure at the end of the trail. Brad would have wanted it that way. After all, he sent me that e-mail. And it must be important to Melanie, too, or she wouldn't have let us come back to her house on the very day her husband's body was found.

"So—I have a question," I say. If she's this resilient, she must need answers as much as I do. Closure. "If these documents and files are from your husband's office, Mrs. Foreman, how did they get here? And why?"

She looks up with a wan smile. "Melanie, remember?" She puts a finger between some files to hold her place. "Brad brought them home, piles and piles of papers. I did ask him what they were, but he was unusually dismissive. Just said, 'Oh, nothing, honey.' I should have—"

Melanie's voice catches in her throat. "I should have—" she tries again.

I'm so focused on Melanie's anguish, when the phone rings I almost fall off the couch.

Melanie flutters a pale hand to her throat and picks up the receiver.

"Hello?"

I'm not sure how I can avoid listening. After all, it's probably a private condolence call. I pretend to be looking at files, but I can't resist sneaking a peek at Melanie.

She looks perplexed, and holds the receiver out in front of her as if she could look inside and see who's calling. She brings it back to her ear. "Hello? Hello?" She listens again briefly, then places the phone gently back in its cradle. "One of your colleagues?" she asks with a wry smile.

Franklin laughs, too, as I answer, "Probably a telemarketer, or wrong number," I correct her. "A reporter would never hang up."

The little terrier trots into the room and jumps onto the couch. She gives me an appraising glance, then curls up on the cushion beside me. I reach out to give her a pat, but withdraw my hand when I hear Melanie's voice.

Her smile has evaporated. "Banjo," she snaps. "Get down." The dog leaps from the couch, scampering away. "She's not the same," Melanie explains, her voice softening, "since Brad . . ."

"I know how skittish pets can be," I reply, letting her know I understand. "My cat's at the vet. Apparently there's some feline flu going around and . . ." I stop. I'm trying to be sympathetic, but she must be so fragile, so on edge. I can't help her by sharing pet stories. I can only help her by looking for answers.

Melanie and Franklin, Banjo forgotten, have gone back to the documents, but I realize I'm more than a little unnerved. Dead guy's office. Mysterious phone call. Purloined documents.

Shake it off, I tell myself.

"So?" I ask. "Anything interesting?"

"Hard to tell." Franklin seems perplexed. "There are some Aztratech accounting ledgers. There's a big file of what looks like copies of the newspaper stock tables, all marked up. And this is a stack of 10k's, annual reports from two dozen or so corporations."

"Anything that looks personal? Or confidential? You said—stock tables?"

Franklin hands me a page from the top of the pile. It looks as if it's copied from a *New York Times* stock market page, blurred so much that maybe it's a copy of a copy. There are blue dots and red dots in various places, apparently marking companies someone was interested in.

"Here's an idea," I say, handing the page back. "Melanie, do you know if your husband had a stock market theory? Was he playing the market?"

Melanie frowns. I can't tell if she's thinking about my question, or if I've offended her. Savvy move, Charlie. Ask about the dead husband's finances again. I hope for the best, and keep talking.

Because now I think it's possible our whistle-blowing idea is wrong. Maybe Brad was thinking about quitting Aztratech and going into the market. That's why he brought all his stock research home.

"I mean, if you could predict the market, you could rule the world. But if he proved it worked, obviously, he couldn't let anyone know."

The e-mail. I pull it from my pocket, checking again for some clue I missed. "Which, of course, means I'm wrong." I shake my head and refold the paper, running my fingers along the crease. "If he couldn't tell anyone, he's not going to e-mail a reporter."

Franklin raises one eyebrow and stacks up another file. "Yeah," he says mildly. "That's kind of what I was thinking."

"Could I just say," Melanie breaks in softly, "I'm sure Brad didn't have a 'beat the stock market' idea. But I do think something—or someone—was worrying him."

"You do?" Franklin and I say this in unison. We may have worked together too long. "Why?"

"And, Melanie," I add, mentally replaying this morning's interview, "you told me everything was fine. You said he wasn't depressed or upset."

She sinks into the desk chair, briefly puts her head in her hands. When she looks up, her eyes are filled with tears, and she seems to be struggling for words.

"I know, and I'm sorry if I misled you, Charlie. But I was afraid. I thought if Brad knew something he wasn't supposed to know, maybe someone would think I know whatever it is, too. And I don't know anything."

Franklin puts down his papers. "Why do you think he knew something?"

Melanie fidgets a little in her chair. Brad's chair. "Well, he was just behaving strangely. He came home later than usual, or earlier. He spent a lot of time reading the newspaper.

"I'm sorry," she says, shaking her head. "I sound ridiculous. Neurotic wife, overanalyzing . . ." Her voice trails off.

"No, no . . ." Franklin and I, in unison again, rush to reassure her.

"That's why we're here," I say. "To try to find some answers."

The room is quiet again. I guess we're all thinking about Brad. Whatever he had in the works, things did not go as he planned.

And now, what are we missing? I get up to take another look through Brad's file box.

"There's all that Aztratech stuff, then a series of green folders with a company name on each," I say, moving the files on their metal rack. "Looks like—corporations. Rogers Chalmers. Electrometrics. Then, let's see, Fisher Industries." I turn to Melanie, questioning. "Ring a bell?"

She looks doubtful. "No."

"They're all different kinds of companies," Franklin muses, looking over my shoulder. "Agriculture. Chemicals. Construction. Only a couple of pharmaceuticals. Why would he have all these?"

We pull the files forward, one at a time. Each appears to contain the same kinds of documents: an annual report, stock research and market performance information, and advertising materials. The Aztratech file is especially plump.

After a few moments, Franklin steps back and sits down in a smoky-striped wing chair.

"Okay, this is not so mysterious," he says. He starts to put his feet up on the coffee table, then stops. "He was job hunting. He's researching opportunities. This is unquestionably the collection of someone scouting for new employment."

I tilt my head back and forth, considering. "But didn't he like his job at Aztratech?"

"He never said he wasn't happy with his job," Melanie says. "So I really don't think . . ."

I glance at Franklin, my eyes signaling our tactics. He gives the tiniest of nods—he understands. I'm going for it.

"Um, Melanie," I begin. "What if . . . Could your husband have been researching, say, price fixing of some kind?"

"Does he have other documents? That could be his, well, ammunition?" Franklin adds, moving in for the follow-up. "Evidence he was going to use as proof of corporate collusion? Or something like that?"

Melanie slicks back her hair, stares off into the distance.

Damn it. We may have pushed too hard. Lost her. Franklin's giving me a worried look. I raise a hand, signaling again. Hang on.

Melanie sighs. "I suppose it's possible," she says softly, still looking away. "He never told me anything about—anything like that." She turns to us, eyes moist. "But as I said, it's possible."

She opens a maroon lacquered box on the desk and takes out a thin cigarette. She holds it up silently, and when we don't object, she lights it with a heavy silver lighter and puffs out a narrow stream of gray smoke.

"We did have money problems," she says finally. "Bradley was desperately trying to refinance. This house used to be my mother's. She gave it to us when she moved to her condo."

The jangle of the phone interrupts us again.

Melanie tilts her head back and her shoulders drop. She looks exhausted and overwhelmed. She picks up the receiver. "Hello?" she says quietly.

This time there must be someone on the other end. I watch Melanie's face register emotions: recognition, confusion, annoyance, concern. And then, do I see fear?

Melanie regains her composure, but I still think she looks uncomfortable. "No, nothing at all," she says, glancing at the stack of ledgers and paperwork, and then at Franklin and me. "I'm sure it'll be fine."

She hangs up and takes another drag on her cigarette, stubs it out. I wait, figuring if she wants to explain, she'll explain.

"That was someone from Brad's office," she says. "Asking if Brad had brought anything home." A puff of gray smoke. "I said no, because it just didn't seem right. What business is it of theirs if Brad brought papers home?"

"I suppose if they're Aztratech property," I say slowly, "they legally belong to the company. If Brad took them without permission, you may be obligated to give them back."

Melanie opens the lacquered box again, lights another cigarette. I can see the flame flicker in her trembling hand. "What if they're sending someone now? To get them? I don't have time to shred all this, or burn them," she says, looking at us helplessly. Her voice rises, and she twists that rock of a ring around her finger. "They could find everything, all these files. I can't risk—"

"If you still had them," I say slowly.

Melanie's expression changes, her chin lifts, and she looks at me through narrowing eyes. "You're suggesting . . . I give them to you?" She pauses, then shakes her head. "I think—that's not the best idea."

"But if they weren't here . . ." I pause, hoping Melanie will fill in the blank. She doesn't, so I do. "They couldn't find them. They'd never know. You could protect Brad."

Melanie taps her cigarette thoughtfully into the ashtray. Taps it again and again. Finally, she almost smiles. "And you'd never tell, of course, if I gave you the files. Reporter privilege, is it called?"

"We never reveal a source, Mrs. Foreman," I say formally. "And we'll never release documents. You can take that to the bank."

"So that's fantastic," I say to Franklin, fastening my seat belt. A car arrives at the entrance to Melanie's driveway, its headlights flashing in our mirror. Must be a relative or someone to comfort her. Good. She shouldn't be alone. "We get a boxful of documents that could be the key to who knows what."

"Yeah," Franklin replies. He steers the car out the landscaped gravel loop of Melanie's driveway. "We'll just take these puppies into the safety of our office."

"And then tomorrow, we'll try to figure how they connect to the e-mail Brad sent me."

"Right. What was in that file you had, by the way?" he asks.

The folder I kind of swiped is still in my tote bag. Melanie will never miss it. I yank it out and flip through. "Spam," I say, as bewildered as I was when I first saw the papers inside. "Weird." I flip through them again. "All spam. And all about refinancing. Although the subject line spells it r-e-f-i-g-h. Very weird."

"Not weird at all," Franklin pronounces. "Brad was looking to refinance, Melanie said so. So those spams make perfect sense." He takes the exit toward Boston. "Want me to just drop you at home?"

"Oh, no," I say, fluttering my eyelashes dramatically. "Drop me at Excelsior. On Boylston Street. I can have a couple of martinis before Andrew arrives. You know, he's that incredibly handsome and successful first-amendment lawyer I've been dating." I trill a little giggle and fluff my hair.

Franklin doesn't bat an eye.

"In your dreams," he says. "Home it is."

We drive in silence for a few moments, me contemplating my actual evening of frozen no-fat zucchini lasagna and TV. Which, despite Maysie's urgings and Franklin's loud silence, sounds terrific.

"Unless," Franklin begins again, "you'd be interested in joining me and Stephen for dinner. Our place. It'll be fine. He's a fabulous accountant, but he can never estimate how much food he's making. There's always way too much, and I know he'd love to see you again. Get to know you better."

My heart fills with affection for Franklin, a relative newcomer to my life, clearly happy with his own, and yet . . . trying to take care of me.

"Oh, no, I'll be fine," I begin to demur. Then I think—why the hell not? Friends are good.

Franklin's cell phone rings as he's setting the table. He cradles the phone between his ear and shoulder, placing forks and napkins as he listens, then hangs up.

"I'm so sorry, you two," Franklin says. "Charlotte this morning, me tonight. Gotta head to the airport and pick up a soundbite. Some bigwig flying in, no other producers to grab it." He looks at his watch. "They promised I'd be finished before nine."

"Who?" I ask. "Somebody good? Should I go with you?" I turn to look for my coat. "I should go with you."

Franklin grabs his jacket, pecks Stephen on the cheek, heads for the door. "Nope, you stay," he instructs me. "Bond. Have some more wine. Save me some—whatever that is. I'll be back before dessert."

The door slams, and Stephen and I are alone. I pull a wicker bar stool up to the kitchen counter and lean on my elbows as I watch Franklin's partner stir the contents of a bright-blue enamel pot.

"How do you manage it?" I have to ask. "You've planned this elaborate dinner, and he runs out. Do you feel—?"

Stephen cuts me off with a smile. "It's Franklin's job. He loves it. I love him. Not many emergencies in the accounting biz—chop this parsley, okay?—except around tax time. So we balance." Stephen pulls a glistening chef's knife from a chrome-and-granite rack and hands it to me. "He's coming home, and that's all I care about. Besides, beef bourguignon always tastes better reheated, right? So it's a win-win."

For a moment, I sip and chop. The only sounds are the bubbling concoction on the stove and my knife cutting through the green leaves. There was not a twinge of impatience or annoyance in Stephen's voice. No wonder he's certain Franklin's coming back. Who wouldn't want to be so—respected? Admired? Loved? Their high-ceilinged brownstone is full of flowers and framed family photos, a white cat curled contentedly on an asymmetrical red leather chair. Their place is as contemporary as their relationship, but there's something serenely old-fashioned about their commitment. Nothing temporary here.

"So." Stephen interrupts our silence. "Why are you alone?"

I look up, bewildered, midchop. "I'm not alone."

"You know what I mean," Stephen persists. "Were you ever . . . married? Engaged?"

Only Stephen could get away with going so Oprah, I suppose. My past is none of his business, but his love partner is my work partner, so maybe that makes us—cousins or something.

I take another sip of wine. "Oh, you know, married once at twenty," I begin. "Divorced. Since then? Never met the right guy, I guess. Work is . . . well, you know. There's always the next story. They chew up the days. Time disappears. Deadlines, all that."

"So you're thinking you're done? Listen, you have, what, half your life to live still? Maybe forty good years, if you're lucky?"

I should have gone home. "You're a fun guy," I say, trying for a light tone. "I can see why Franklin sticks around."

Stephen points a spoon at me. "I'm just saying." He gestures, and a gathering drop of burgundy sauce threatens the kitchen parquet. "Counting on TV is like counting on nuclear power. It works great till it blows up in your face." He goes back to stirring, looking at the stew, talking to me. "Ever think your life story is right out of a made-for-TV movie? The 'before'?"

I have to defend myself here. "Well, I help people," I pronounce. "I—fix things. Dig up the scoop, you know? Action news gets action, all that?" I attempt a little laugh. This conversation is getting a little close to the bone.

"I know that," he replies. "But I'm asking, what's the scoop on *you?* Not TV-you. You-you. Franklin says you never talk about friends. Love. You're all about work."

"You've gotta make choices," I say slowly, thinking this over. "TV is relentless. Inflexible. You want nine to five? Sell shoes. Someone who doesn't understand you have to feed the beast—well, they'll fail. I refuse to fail."

Stephen nods. "So you sacrificed . . ."

"Not 'sacrificed,'" I correct him. "I didn't really 'give up.' I—got."

"Got what?" Stephen persists. "Some Emmy statues on your bookshelf? That's all good, of course, but they're not going to be much comfort in the long run. And, from what I hear," he says with a smile, "they're not terribly obliging in the romance department."

Whoa. I look around for an exit, or at least an exit strategy. I decide, again, on diversion.

"So how did you and Franklin meet?" I ask.

Stephen bursts out laughing. "Good try," he says, nodding. "You don't want to talk about it, we won't. But you should know Franklin thinks you're special. And he worries about you."

Silence again. A plume of winey steam wafts from the pot as Stephen adds a second cup of burgundy. I stare into my glass, trying to think of something to say. But it's Stephen who continues, now looking a little sheepish.

"I'm sorry, Charlie," he apologizes. "I'm too nosy for my own good. I should work for one of those tabloid shows, or something. But I feel like I know you, now, because of Franklin. And since you—TV hotshot and all—are basically a loner, I can't stop myself from wondering why." He shrugs. "Just ignore me."

Good idea. "Maybe I'll get it right next lifetime," I reply. I hand Stephen the pile of chopped-up greens and pour myself another glass of pinot noir. Time to change the damn subject.

CHAPTER FIVE

"Hi, it's Charlie McNally. I'm away from my office or on the other line right now. Leave a message after the beep, and I'll call you back."

Beep. Call received today at 9:01 a.m.

"Ms. McNally, this is the nurse at Metro Cat Hospital. I know you planned to pick Botox up this evening, but we want to keep her a little longer. She's fine, don't worry, but we can get her temp down more quickly if she's here. When she's fully recovered, we'll drop her off at your apartment, as usual."

Poor little Toxie. I ESP her a quick kittie-get-well message, then punch in my code to retrieve the next voice mail. I instantly regret it.

"Charlie," Angela's voice rasps through my speakerphone. "Ratings, ratings, ratings! Tick, tick, tick. It's 9:06. Where are you? What's your story? Call me."

There's an inspiring way to start a workday. I glare at the phone, seething. I can't imagine anyone more irritating.

"Begone, you have no power here," I say, pointing dramatically at the receiver and channeling my best Glinda. Unfortunately we're not in Kansas, the phone does not explode and I know the wicked witch of the newsroom does indeed have power.

I stare at the phone as if it's a living creature. I wouldn't put up with this in a relationship. Someone who's disrespectful. Critical. Demanding. Unappreciative.

I'd have read the signs long ago if it were a guy.

And what would I do? I'd just dump him. Before he dumps me. So why not just handle this job the same way? I can still be married to journalism, sure. But maybe it's safer to find myself a new little love nest where the honeymoon's just beginning.

Another station, maybe. My eyes narrow, plotting. Follow your bliss, they say. Well, I did that, and apparently followed it right into a brick wall. Maybe I should just follow it another direction, let's say, across town to Channel 8. Big promotional coup for them, getting me, the award-winning et cetera, and I can give the old "sorry, Charlie" tuna line back to Angela. I smile for the first time today, imagining it. That would be so richly rewarding.

I plummet back to reality. Ten years ago, maybe. Five. But now, it would probably be the same over there. A management calculation, then a respectful but definite rejection. *She's good, of course,* some exec would say to the other. *But she's not what we need now.*

Maybe Stephen's right. I open Google and slowly type in the name. James. Elliott. Rayburn. With one more click, I could find out if Sweet Baby James is still in New England. Married? Or available?

I stare at his name. Then, deliberately, I hit Delete. Again. And again. I erase one letter at a time, until his name is gone.

My past is not my future. I've got to find a story.

I click on my computer, and my e-mail flashes into life, a flickering list of newly arrived gobbledygook and spam. Vitamins of the Stars, Instant Master's Degrees, Free Facelifts, Wall Street

Secrets to Success. I zap the junk mail almost without thinking, and imagine Brad Foreman doing the same thing.

I'm still somehow haunted by the young couple, looking to refinance their home in Lexington. Brad probably studied refi spams like these, searching for some solution to their financial predicament. Melanie never knew how he struggled. The magic never happened. Fade to black.

I wonder if I'm getting the same spams he did? Makes sense I would, since they're all sent to millions of people. I remember his had that strangely spelled heading—*refigh*—so I click down the row of e-mails, searching. And there it is.

Hello, the subject line says. *A new re-figh deal 4-u*. Just like Brad's. I click it open—then stare in confusion. The text of the e-mail is not about refinancing at all.

But *re-figh* has to mean refinancing, right? Propping my chin in my hands, I gaze at the text.

Master Bowser, you come in happy times
Here is the villain Bagot that you seek.
All of those jewels have I in my hands
Officers, look to him, hold him fast.

Master Bowser? The villain Bagot? From the language and the meter, it sounds like a play, maybe Elizabethan. I allow myself a mental high five. Mom told me majoring in Shakespeare would never be relevant in the real world.

Still, why is it in a spam about refinancing? Whoever opens it is only going to be confused, or annoyed, and then delete it.

I know all spams don't contain messages like this. This one is different.

I click back to the main screen of unread e-mails and scan down the list, looking for ones that look the same as the "Bagot" spam. I remember it started with "Hello . . ."

There's one. *Hello, a new re-figh deal* . . . I click it open.

It's another peculiar message. And it contains not a word about refinancing.

But when he tried to execute his fell purpose he found that in the order of nature it was appointed that he himself perish miserably in the encounter.

My shoulders sag. This has now lured me so far out of work mode I might as well be playing Tetris. Still, I've got ten minutes until my required appearance at Angela's inevitably mind-numbing weekly strategy meeting, so squandering a little more time in spam-world can't hurt.

I copy the entire "Bagot and Bowser" passage, then plop the whole thing into a Google search. When the results come back, I'm still in the dark. According to this, the e-mail contains dialogue from a play called *Cromwell*, circa 1790, sometimes attributed to Shakespeare. (Applause for me.) But it's nonsense. And certainly not about refinancing.

The other e-mail is from Ambrose Bierce's *Fantastic Fables*. Again, no connection to refinancing.

I stare at my computer screen as the cursor flickers provocatively. *Go on*, it's telling me. But to what?

Two strange unconnected quotes. Obscure and seemingly meaningless. Who's sending these e-mails? And why? Okay, mystery boys. I have another idea.

First, I copy the entire next speech of *Cromwell* from Google and paste it into the reply screen of the spam that sent it. I hit Send. Then I copy the entire next paragraph of the Ambrose Bierce piece, paste it into the other reply screen and zap it right back to wherever it came from.

I lean back in my chair, crossing my arms, considering my now-blank monitor. I've definitely hit the ball back through cyberspace. Question is, who's catching?

By the time Franklin and I make it through the line at Soup 'N' Salad, I've related the highlights of the Angela meeting, then, with more enthusiasm, described the whole spam mystery. Now, we're deep into theorizing what it could mean. As cheap-necktied pols head back to the gold-domed State House across the street, we snag a booth by the window, and I wait, balancing my tray, as Franklin wipes off the table with a pile of napkins.

Turns out, my salad is a disaster. "I told the guy, no croutons," I mutter, shaking my head in annoyance. "And no carrots. Can you believe this? This salad is a carbohydrate minefield."

Franklin is already chomping on his cheeseburger, ketchup spurting out the side of the seeded bun. "Ever worry about your food issues?" he asks.

"I'm not having the carb conversation again," I insist. "TV adds ten pounds and ten years. I'm not going to help it." I stab an olive with my fork and gesture at Franklin with it for emphasis. "Back to the e-mail. What about those quotes? Someone had to put them there on purpose, didn't they?"

Franklin's cleaning his hands with an antibacterial wipe. "Well," he says slowly, tossing the used wipe toward a trash container and hitting it with an effortless swish. "It could be your computer settings. Newer systems click you instantly into graphics and pictures. Does yours?"

I frown, picking through my lettuce to avoid the brown pieces. "Graphics? I never see graphics and pictures in my e-mail."

"Really?" Franklin purses his lips, considering. "Then it's your e-mail setup—it's probably on 'plain text.' That's why you're seeing those quotes. Most likely, some low-level spam prole is amusing himself by using gibberish to fill up a screen that hardly anyone will ever see—like a private e-mail joke. When we get back to the office I'll check your settings and see if they need to be corrected."

The light goes on. I understand it now. Those quotes were only revealed because my computer setup is so antiquated. Like that's my fault. But I still don't know what the quotes mean. If they mean anything. Maybe Franklin's right, they're a joke.

Yet I can't shake the feeling that it's more complicated than that. Why would someone take the time to insert obscure quotes and dialogue? And I can't be the only one with a prehistoric e-mail system, so it makes sense that someone would see it. Maybe—is even *supposed* to see it.

Whatever. We won't find any answers in Soup 'N' Salad. I've got to go back to work. Like they say, just *do* it. And instantly I see what to just do. The message light on my cell phone is flashing, so I punch in the code to get my messages. I hear the beep and then the voice.

Melanie.

"Hello, Melanie," I say, voice on a tightrope, attempting to keep the worry out of my tone. To be safe, I decided to come back to the office to call her. My cell-phone battery hates me, and I refuse to give it the satisfaction of dying in the middle of my conversation. "It's Charlie McNally, returning your call. Is everything all right?"

"Thanks, Charlie." I hear a little exhale, as if maybe she's smoking. "Do you have a moment?"

"Of course," I say. Melanie has something to tell me. Maybe it's something good, like Brad's big secret. But maybe it's something bad, like Aztratech lawyers with a federal warrant demanding the box of stolen files.

"Well, I was going through some of Bradley's things, you know?"

"Yes," I say, relieved. No warrant. "Go on."

"I finally got into his e-mail," she begins again. "He had a separate password. I hadn't known about it. But I tried—" she pauses "—I tried 'Moondance.' It was our wedding song. And that was it. So I suppose I was just looking to see if . . . I don't know. But I found a copy of that e-mail he sent you," she continues. "And it appears he sent copies of it to two other people."

My heart revs. He'd better not have e-mailed any other reporters.

"Two other people?" I say, trying to keep my voice level. What if he sent it to other reporters? "Can you—just tell me their names?"

A pause. "Well, Charlie, I don't know," she says. "If Brad wanted to keep it private, maybe it should stay that way."

I slap my palm against my forehead in frustration, and try to transmit persuasive telepathic messages to her through the phone wires. Tell. Me. The NAMES.

"Whatever you say, Melanie," I begin out loud, trying the reporter's faithful reverse-psychology ploy. "No pressure." Shifting gears, I move in for the takedown. "But I thought you wanted to know what happened to your husband, and I was just thinking those other two people would have some ideas. In fact, maybe they could really help you." And me, and our possible big story, I don't add.

Melanie doesn't answer, and I hope she's considering my unassailable logic. Finally, I hear a little sigh.

"Got a pencil?" she asks.

I sit up straight and hold the phone to my ear with one hand. With the other, I write the names I'm hoping will be our key to success.

"Okay, got it," I say. "Let me just repeat to make sure I'm correct. You said, Joshua Gelston? And Mack Briggs? *Briggs* with two Gs? *Mack* like Mack truck?"

"Right," Melanie confirms.

"Do you know who these people are?" It could be they already know what Brad wanted to tell me, that's for sure. I'll just get in touch with them, and the mystery will be solved.

"Pssst." I cover the phone mouthpiece and hiss to get Franklin's attention without letting Melanie know. "Mel-a-nie," I mouth her name noiselessly.

Franklin wrinkles his forehead; he doesn't get it. I scrawl her name on a piece of paper and hold it up. Now Franklin's interested. He gets off his phone call and rolls closer to my desk.

"What does she want?" he whispers.

I glare at him. Why do people think it's easier to have two conversations at once if one person is whispering?

Meanwhile, I've missed part of what Melanie is trying to tell me.

"I'm so sorry, someone came to the door," I fib. "You said, what again?"

"Briggs, no, I've never heard of him," Melanie answers.

So much for the easy solution.

"Josh Gelston, though," she continues. "I think he's someone Brad met at a dinner party. A teacher, or something."

"Can you read me their e-mail addresses?" I ask.

I hear some clicking on the other end.

"I apologize, Charlie," Melanie finally says. "But I don't see any addresses. Do you honestly think you could find out if these people know anything? I'd be terribly grateful if you could tell me what Brad may have confided to them."

Her voice sounds so beseeching, so needy. Of course, she's still deeply in mourning. Looking for explanations. And I'm thrilled to be able to help her. I feel just like Nancy Drew, only a whole lot older and without the blue roadster. I can't wait to start working on this.

"Give me a little time," I reply. "Let me see what I can come up with."

Charlie McNally, girl detective, on the way to get some answers. I'm buzzing up the turnpike, high on journalism, wishing my Jeep had a convertible top to put down.

There was no Mack Briggs in my Internet database, but there was an instant hit on one Joshua Ives Gelston, no DOB listed, head of the English department at the oh-so-exclusive Bexter Academy. I know that's the revered alma mater of countless moguls, hotshots, corporate patricians and even a few presidents. The school's website says he's been on the faculty for years, adviser to the honor society and Latin club, and director of the school's drama program. Sounds like an interesting old coot, but his world seems completely alien to Brad Foreman's accounting/pharmaceutical universe. Wonder what they have in common?

I carefully lift my steaming latte-to-go from the Jeep's cup holder and take a few sips while I plan my approach.

Obstacle number one: this Mr. Gelston has no idea I'm on the way. If Bexter Academy has guards, or a locked gate, that may present a problem. I'm envisioning driving blithely in, parking somewhere, sauntering into some easily recognizable building and finding Gelston's office. My plan doesn't include rent-a-cops.

Obstacle number two: this Mr. Gelston has no idea I'm on the way. So even though it's a school day, it's possible Gelston's not even there. I shake my head, dismissing the negative vibes. My plan doesn't include disappointment.

I put my latte back, carefully keeping my eyes on the road the way you're supposed to, and wonder yet again whether I should have called first. But, after debating the issue with Franklin, I decided to take my chances.

Giving a quick glance in my rearview mirror, I turn the Jeep up Bexter's winding maple-lined driveway. I have to drive slowly, the draping canopy of crimson leaves making it more like dusk than daytime. As I emerge from the shadows, a blast of sunshine flares into my line of sight.

When my vision clears, I've obviously been teleported into a photo shoot for some documentary on the lives of the rich and preppy. Impossibly adorable mop-haired teenagers perch on artfully whitewashed fences; other youngsters sprawl fetchingly on the manicured lawn. I wince in momentary confusion, startled, as something metallic shimmers just over my car's path. It's a Frisbee. A tawny-haired, argyle-sweatered boy lifts a languid hand as he retrieves it from beside the road.

Still a little unnerved from the close encounter, I steer the Jeep into a space marked Visitors. I push the gearshift into Park, which knocks the lid off my latte, spilling the last dregs of my coffee onto the passenger seat.

I scrounge into the console for my stash of napkins, remembering, too late, I used the last of them after Botox threw up on the way to the vet. All that's in there now is my disposable camera (for insurance purposes in case I get in a crash), and about a million forks and straws. In case I'm stranded someplace where they don't have forks and straws. As I'm cleaning up with a page from my reporter notebook, there's a knock at my car window.

As I buzz it down, I see Frisbee Boy (even more photogenic close up) leaning in and looking repentant. "Sorry I almost nailed you," he apologizes engagingly. "Can I help you with anything?"

And that's why, a few minutes later, I'm knocking on the burnished oak door of Landman Hall, room 117.

"Come in!" I hear. My stomach gives a little maybe-there's-a-good-story flutter. I step into possibility.

Gelston has his back to me as I enter his office. "May I help you?" he says, without turning around. He's standing behind a battered but beautiful old wooden desk, and looks as if he's trying to find something in a floor-to-ceiling bookshelf.

"Hello, Mr., uh, Professor Gelston?" I put on my humble and needy voice. "I'm Charlotte McNally from . . ."

He turns around.

It's Gregory Peck. Not old, scary Gregory Peck in *Moby Dick*, or slimy, devious Nazi Gregory Peck in *Boys from Brazil*, but the tweedy, noble, taller-than-I-am lawyer Gregory Peck in *To Kill a Mockingbird*. My favorite movie.

I take a step backward. This is not the doddering old-fashioned schoolteacher I expected.

Gregory, I mean Gelston, smiles inquiringly, charmingly, adorably. He's now giving me his full attention.

"Oh, I thought you were a student." He walks around his desk and holds out his hand. "Josh Gelston. Sorry, I'm just researching something, and . . . Well, it doesn't matter." His eyes twinkle at me. "So, Charlie McNally," he goes on. "Of course I know who you are." He looks briefly perplexed. "But—did you have an appointment?"

"Um, no, I don't—didn't." I make a valiant attempt at composure. "I know this is an unusual request, but I'm researching a story, and I think you may be able to help me with it. Do you have a moment?"

He waves me to a forest-green leather chair in front of his desk, and he sits in the one beside me. "Of course," he says, "and you have me curious. What could bring a TV reporter, with no camera, out to our neck of the woods?"

He crosses one ankle over the other knee, leaning back in his chair as if we're old friends, and looks at me expectantly. I catalog salt-and-pepper hair, tasseled loafers, broken-in corduroy pants, tattersall oxford shirt, maroon crewneck sweater with just a hint of a tie sticking out. I expect an Irish setter to come sit at his knee, a fire crackling in the background, a little Ella on the stereo. I sneak a look at his left hand. No ring.

I can't believe myself.

Then I remember. Gelston may not know about Bradley Foreman's death. Am I going to be the one to tell him a friend has died in a car crash? Although Melanie indicated they weren't exactly friends. But then again, they were e-mailing each other. Or maybe they weren't; maybe Brad just sent him that one e-mail. Why, why, why didn't I think about this in the car?

Too late now.

"I've been talking recently with Melanie Foreman," I begin carefully. "Have you . . . Did you . . ."

"Yes, I heard what happened to Brad." A shadow passes over his face, and his hazel eyes close briefly behind his tortoiseshell glasses. "I'm sure Melanie explained we were acquaintances. It's very sad. From what I know, he was a great guy." It looks as if he's going to say something else, then he stops.

"Right. That's exactly how she described your relationship." I decide to explore a little further. "But he sent me an e-mail, just before he died. You know that, correct?"

"Yes, I know that." If you like the studious English-teacher type, which I do, he's incredibly attractive, but he's giving me nothing. My turn again.

"And, well, it's kind of complicated, but I didn't read his message until after the accident. And now I'm wondering, and Melanie is wondering, what was it he wanted to tell me? I thought you might have an idea, since he sent you a copy of it."

His turn. Now he's going to spill it. Or throw me out.

Josh walks back to his desk, where, I just happen to notice, there's not one family-looking photo of any woman. Or man. When he turns around, I'm—luckily—no longer looking at his romance-free desk, but looking right at him.

"I wondered what would happen about that," he says. I can't tell from his expression what he's thinking.

"And?" I ask.

He sits back down, takes a leather book from his desk and holds it on his lap. "Well, a few, oh, weeks ago, I guess, I got a call from Brad. I did remember him from a big dinner party we both attended. We really just met in passing. So I was a bit surprised when he called. Anyway, he said he had a box of files he was going to send to my home, and some references he wanted me to check."

"References? Check?" I'm confused, then realize maybe Franklin was right. "Like job references?" I ask.

"Job . . . ? No. Not like that." Josh smiles and points to his own chest. "English teacher, remember? Literary references. So I said, sure, I'd be glad to try to help him. He read me the lines, though, and they weren't familiar, so I asked him to e-mail them to me. I never figured out why he didn't research them himself. Anyway. I looked them up, and e-mailed him back the results. It happened a couple of times, maybe three. And that was the end of that."

I take out my notebook and flip it open. "Do you mind telling me what the quotes were?"

"I guess it's fine," Josh says slowly, apparently weighing any possible consequences. He holds up the book. "In fact, I was looking back on one of them now." He runs a finger down what I guess is the table of contents, hunting for the page.

"Here's the last quote he sent," Josh says. He begins to read:

"The cloud-capped towers, the gorgeous palaces,
The solemn temples, the great globe itself,

Yea, all which it inherit, shall dissolve;
And like this insubstantial pageant faded,
Leave not a rack behind."

He puts a finger in the book to mark his place and looks up at me, starts to say something.

I can't help but interrupt. "*The Tempest*, huh?"

And then, I almost burst out laughing. I don't think I've ever actually seen anyone's jaw literally drop. But Josh's jaw does, and now he's trying to recover.

"I'm sorry," he says, eyes widening. "Of course I've seen your investigative stories, but I didn't have you pegged as a Shakespeare buff."

He is so very, very cute. And so flatteringly sweet, remembering me from TV. I know it's a big journalism "don't" to flirt on the job, but there can't be any harm in being friendly, right? Well, there actually can, but I'm promising myself I won't cross the line.

"My mother always warned me my major in Shakespeare would make me unemployable," I tell him, attempting to look charming and well educated, but not too self-satisfied. "But from time to time, it comes in handy."

"Impressive," he says. He clamps the book closed. "But anyway, that was one of the quotes. He wanted me to identify each one and then tell him the next two lines."

"'We are such stuff/As dreams are made on, and our little life/Is rounded with a sleep,'" I quote back. "That's what's next, isn't it?"

"Very good." Josh nods in professorial admiration. "Who knew you TV types had hidden depths?"

I can see little laugh crinkles behind his glasses, and he absently brushes away a shock of barber-needy hair that's fallen onto his forehead. I calculate there's more salt than pepper, and that he must be early fifties, maybe mid. I can feel "the line" getting fainter and fainter.

"Wait," he says. "Let me show you another quote he sent. This one's tougher."

I watch as he gets up and turns back to the bookcase, moving his hand slowly across a shelf of multicolored covers. There's laughter out in the hallway; somewhere a door slams. It feels . . . familiar.

I've been here before? No. It was years ago.

It was the day I met James. Sweet Baby James.

My hair was still dark brown back then, parted Steinem-style down the middle, pulled back into a ponytail. My skirt was unimaginably short. Not that it mattered. I was Charlotte Ann McNally, radio reporter. First real job out of college, no contract, five dollars an hour. My mind was racing with my looming deadline, wondering how I could explain the state's newly passed clean-water law in a thirty-second story.

Then, I heard laughter out in the hallway; somewhere a door slammed. I felt someone enter the room, and turned around. Even now, I remember I had to steady myself on the back of my chair. Cheekbones. Pinstripes. A smile that wrapped me in promise. I hadn't even heard his voice. And who cared what he said in the interview. Deadlines melted, time evaporated, sound disappeared.

I wore a pink Ultrasuede suit and white stockings to our wedding—just a few months later—in a fluorescent-chilled clerk's office at City Hall. I could see nothing in my future but that handsome face. For months, his astonishing looks distracted me from what I decided was his astonishingly manipulative lifestyle. Eventually, as I got into the book behind his glossy cover, I found it was less a romance and more an autobiography. All about himself.

Half-empty/half-full? Life with James, I soon decided, meant it was always half-empty, and my responsibility to make it full again.

He wanted to change the world, except for the part behind our apartment door.

His work? Valuable and worthwhile. My work? Fine as long as I was home to make dinner. His long hours? Valuable and worthwhile. My long hours? Proof I only cared about my career. My hard-won job interview at Channel 3? A pitiful attempt to match his public success. My Sweet Baby James turned out to be just a baby. I grew up and he didn't. Which is exactly what I told him.

He told me I was married to my career, not to him. He wanted children; I wanted to wait. Which of us, he sneered, was the grown-up?

As it turned out, I left behind the array of trendy appliances I'd purchased to prove my homemaking prowess. I kept my collection of Tina Turner albums, Gramma's good china, and my dedication to journalism. Every time I placed a new Emmy on my bookshelves, it was a shining reassurance I had made the right choice. Career. Success. Still, tucked into my emotional hope chest, I always thought I preserved the right to choose again. Now I wonder—was I wrong? Now I wonder—has *for now* turned into *forever?*

What would happen, I find myself speculating, if I just glide into happy talk with this guy. What if I forget what happened to Brad, forget about Franklin back at the station, forget about wrinkle-free Cyndi from Cincinnati who's no doubt packing her extensive hair-spray and eye-shadow collection in preparation for her foray into my job territory. Get out while the getting's good. While it's still my decision.

CHAPTER SIX

Just as I'm considering whether a second marriage at my age means no bridesmaids, Josh brings me back to reality.

The moment he begins to read the quote he looked up, it's *my* jaw that drops. If I hadn't been so distracted by my theoretical future with a certain schoolteacher, I probably would have predicted it.

"Master Bowser, you come in happy times . . ." Josh is saying.

It's Bowser and Bagot.

My brain begins racing faster than my mouth can form the words, and I know I'm not finishing any sentences.

Josh has turned his chair to face me, and his eyes are locked into mine. He nods intently, listening, as I spill out what I know: Brad's collection of company files; the refinancing spams; the obscure quotes, including Bagot and Bowser; my search through Google and my experimental e-mails in reply.

"And here's what makes it even stranger." I'm winding up now, hoping I'm making sense. "I checked the new e-mails I got back, and each of the spam addresses I sent a quote to sent me back another e-mail. With another quote."

"But it's spam, isn't it?" he asks, looking perplexed. "The whole essence of spam is that it's random, nonspecific. Blasted out to everyone, like junk mail. Everyone gets the same thing."

I nod in agreement. "Absolutely. It doesn't make sense."

We both pause. The room is quiet; the golden afternoon light filters through the walnut-rimmed windows, lighting the thick dark-green rug with a patch of color.

"Let's go back to the beginning," I suggest. "I sent back the completed quotes as sort of . . . a lark, you know? I didn't really think I'd get a reply."

"Right," says Josh.

"So . . ." I pause to get my thoughts in order. "I'm wondering if that's what Brad did, too. And if he did, whether that's when he discovered something."

"Discovered what?"

"Well, that's the question." I get up and start to pace around the bookshelf-lined office. I focus on the thick carpeting, thinking.

When I look up, Josh is staring at me. Good staring. Over-the-journalism-line staring. He fidgets, caught, then pretends the moment never happened.

"All right, let's see," he continues. He's ticking off points on his fingers. "Brad had a cache of files. He asks me to dig up some obscure quotes. He writes to you, apparently with something to reveal. Then, there's a car accident. Police think it's suicide. And his wife tells you her husband was worried about something." He shrugs. "That's as far as I get."

From somewhere, I hear the theme music from *To Kill a Mockingbird*. And then, from somewhere, I get an idea.

"Josh," I say, "do you know a Mack Briggs?"

Josh raises his eyebrows. "Mack Briggs? Like a Mack truck?"

"Far as I know," I answer. "At least that's what Melanie said. She told me Brad sent this 'Briggs' the same e-mail he sent us."

But Josh shakes his head. "Never heard of him."

Every door in the journalism universe simultaneously slams shut. Maybe Brad's secret just died with Brad. But I have to ask one more question.

"Back to why I'm here," I say. "Did Brad ever mention any, say, inappropriate or illegal financial dealings at Aztratech?"

Josh looks surprised, and then surprises me by laughing.

"Well, there's a bombshell." Josh pretends to do a double take. "Where'd you come up with that one?"

I'm clearly putting my full hand on the table now, though I can't quite remember when I decided to go all the way. Within a few minutes, he hears all about Franklin's research, the lawsuit against Aztratech and our theory that Brad might be a whistle-blower.

His face evolves from skeptical to impressed. "Sounds . . . plausible," he finally says. "But did you ask Melanie? I mean, if Brad was ready to rat out his employer to the feds, as you so colloquially put it, wouldn't he have told his wife?"

"You'd think so," I reply. "But she says no."

Both of us pause, and in that quiet moment, I swear I hear bells. In fact, I know I recognize Beethoven's Ninth Symphony. Then I realize Josh hears it, too.

"'Ode to Joy.'" He waves a hand toward his window, smiling. "On the school's carillon. Means classes are over for the day. Time for all good students to head for the dorms. Or the football field, or wherever."

"And time for me to go, too, I guess." I rummage in my purse for a business card. I also send a swift prayer to Saint Maysie, patron of happy romantic endings. "Here's my number if you think of anything," I say. "Thank you so much."

He takes the card. And Saint Maysie answers my plea.

"Um, Charlie," Josh begins, coming around from behind his desk. "You know I'm the adviser to the drama department?"

I'm gratified to see he's now the one looking uneasy.

"Anyway," he continues, "this Thursday, we're having our student performance of 'The Gold-Bug.' Edgar Allan Poe, remember?" He hands me a black-and-white playbill, its cover amateurish but adorable artwork. "It ain't Shakespeare, but you still might get a kick out of it. I hope this isn't out of line, but the kids have really worked hard and . . ." He looks at me quizzically. "Can you make dates with people you interview?"

Franklin jumps from his chair, following me to the coatrack as I hang up my jacket. I'm still floating in a romance-novel haze, but the usually perceptive Franklin seems focused on his own agenda.

"What in hell were you doing?" he grills me. "What the hell took you so long?" His accent transforms *hell* into *hay-ull*, which makes it somewhat less threatening. Anyway, I know he's not really angry—this is his "I have something interesting to tell you" mode.

"I'll give you the lowdown," I promise, "but what's up with you? You look like you're sitting on something hot."

"It's not me, it's one Mr. Wesley Rasmussen who will soon be in the hot seat," Franklin says.

"Wesley Ras . . . ?"

"Rasmussen, Rasmussen," Franklin repeats, grinning. "CEO of Aztratech. And here's the scoop. He's going to do an interview with you about the pharmaceutical whistle-blowing case."

"No way," I say, plopping down in my chair. I swivel toward Franklin. "It's in litigation. His lawyers wouldn't allow it." I urge my brain to move faster, consider the options. "I mean, he's got nothing to gain, right? Sure, he might want to tell his company's side of the story. But if the feds think Aztratech is ripping off taxpayers, going on camera seems like a losing proposition."

"Here's what happened," Franklin says. "I called him, said we were doing a survey of all local pharmaceutical companies. Research on drug pricing, whether drug companies may be overcharging the government. He's huffy and dismissive, says, 'Oh, that's all nonsense, media hype.' So I'm all apologetic, yeah well, da da da, our bosses say we have to do this story."

"So he doesn't know we know about the lawsuit," I say, realizing what Franklin didn't tell him.

"Right." Franklin smiles. "I figured we don't have to give him everything, you know? It's not like it's news to him there's a lawsuit. You start out with one of your wide-eyed-little-girl interviews, see what he tells us. Then hit him with the big one."

Course they don't teach in J-school: Getting the Interview—The Art of Omission.

"Ask if he knows who the whistle-blower is." I nod. "Sure. It could work. When's the interview?"

"I'm hoping today, even though it's late-ish. Calling him now to confirm it." Franklin turns to the phone.

While Franklin calls Aztratech, I do a quick spam check. It looks as if every one I answered sent me a response.

Franklin had updated my computer settings and showed me how, with my monitor set properly, the same weird spams display fancy graphics of dollar signs and houses for sale. I switch my system back to the old way. I want to see the quotes instead.

I click on the first *Hello, a new re-figh deal for you* . . . With a flash of white, the screen changes to the now-familiar typeface, and this time, what's clearly part of an address.

Vermont Songwriters Association, RD 2 Box

Fine. I know the drill. Into Google it goes, and out comes *Vermont Songwriters Association, RD 2 Box 277 Underhill VT. 05489.*

I am one hundred percent mystified. Am I playing a game? Or is someone else playing a game? Or is there even a game?

I copy and paste the full address, and send it back. Just one more, I promise myself. I click on the next *Hello, a new re-figh deal for you.*

The hard drive spins as it pulls the e-mail from cyberspace. A blank screen, followed by words. And then, a trapdoor under my chair opens, and I spiral though the blackness, rabbits with pocket watches going by, Mad Hatters, dormouses. Dormice. At my desk, things get curiouser and curiouser.

The cloud-capped towers, the gorgeous palaces . . . It's *The Tempest.* The same quote Brad sent Josh.

My fingers still resting on the keyboard, I stare at the monitor. It hums tauntingly, daring me to understand.

The only thing that's clear: I've gotten exactly the same e-mails Brad did. I sent back the second half of a quote, and whoever got it sent me this in reply. Just the way, I bet, they did to Brad. Was the bottom of Brad's rabbit hole a miserable rain-soaked morning and the crash of metal? Suicide because of what he found? Or something else?

I sit up and shake my head to clear it. There's no rabbit hole. Spam is just spam. But I cut and paste the rest of the *Tempest* quotation just in case. *We are such stuff as dreams are made on.* And once again, I hit SEND.

Franklin clatters down the phone and hands me a piece of paper. "Here's the directions to Aztratech," he says. "Rasmussen's all set. Your photographer is Walt." He looks apologetic. "Sorry. No choice. He'll meet you in front of the station in five."

I gather up my stuff and turn for the door. "This'll be good," I say enthusiastically, tucking a notebook in my bag. "Even with Slo-mo Walt. I'll call you as soon as it's over."

"Hey," Franklin calls after me.

I turn around, impatient. "What? I'm all set. I'm outta here."

Franklin is standing by his desk, hands on hips. "Before you head to your big 'get,'" he says, "you want to tell me about whatever it was that happened at Bexter this afternoon? Whatever secrets you're keeping from me?"

"No secrets," I sort of lie. "I, uh, just interviewed Professor Gelston, who's really not that much of a geezer, turns out. . . ." I trail off, tongue-tied even trying to explain it.

"You're blushing, girl," Franklin reports. "'Nuff said."

I know Tyra Banks can't possibly work at Aztratech, but the lanky fashionista emerging from the elevator's polished doors into the high-tech lobby is a real-life photocopy of the supermodel. Her carefully cropped hair, with just a smattering of silver, her got-to-be designer suit with its black ribbon belt tied artfully around the waist, her charcoal suede pumps.

"Charlie McNally? I'm Gwen Matherton, Mr. Rasmussen's assistant." She looks at her sleek watch. "He's running a little behind today, I'm afraid," she adds, with a look I translate as *he's really an important, busy guy, you're lucky to see him, you're not going to be allowed much time.* "So set up your equipment, then I'll bring him in."

Fifteen stories up, Wes Rasmussen's mahogany-and-steel office looks like a movie set, skillfully designed to suggest Big Commerce. Big Responsibility. Big Money.

Gwen leaves us alone, saying she'll be back in ten minutes. Walt, with much exaggerated clanking of equipment (clearly to prove how hard he's working), sets up his lights and clicks his camera onto the tripod.

I survey the room, looking for insight into this mogul. Awards, degrees: none. Family photographs: zero. Desk mountained with papers, and a leatherbound row of books held up by snarling brass lions. Nothing personal—no, wait. Recessed into the paneled wall in front of me is one cabinet, pin-spotted to show off the one thing it contains: a fantastically intricate model of a wooden sailboat, canvas sails unfurled. Before I can check it out, I hear the door open.

Now I know why Wes Rasmussen, CEO of one of the most go-go pharmaceutical companies in New England, is pressed for time. He's obviously got an important meeting coming up—in the clubhouse. He's wearing a yellow polo shirt, khaki pants, boat shoes with no socks. For someone whose corporate power is legendary, at least according to the background material Franklin gave me, this guy looks like someone who can't wait to get out of the office and into a comfortable golf cart.

I shake his wooly-mammoth hand as we introduce ourselves, and he waves me to a chair. He pushes a button on his desk and a panel in the wall slides open. He pulls out a navy blazer, putting it on over his knit shirt, as the hidden closet slides shut.

"This'll do for TV, won't it?" he asks. He has the air of someone who's not used to anyone saying no. "You don't want much from me, I imagine." He sits behind his desk and looks at me inquiringly. "Now, what can I do for you?"

Walt clicks the microphone onto Rasmussen's lapel, then goes back to his camera. "Rolling," he announces.

"Okay," I begin with a benign smile. "First, Mr. Rasmussen, how would you characterize the current pricing controversy?" I always ask easy, noncontentious, open-ended questions first. Brings their guard down.

Rasmussen spreads his arms expansively across his desk. "Ms. McNally," he says, "the pharmaceutical industry is one hundred percent focused on keeping America and the world as healthy as humanly possible. We partner with the federal government to provide life-saving medications to underprivileged folk who can't afford them. It's a system that works to everyone's benefit."

He smiles at me, as if I'm some fifth-grader, and starts to stand up. "Got it?"

"Mr. Rasmussen," I say, smiling in pretend apology, and gesture to him to sit back down. "Forgive me, just a couple more quick questions. My producer told me to ask you, you know?" My trusty "just an employee" technique.

He puffs with noblesse oblige, deigning to give the girl a chance.

"So to clarify," I say. "How would you answer criticism that pharmaceutical companies like yours are making an unsuitable profit on government contracts, all at taxpayer expense?"

I get the fifth-grader expression again. "Ms. McNally," he says, "the pharmaceutical industry is one hundred percent focused on keeping America and the world as healthy as humanly possible. . . ."

He continues, giving word for word the same answer he did the first time. I almost laugh out loud. Obviously, Rasmussen has a prepared statement, which he's memorized and tried to make sound spontaneous. That doesn't work so well when you give the exact same statement a second time.

"As you said before," I acknowledge. "But what I'm asking is, does your company, in order to increase profits, charge excessively high prices for government contracts because taxpayers foot the bill?"

Rasmussen scowls, and I can see him assessing how to handle this. He'll look guilty if he throws me out or cuts off the interview with the camera rolling.

"Ms. McNally," he finally says, "the pharmaceutical industry is one hundred percent focused on . . ."

I interrupt. "Mr. Rasmussen, thanks so much, we have that." Time to pitch him the biggie. "But what's your specific answer to the allegation that your company is defrauding the government?"

"Uh, Charlie," I hear from behind me. "Wait a second." It's Walt.

What the hell now?

I smile brightly at the increasingly uncomfortable CEO. "Technical difficulties, I think," I say, acting as if this is nothing.

Walt's moved away from the camera. "Camera battery's dead," he says. "Gotta get another one."

"There's one in your bag, correct?" I am going to kill him if there isn't.

He shakes his head. "Gotta go to the car."

As he saunters away, I realize a new battery is fifteen stories down, fifteen stories back up. If I can't keep Rasmussen at his desk, the battery isn't the only thing that's dead. So's this interview. And my career.

"Mr. Rasmussen," I begin, life-support systems full throttle, "let me just give you my condolences for your employee Brad Foreman."

Rasmussen leans back in his chair, props an ankle over a knee. "Well, thank you, yes. We were all very surprised, of course."

"Did you know him well?" I continue. It's a tacky question, but I'm a reporter and he certainly thinks we're all tacky anyway.

Fifth-grader look again. Fifth-grader on the way to the principal's office, if I read him correctly. He actually harrumphs.

"Not really," he says. "One of my headhunters found him in a search for second-tier employees. Office wasn't on this floor, of course."

Rasmussen is obviously putting as much space as he can between them. But I'm thinking if he suspects Foreman is the whistleblower, he'll characterize him as some sort of know-nothing, someone with no access and no possible knowledge of pricing practices.

The CEO doesn't disappoint me.

"Foreman wasn't a decision maker by any means," Rasmussen continues. He gives a patriarchal wave. "Just a number cruncher. But you know, there's always room for worker bees. Sorry, of course, about what happened to him."

He pauses, then his tone changes. Very cagey. "I understand police think it was suicide. Have you heard anything?"

Oh, right, Mr. CEO, you're my best friend now. You're pumping me, trying to find out what I know. That means there's something to know. I just don't know what it is. Yet.

"Oh, goodness, no, I don't know anything about that." Where the hell is Walt? I can't really vamp much longer. "Anyway, let's see . . ." I pretend to flip through my notes.

"Rolling," I hear from behind me. The return of Walt. Saved.

"Anyway, Mr. Rasmussen, we're taping again." I gesture to him that we're beginning. "Let me ask you about the lawsuits filed against Aztratech. . . ."

His eyes go icy. He does not like this question. And that means it's a very good question.

"Ms. McNally, I have no idea what you're referring to."

"The whistle-blower suit which charges—"

"If there were a lawsuit," he interrupts, "I would not discuss it. Hear me now, I'm not saying there is a lawsuit. But if there were, I would say nothing about it. And if your colleague had been honest enough to tell me the real reason you wanted this interview, I would have certainly said no."

He shakes his head in infinite disdain. "Television," he says, sneering at me.

I can take it. "Well, let me show you this, Mr. Rasmussen." I bring out a copy of the lawsuit, placing it in front of him. "In this complaint against your company, a whistle-blower claims to have invoices that prove—"

Rasmussen stands up, the microphone cord yanking down the lapel of his jacket. I love this. If he rips off the mike and storms out, it'll be great TV.

Do it, Wes.

He doesn't.

"Let's just turn off the camera, shall we?" he asks, sitting back down.

Here we go again. Clearly I'm hexed by some sort of journalism jinx.

I turn to Walt and slash my neck with a finger. "Cut," I mouth the word silently.

"Good." Rasmussen regains his composure, leans back in his chair. "Now, Ms. McNally, this is one hundred percent off the record. But let me assure you it's for your own good."

He steeples his fingers in what he probably imagines is a power gesture. "These so-called whistle-blowers," he says, "are simply con artists. Blowing whistles? I say they're blowing smoke." He smiles, at his own clever wordplay, I guess.

"Allow me to give you some advice, Ms. McNally," he says conspiratorially. "I admire your work, and I don't like to see you wasting your time, let alone being misled by some crackpot lawsuit. Anyone can pay some lawyer to file a stack of papers in court, but if some number cruncher says we're in any way involved in improper pricing procedures, well, hear me now, he's wrong. Dead wrong."

Rasmussen unclips the mike from his lapel and puts it on his desk. Smart guy. He knows Walt's camera is still off. This time he stands up and stays up. "We're done here, Ms. McNally."

CHAPTER SEVEN

The entire dayside crew has gone by the time I return to Channel 3, but faithful Franklin is waiting for me, standing at the video screening machine outside our office. I'd filled him in on the interview from the car, including my suspicions about the wily Mr. Rasmussen. Now I slide in the interview tape and push Rewind.

Numbers on the digital counter fly by in reverse as the videotape rolls back. At zero-zero-zero, I push Play.

"Wait a minute." I squint as an unexpected scene pops into view. "I didn't know Walt shot this. Must have been when I was hanging up my coat."

The camera pans Rasmussen's entire office, the glass door, the monolith of a desk, the sleek paneled walls. We see the piercing blue light illuminating the glass-encased sailboat. As the boat comes center screen, the camera movement stops.

"Shit. Son of a bitch."

Franklin and I look at each other. The room on tape is empty. And neither of us has said a word. Then it hits us simultaneously and we burst into laughter.

"It's Walt," I say, still giggling. "He forgot the camera audio was recording."

"Son of a bitch," we hear again. Walt's behind the camera, of course, so we don't see him. Then we hear something unzip, some bumping noises, then a zip again. "Well," the voice says, "she'll just have to talk fast. I'm sure as hell not going to go all the way back down there to get another battery."

"I can't stand it," I moan. "He knew, he knew all along he didn't have another battery."

The video continues, but I push Pause. "Look right there," I say. "Hard to see, but there's a closet hidden in the wall. Rasmussen hit a button on his desk, and it opened right up."

"Neat." Franklin takes off his glasses to look closer, then pushes Play again.

The camera continues around the room, and lands on the sailboat again.

The camera goes infuriatingly out of focus.

"Even with the rotten video," he says, "you can tell that boat's a beauty. Expensive, too. You know, I've seen some articles about this—social-climbing corporate execs buying elaborate boats. Apparently yacht racing is the new polo."

"You think it belongs to Rasmussen?" I ask, an idea slowly coalescing. "If it does, where'd he get the money to buy it? Or listen, what if he's actually the whistle-blower himself?"

"That'd be a cool twist," Franklin agrees. "Great story, too."

"Okay, look," I say. "It's easy enough for us to run down the ownership trail of this beauty, right? And then who knows? Is the name of the boat visible?"

Franklin puts his nose up to the screen, then pulls away. "It's just too fuzzy. But you're right—if we could track down who owns it, that could be a gold mine."

"Hey, yo." I hear a voice behind me as the doors to Special Projects click open.

Teddy Sheehan, Red Sox cap turned backward on his head and

wearing his usual coffee-stained khakis, lumbers toward us. He's the morning producer, but Franklin thinks he never goes home. I think he may be so in love with TV news, he'd rather live at the station. I've never been here when he isn't.

Teddy sets down the black plastic box of videocassettes he's returning to our archive shelf, and steps closer to the screen. "Cool," he says. "The *Miranda.* Video sucks, though," he assesses. "Don't bring that junk into the edit booth, dudes."

"The—are you saying you recognize this boat?" I ask.

"Hell, yeah. The *Miranda.* Sleek and fast as hell. Cost millions. She almost won the America's Cup last go-round. Got beat in a close heat by the Australians."

"You sure?" Franklin persists.

"Watched start to finish on ESPN," Teddy assures us. "What else can I do you for?"

Franklin and I exchange glances. We've gotten an answer, I guess. Not that we know what it means.

"Well, you're certainly a full-service producer," I say, giving Teddy a thumbs-up.

He turns his cap around, putting the bill in the front, and then tips it at us. "No prob," he says. "TV is my life."

As he picks up his batch of file tapes and heads to the library shelf, I pop our yellow cassette from the viewer and hand it to Franklin.

"First thing tomorrow, we're doing *Miranda* research," I say. "But now, I vote we head out. I've got a date with some leftover Chinese food."

Not again.

Even though I'm pretty sure it's a false alarm, my heart flutters in fear as I arrive home. There's a lineup of fire trucks, scurrying firefighters, swirling red lights. They're in front of my building on the flat of Beacon Hill, a graceful but quirky brownstone tucked behind the old fire station where they filmed the old *Spenser: For Hire* TV show.

I scan for smoke. Flames. Nothing.

I hurry to join the cluster of my evacuated fellow condo dwellers gathered behind the fire trucks converged on Mt. Vernon Square. Most are focused on the building, others are trying to keep their kids off the gleaming yellow ladder truck, one teenager struggling to control a squirming puppy.

No firefighters are running. Good sign.

Still, this is when it would pay to know your neighbors by name. My mental Miss Manners jabs me with a reproving elbow as I approach—I think it's the woman in 2B, Mrs. Milavec?

"'Scuse me," I say. "I just got home. Please tell me it's the—"

"Yeah," she replies, looking annoyed. "Again."

I can't take it. Every time our astonishingly oversensitive smoke alarm blares the building into panic, I frantically grab all that's precious—Botox, my photo albums (including the one existing snapshot of my wedding, which I can't bring myself to destroy), Gramma's jewelry box and Cinnamon, my battered little stuffed pony, faithful friend since age three and crucial good luck charm. If they don't fix this thing, I'm going to store all my valuables in a box by my front door.

"All clear, folks." A white-helmeted deputy signals we can go back inside, as the firefighters clamber onto their trucks and the engines rumble away up Charles Street.

I join the muttering crowd trudging into our building and hear the slamming of doors closing each of us back into our separate lives.

Finally.

Once inside, I scoop up the latest pile of bills and junk from the floor, and make today's contribution to the expanding mountain of mail and *New Yorker*s on my dining room table. As I toss my coat over a dining room chair, I wonder again why I spent so much money on furniture that I now only use as a spare closet and junk-mail storage.

My living room's gorgeous, too.

Deep-cushioned navy leather couch. Cozy. Sexy. Voluptuously upholstered wing chairs. Casually elegant glass coffee table placed perfectly in front of the fireplace. All artfully arranged to create the perfect backdrop for a woman-about-town. That's what Decorator Don told me, at least. And it's even possible that someday, that'll all be true. Botox loves the chairs, at least.

I pad back to where I really live—my combination study and bedroom. Double rows of books crammed onto the shelves, more stacks of magazines, an array of framed photographs covering one wall—Dad when he was a cub reporter, Mom's sorority, Gramma and Grampa's Gatsby-looking wedding, a few Baby Charlies, a chubby adolescent gap-toothed me with a pony and grown-up me with a couple of movie stars, a general and two presidents.

I stop to examine me with the general, calculating it was taken, what? Five years ago? I analyze my jawline, my waistline, the lines in my face. Why didn't I realize I looked fine back then? I always thought I could look better tomorrow. Now it's tomorrow, and I forgot to be happy yesterday.

I punch my code into the speakerphone on my desk as I peel off my sweater and toss it in the dry-cleaner pile. Messages.

"Beep. Message received Tuesday at 7:45 p.m."

I click my skirt onto its hanger, but before I can put it back into the closet, I stop, midhang, focused on a voice I instantly recognize.

"Hey, Charlie, it's Josh Gelston. Just checking in about Thursday.

Hope we're still on. You can meet me at Bexter Auditorium, as we planned, and you can sit backstage. There's a cast party after. See you around seven."

The machine begins its whir toward the next message, but my mind, swirling with memories, is rewinding to this afternoon. And then forward, to Thursday around seven.

And then, back to reality.

"Beep. Message received Tuesday at 8:02 p.m."

"Charlie, Angela. The promotion department tells me you haven't submitted your sweeps schedule. We're up against a deadline, you know. We'll continue this tomorrow."

I sit up and punch the speaker off. I'm home. There's no fire. I have a date with a real possibility. With a flutter of memory, I dig in my bag for the "Gold-Bug" program Josh gave me, smoothing the cover, then scanning for his name. *Professor Joshua Ives Gelston*, I read. *Producer and Drama coach—Board Member, Bexter Academy.* I feel myself smiling. Maybe we can produce some interesting drama together. Wonder what Maysie will think.

With a flourish, I delete the last phone message. Angela can wait.

CHAPTER EIGHT

My desk phone is ringing, an incoming text is pinging and the intern twins from the promotion department are hovering at my office door. Franklin doesn't take his eyes off his computer monitor as I arrive for work, but he sticks out one arm, pointing toward the hallway. "Printer," he says.

I recognize this as Franklin's shorthand for "I just printed something interesting and since you're out there, go pick it up." This definitely trumps the phone, the text and the twins.

I turn to retrieve Franklin's stuff, but the interns are faster.

"We're here to get the list of your sweeps story ideas," says the one in the lavender angora. She runs a tiny hand through her strawberry-blond mop, flipping her too-long bangs briefly out of her face.

I notice the pink peek of skin between the sweater and her low-rider cargoes and wonder if she has a full-length mirror in her dorm room. Her sidekick is resplendent in pale blue nail polish, and with an equally dress-for-access tummy. They're both wearing sandals. In October.

"They told us to come pick it up?" she puts in. "That, like, you'd have it for us? It was due, like, today?" She looks at me as if I'm supposed to know what she's talking about.

The energy of the room suddenly goes dark, and I see the twins scoot closer together, huddling like delicate forest creatures sensing danger. Franklin looks up, questioning. And then, without a sound, Angela appears in our office.

"I've come from the meeting," she says quietly. She says it like "THE MEETING." The forest creatures cringe farther into the corner.

"We're all wondering," she goes on, her voice brittle with power, "about your sweeps story ideas." She looks down at her clipboard, apparently ticking off some list. "Healthcast sent in their proposals, so did Sports, Envirobeat and Dollarwise. But we can't plan our ratings book schedule until we hear from you, Charlie. I texted you. I called you. Is there—a problem?"

She looks as if she hopes there is.

"I, um, we're . . ." I know I can finish this sentence. I just have to decide on my tactics. And fast.

Thank goodness Franklin is faster.

"Printer," he says again.

"As I was going to say," I continue, praying I understand Franklin's shorthand, "we've just finished with the story list, and it's on the printer."

"Ten copies," Franklin adds.

The news bunnies perk back into life, puffing up their angora and tossing their hair.

"We'll—" one chirps.

"Get them," says the other.

They're gone, leaving only the faint scent of some trendy perfume behind.

Angela's curls briefly turn to serpents, just long enough for me to notice, then back to her ordinary tangle.

"Thanks, Charlie," she says. "I'll let you know what we decide." She turns to go, then turns back, with what apparently is supposed to be a smile.

"We're counting on you, you know," she says. "If your stories are good enough, we could have a solid win this time. No pressure, ha-ha." Angela waves her clipboard and gives her patented exit line. "Ciao, newsies."

I flop into my chair and deflate in frustration. *My* stories? They're making *me* responsible for the ratings of the entire TV station?

"Wow, Franko," I say, remembering my manners. "Great move."

"No problem," he says, waving me off. "My job."

"But listen," I say. "What did you put on that list, anyway? Stories we can actually do?"

"Definitely," Franklin replies. "You had most of the ideas, as usual. Trucking safety, off-campus housing, those newsbreak stories you were talking about the other morning, remember?"

"Good work," I tell him. "Did you include the whistle-blower story?"

Periwinkle Toes is back at our door. She's carrying a piece of paper, looking back and forth between me and Franklin.

"Like, um, here's some other stuff that was on the printer? For you guys?"

"I'll take it," Franklin says, holding out a hand. He glances at the paper and smiles. "This is what I was trying to tell you before storylist-gate. I think there may be something going on at Aztratech. Something Brad Foreman may have latched onto."

"What? How? How do you know? Can I see? Show me the . . ." I begin. Then there's a little tap on our open door.

"Um, Miss McNally?" The intern is still hovering. "I'm Hayley Coffman, I'm a senior at BU?"

Of course you are, dear. Majoring in what, Abs 101?

"Yes?" is what I actually say, looking up at her. Ten seconds, she's got ten seconds.

"I hope I'm not taking up too much of your time, but I was wondering if I might interview you. For a paper I'm doing on how successful women journalists began their careers? Like what obstacles they had to overcome, that kind of thing. You're so—like, I mean, I've watched you ever since I was little. Professor Shaplen shows your tapes in class all the time." She gives a little gulp. "And I want to be just like you."

Franklin swivels out of the conversation, and I feel my eyes—and my heart—go a little soft.

Hayley wants to hear about obstacles. She doesn't know it, but she just encountered her first. And I'm responsible for it. I'd written her off, based only on her toes and her tummy.

She's certainly intelligent enough, confident enough, to ask for advice. I've been whining about how unfair it is that your TV face dictates your TV future. So what do I do? The same thing in reverse. If I can do it to her, why am I surprised when they do it to me? What's even more disconcerting—have I become what I fear?

"Of course I'll do an interview," I tell her. "I'm flattered and honored you would think of me." This rings disarmingly true, and somehow bittersweet. "Here's my direct phone number," I say, handing my card to the younger generation. "I'm happy to help." This is true, too.

With a shy smile, Hayley tucks my card into her jeans and skitters away into her world full of possibilities.

"She was kind of adorable, really, wasn't she, Franklin?" I say, getting up to watch her go. I turn back to face him. "And, you know, so earnest and eager? Like me, kind of, back in the day."

Franklin logs off his computer, glances at me sideways. "I'd have loved to see you in that getup, if that's true," he says.

"That's not what I mean, you—"

Franklin goes on talking. "If you're finished with the Charlie fan club meeting," he says, "we need more info on the ownership of the *Miranda*." He tucks a piece of paper in his back pocket. "And here's how we're going to get it."

"Boat ownership, sure," I reply, cutting him off. "Coast Guard. But aren't those records in D.C.? Or Annapolis, or someplace like that?"

"Not anymore," Franklin says with a raised finger. He makes a mark in the air. "Score one for the producer kid. And as a result, you're gonna have to get your coat—and trust me."

"Miss?" A gray-uniformed officer points me to the metal detector, gesturing me to put my purse on the conveyor. When Franklin announced we were researching the *Miranda*'s ownership at the Coast Guard's waterfront headquarters, I forgot we'd be X-rayed and patted down.

I do a warp-speed inventory of what's in my bag, in case there's anything embarrassing (feminine hygiene), or illegal (my contraband pepper spray) or both (the Oxycet I hoarded after my last bout with the periodontist). I glance at the young sailor, doing a warp-speed inventory of his bodybuilder shoulders, steely eyes and white-gloved hands. Wonder if he does the patting?

"You're fine, ma'am," the officer says. You are, too, I don't say back, even though in a nanosecond I've somehow aged from *Miss* to *Ma'am*.

Once the armed services are satisfied we're not out to bring down the government, Franklin and I push through the brass-eagled handles of the double glass doors, past a series of oil paintings showing stern-faced officers in fancy dress uniforms, and follow a red-white-and-blue arrow down the stairway marked Records. We're headed underground, I can tell, as the musty smell of basement overtakes the salt air of the high-windowed harbor-side reception area upstairs.

A line of olive drab doors stretches out in front of us. Franklin walks determinedly ahead, double-checks the directions, then turns into an open doorway.

Behind a dingy Formica counter, a uniformed officer, this one looking more like someone's seafaring grandfather than the movie-star material manning the metal detector, adjusts his glasses and peers at me. His face crinkles into a beaming smile and he gives a little salute.

"Charlie McNally," he says. "I watch you every day. Your assistant told me you'd be with him, but I just didn't believe it."

I can almost hear Franklin wince at the *A* word, but he keeps quiet. No one outside the biz really understands what producers do.

"Hello, sir," I say, coming toward the counter. "You're . . ."

"Chief Petty Officer Paul T. Rabb," he answers, standing at attention and saluting again. "Retired. You did that investigation on port security—got us lots of good new resources. When your assistant called, I thought the least I could do is grease a few skids. You could get this paperwork anyway, eventually, but the red tape'd choke you first."

Franklin holds out a hand. "I'm Franklin Parrish," he says, "Charlie's produ—"

Before he can get his title corrected, Rabb hefts a stack of manila file folders into Franklin's arms.

"Oof," Franklin grunts, staggering back a step under the weight. The papers inside threaten to slide out, and Franklin pulls a quick juggle maneuver to keep everything together.

I twinkle at my new pal. "He's up for some weight training, I guess," I say. Franklin will know I'm teasing. I hope.

“Would you like some coffee while you look at the ownership records?” Rabb offers. “I could show you the officers’ mess.” He’s looking at me, not at Franklin. Of course *he’s* smitten, but not my sailor boy upstairs.

“Oh, no, thanks,” I begin. “I’m—”

“She’d love some coffee,” Franklin says. I get it. Payback for the weight-training crack. “In fact, you two just go have fun, and I’ll look through these.”

“You owe me, Franko.” I’m back with my armed-services coffee and I want information. “What are you . . . ?”

Franklin’s sitting at a government-issue metal table, tucked at the back of the records room; he’s sorting the files as if he’s dealing some oversize game of solitaire. After a moment, he taps the largest pile with his pencil.

“Carlo Bronizetti of Exotel,” he pronounces. Another tap. “A. Grimes Brown, CEO of Rogers Chalmers Enterprises.” Tap. “The Islington brothers, Alexander and Sam.”

He looks up at me. “According to these Coast Guard boat registrations, so kindly provided by your very own salty dog, they are all co-owners of the sleek sloop *Miranda*. And guess who the other owner is?”

I know the answer, of course. A certain arrogant, golf-playing, double-talking CEO.

“Wes Rasmussen,” I say confidently. “Am I right or what? Wes Rasmussen. Like I said.” I punctuate each word with a little hip-hop dance move, and then try to give Franklin a high-five. He rolls his eyes and ignores me, but he can’t hide his enthusiasm.

“Yeah, pretty cool, huh?” He’s actually rubbing his palms together. “So, turns out our Mr. Rasmussen is very hooked into the big-money fraternity of international yacht racing. And here's my theory," Franklin continues. "Tax shelter. Yachts are terrific tax write-offs. Especially if the boats lose races."

But I'm still staring at the stacks of papers. "Wow," I whisper, suddenly worried someone will overhear. "Islington brothers. Rogers Chalmers. Exotel." I pause. "We wondered how the companies in Brad's files were connected. And now, right here, are four of them. All in Brad's files, their CEOs owners of the *Miranda*. That cannot be a coincidence."

"This has got to be the key," Franklin agrees, his voice low. "We just don't know to what."

"Maybe," I say. "Maybe the officers of the companies in Brad's files own other stuff together. Other boats. Or, you know, hotels. Shopping malls. Golf courses. Race cars."

"Charlotte Ann McNally," he says, grinning. "You deserve a huge latte, girl. Those people who wonder why you win all the Emmys, this is why."

I'm instantly concerned. "Who wonders why I win all the Emmys?" I demand. "Did someone actually say something about it? Who?"

"I'm never going to compliment you again." Franklin waves me off. "Nobody's questioning your Emmys. Jeez. I hope tonight's your meeting of approval addicts anonymous."

"You got me," I admit. "Report-card mentality. Mother's fault, you know? Still trying for all As." I secretly think that's an asset, not a personality flaw, but I know it's probably a conversation to avoid. "So back to the world of big-money buying. We could do a wider search, couldn't we? Databases of . . . car titles. Excise tax. Registration. That sort of thing. See if—"

Franklin puts one hand up to interrupt me. "What I'll do . . ." he says slowly, ". . . is set up an ownership cross-reference from all those sources. . . ."

"Let me ask you this, Charlotte," Franklin says. Back at the station, we've shared some Tu-Your-Door brown-rice sushi and non-fat milk shakes. Blood sugar surging, we're both feeling more optimistic. "What are the three little words you love to hear the most?"

"What are the three—what?"

"Come on, think about it." The beginnings of a smile. "This shouldn't be a toughie."

What three words? Time for lunch? Angela's been fired? A potentially delicious thought occurs to me. Message from Josh?

"Are you trying to say you love me?" I ask. "What will your adorable Stephen do?"

Franklin throws a pencil at me, which I know he doesn't mean to hit because it doesn't. "Think, Charlotte," he urges.

"My three . . ." Suddenly, I get it. "I was right!"

Franklin points to his nose. "Correct," he says. "This database shows four CEOs, including Rasmussen, also own at least one other boat."

"That's great," I say, eyes widening. "Anything else?"

"That's the bad news," Franklin says. "The database search is still churning away. Matching millions of records. I told you it was going to take a while."

"Let me know the minute you have a hit," I insist. "I'll check for new spam." With a little computer-music fanfare, dozens of new arrivals are displayed from top to bottom of my screen. And some are just what I was hoping for: *Hello, A new re-figh deal 4-u, a good time to buy.* Possibly they're written that way to get past the spam filters. Maybe it's a mistake.

I click open the first of the "re-fighs." Inside, it again says, *Hello, A new re-figh deal 4-u, a good time to buy.* Then it says, *Numbers 4:55-56.*

I copy and paste it into Google. I'm almost bored now. I know what's going to happen. Some Bible verse is going to pop up, I'll send it back and I'll get something else in return.

I prop my chin on my hands as Google thinks.

After this, I decide, I'm not going to play anymore. It's a waste. And probably will wind up being a gimmick. At the end of these mysterious back-and-forth e-mails is going to be some legitimate offer to refinance my condo or something. That'll be truly, truly annoying.

A flash of white screen, then up pops the results page. One entry only, I see, and it's not from the Bible.

It's which buses you can take to get to some martial arts school in London.

This is perplexing. Why doesn't it show a Bible verse?

"Hey, Franklin?" I say. He's told me from moment one this refinancing trail is going nowhere, and I guess he's right. "It's your turn to hear the three little words." That'll get him.

Of course he looks up. "What am I right about?"

I show him the latest e-mails and the Bible verse.

"See? This is definitely a Bible citation, anyone could recognize that. But when I did the search, it comes up with this London address. So you were right. This re-fi e-mail is nothing but a huge time-sucker."

Franklin, ignoring my admission of defeat, reads it out loud. "Numbers 4. Fifty-five to fifty-six." He tilts his head, thinking, then looks as if he's counting something on his fingers.

"What are—" I begin. Franklin stops me with a glare. I've apparently made him lose track of whatever he's counting. He starts again.

"This isn't a Bible verse," he finally pronounces.

"Not a Bible verse?" I reply, unconvinced. "Sure it is."

"Nope." Franklin sounds confident. "It's not. Anyone who went to church as much as I did when I was a kid back in Jackson knows this chapter and verse you showed me ain't gospel. Numbers Chapter 4 in King James? Only goes up to Verse 45. So there is no Verse 55 and 56."

"Franklin, that's impossible," I argue. "Besides, how could you possibly know the verses in the Bible?"

Franklin touches his temple and bows slightly. "Some guys know baseball stats, I know the Bible. My father was also my Sunday school teacher, remember?" he says. "But more to the point here, if the e-mails were designed to get you to complete a quotation, why would they send something that's impossible to complete?"

"What do you mean, 'designed'?" I demand, pointing at him. "You told me you thought these e-mails were nothing. A 'junk-mail joke,' if I remember correctly. So now you've changed your mind?"

"Well, I'll admit, after looking at these—Bible verse things—I'm not sure. And I can't forget Brad asked Josh Gelston about exactly the same quotations you got. And maybe he asked Mack Briggs, too. Whoever that is. It all seems too complicated to be a coincidence, you know?"

I knew I was right.

"And you know what we forgot?" I say. "That phone call Melanie got from the Aztratech lawyers, asking if Brad brought home documents. So what was it they thought he had? And if it's what we have now—" I gesture to the box "—what is it we don't understand?"

Franklin and I turn to look at the brown corrugated cardboard box. Inside, a metal bracket, with tabbed green file folders hanging from the frame. The first tab says Aztratech, then Azzores Partnership, then Dioneutraceutics. A dozen or so. Alphabetical. Organized. And completely meaningless.

"I have an idea," Franklin says. "Go to the re-fi spams you received. The ones with the weird spellings. Print them all out, okay?"

Turns out there are about ten "re-figh" e-mails, and each one contains what still looks to me like the citation for a Bible verse. The book Numbers, then chapter and verse.

Franklin starts counting on his fingers again.

I hope he has a plan because I'm not going to be terribly helpful with Bible verses. My college comparative-religion class was at eight in the morning, and no question I rarely made an appearance. And even if I'd had perfect attendance, I couldn't possibly remember how many verses there were in whatever books of the Bible they were teaching.

"Earth to Charlotte." Franklin pokes me in the shoulder. "Earth. To. Charlotte."

"Ow." I wince. "Cut it out. I'm just thinking about Bible verses."

"Here's the deal," Franklin says, pointing to the sheaf of papers. "Some of these are Bible verse citations—but some aren't. This one, for instance, refers to Numbers 10, Verse 73 to 74. The real Numbers 10 ends at Verse 36."

"I'm still beyond impressed that you know this," I say. "But, given that you do, why would someone send—"

"I have no idea," Franklin interrupts. "But it's late, and I'm out of here. Why don't you e-mail back the address of the martial arts school, same way you've always responded to the spams. Just to see. Then tomorrow, we'll move to plan B."

"Great," I say. "Plan B." Whatever that is.

CHAPTER NINE

"Beep. Message received Thursday at 7:42 a.m."

"I'm looking for a . . . Charlie McNally? If this is the correct number, please call me—617-555-3413."

Mystery caller, huh? Fine. Just in case it's another Watergate or Monica, I'll call back. Reporter's credo. I hear a machine click into answer mode. No clue in the outgoing message about who I'm calling.

I leave my name and number, plus my e-mail address to prove I'm sincere, and I'm done. Tag, you're it. I've returned the call, just the way they teach you in J-school.

I tap my computer keyboard to open my e-mail for the day, smiling in self-approval at my continuing commitment to journalism. The monitor flashes to white, then whirs up into my New Mail Received screen. I scan for more "re-figh" e-mails. Nothing.

My smile turns to a pout of bewilderment as I check again. No refinancing spam of any kind. I click Refresh. Nothing. I click Update. Nothing. No refinancing e-mails. Not one.

Maybe the e-mail has crashed again.

Then, as I stare at the screen in consternation, a new e-mail pops up. My eyes and my brain struggle through a moment of disconnect: the subject line says *From Mack Briggs.*

Mack Briggs. Mack Briggs. Mack Briggs is sending me an e-mail. Why?

I click on Open.

Dear Ms. McNally, the e-mail begins. *I just received your voice mail message and decided it might be more efficient, initially at least, to correspond by e-mail.*

I'm mesmerized. Mack Briggs was the mystery caller. What if I hadn't called him back? I murmur a thank-you to the news gods and keep reading.

> *I have been out of the country for the past week, and it was only when I returned to my home in Vermont that I was notified of Bradley Foreman's death.*
>
> *As you know from the e-mail he sent you, there were issues he was eager to discuss. He told me he had seen your article exposing the prices of pet medicines, and decided you might be interested in another story about the pharmaceutical world.*

Ha. I was right.

> *Brad gave me some documents to examine, but now I have no need to keep them, so I'm having them delivered to your office. If I can be of any help, feel free to let me know.*
>
> *Best, Mack Briggs*

Blinking at the screen, I print out a copy of this bombshell. And then I print out another one, just in case my computer crashes and everything is destroyed and I lose the first copy.

So. The elusive Mack Briggs is found. And his little jewel of an e-mail answers a couple of questions at least.

One—what took him so long. Even though we couldn't find Mack Briggs, I always wondered why he didn't try to find me. Now we know he was out of the country.

Two—Franklin and I must be right about the pharmaceutical whistle-blower story. The e-mail certainly alludes to it.

So, we're on the way. When the documents arrive, we may get some more answers. Like who is Mack Briggs, anyway? And why did Brad send him a copy of the e-mail?

I swivel contentedly in my chair, savoring the possibilities. And, I remember with the tiniest of smiles, there's a critical decision ahead of me. As soon as I get home.

This is harder than it was in high school. More complicated than a job interview. I make a face at no one, making fun of my own melodrama. It's just a date.

I perch on the white wicker footstool tucked into the corner of my walk-in closet, and scrutinize the selection that's usually so obvious. Suit—too formal. Unless I pretend I just came from work. Which I didn't. Jeans—too casual. Don't want to look like I'm trying too hard. I sigh with a defeat that shudders through my evaporating confidence. Does it really matter what I wear? This Josh is going to like me, or not like me, based on our chemistry, not my clothing.

I guess.

I choose a maple-red corduroy blazer and crisp white shirt, and pull a pair of black pants from the rack. I stare at the outfit, each piece pristine on its padded hanger, as if it could reveal some answers. And then, it does.

It means safe. Serious. Boring. And, I decide as I hang it all back in place, it might as well be body armor. Am I protecting myself from something? I wonder, as I scour my closet for perfection, if this might be the night to go for it. My almost-too-tight black turtleneck dress beckons from its back-of-the-rack spot. If not now, when?

Maybe Maysie has a point. Maybe I'm out of practice.

I purse my lips . . . and dare myself.

"Marjorie?"

"Here."

"Margaret?"

"Here."

Josh Gelston, holding a clipboard in the backstage darkness of Bexter Auditorium, confirms his "Gold-Bug" cast is complete. Two teenaged actors, heads bent close together, softly rehearse their lines for a final time. The younger kids, seated in a row on a fraying couch, whisper and giggle, unable to keep still. Perched on a high stool in a corner, I watch the swirl of precurtain chaos, the backstage performance a show in itself. Especially, I notice, my charming and charismatic leading man, looking very off-Broadway in a black T-shirt and tweedy blazer.

A wide-eyed little girl, all ruffles and laced-up boots, comes up to clutch Josh's hand as he continues his preshow preparations. She can't be more than six years old, and looks at her teacher adoringly.

"Five minutes to curtain," Josh whispers and then kneels to face the girl beside him. Giving a final adjustment to the silky bow on her bonnet, he points her to her mark onstage. She turns to go, then apparently changing her mind, comes back to give Josh a quick hug. He smiles after her as she trots away to take her place—then he looks up at me.

"Okay?" his eyes ask.

I clasp my hands in front of me, pantomiming delight. This is beyond charming.

And so is Josh.

Someone starts a fog machine, and gray puffs float across the stage. Suburban teenagers somehow become Victorian townspeople, as Josh pulls up a high stool next to mine and holds up crossed fingers. At that moment, the mysteries of the spam and expensive yachts and pharmaceutical prices and documents to arrive tomorrow by overnight mail evaporate. Applause fills the theater, the stage lights go up and the curtain opens on the Bexter School production of "The Gold-Bug."

The night is clear and the sky is cascaded with stars. Our words puff into clouds of cold as we slowly walk from the auditorium. Even in the splotchy parking-lot light, I can see the engaging crinkles around Josh's eyes and read the enthusiasm in his smile.

"And did you see what a tough cookie our little Amy turned out to be? Even when the curtain . . . Charlie?" Josh stops midsentence, turns questioningly to make sure I'm listening.

"I know," I agree. I can listen and dream at the same time. "And she obviously worships you." I take a chance and tuck my gloved hand through Josh's elbow. "All the kids do. And the cast party afterward—everyone was so proud and happy."

I can feel Josh tighten his arm over my hand. And then, just as I'm wondering how I can make this evening last a little longer, we arrive at my car.

Moment of truth. "Anyway, thank you so much," I say. "I had a terrific time. This is my Jeep."

Josh pats my hand, the one I still haven't removed from his arm. "I hoped so," he says, "since it's the only car here."

This stops me. He's right.

"But—where's yours?" Suddenly there's hope for more time with my handsome professor. "Can I . . . May I give you a ride home?"

"Good idea," Josh says. "I don't live far from here."

Josh reaches over to open the driver's side door, which of course doesn't open because I have the remote key.

"Chivalry is dead," I say, beeping the remote. "Killed by technology." After I hop in, Josh goes around to the passenger side.

I quickly chuck my used latte cups and old newspapers onto the floor of the backseat and pump the heater to high. Time for a high-level decision. At some point someone will have to make a move. If he asks me in, will I go? I don't have a toothbrush. Do I need a toothbrush? Isn't dating supposed to be fun? When did it turn into an emotional chess match? Do I even know the rules anymore?

Josh clicks on his seat belt. "Left out of the lot," he says.

I turn the Jeep down a quiet tree-lined street. There's no way to know what will happen until it happens. And you can't win if you don't play.

"Here we are, number 11," Josh says with a smile. "That's me. As I said, thanks so much."

"You live—here?" I say, laughing. I turn off the ignition, but flip the key to keep the heat running. "Some drive home."

"I do have a house up by the Vermont border," Josh replies. "A little place on the Jordan Beach Road. I'm usually there on weekends, especially on my Penny weekends because it's closer for Victoria to drop her off up there. But school days, I stay here at Bexter."

I wasn't surprised to learn he'd been married before. I might have been worried, actually, if he hadn't been. We'd sipped contraband wine in a corner as the cast party of his chattering students flowed around us, and we swapped love-and-war stories about our divorces—Josh's at age fortysomething, from an ambitious doctor-wife who calculated it was more beneficial to latch on to a doctor-husband. His only regret, he'd told me, was Penny, the sweetly sad eight-year-old daughter he misses every day, but only sees every third weekend. I'm crossing my fingers I get to meet her.

Josh unhooks his seat belt, but still makes no move to get out of the car. He turns in his seat to face me and unbuttons his thick navy pea jacket, loosening his tweedy scarf.

Taking his cue, I unhook my seat belt, too. Just a cozy midnight tête-à-tête in my toasty little Cherokee. Not exactly a dream date, but it'll do. And Josh seems to want it to continue.

"So?" he asks. "Any update on the spam saga? When last we met, you were in reporter mode, remember?"

Before I know it, the whole story pours out. The call and e-mail from Mack Briggs, the impending arrival of the documents, the bogus Bible verses, the sloop *Miranda*.

"So you must have been intrigued with that," Josh says. "*Miranda*. Sounds like a clue, doesn't it?"

I don't understand. "You got me," I admit. "A clue?"

Josh waggles a finger. "I thought you were Miss Shakespeare," he says teasingly. "*Miranda*?"

"It's so very late." I go for the sympathy play. "My brain is so very tired. It's . . ." I look at the dashboard clock and surprise myself. "It's two in the morning, did you know that?"

"Don't try to change the subject, Ms. McNally." Josh smiles, pretending to be strict. "*Miranda*. A main character in the play quoted in those e-mails. 'We are such stuff as dreams are made on'—remember? *The Tempest*."

"So you think," I reply slowly, the connection sinking in, "the person who named the boat also sent the spam?"

"It's kind of a funny coincidence if they didn't," Josh says. "You're the reporter, but could that be Wes Rasmussen? Or what's his name? Mack—Briggs?"

I stare at Josh, speechless, and then turn to stare out the windshield into the night sky. My brain is churning, consternation at not having made the *Miranda* connection myself mixing with excitement over Josh's idea.

"So you think . . . hey! Did you see that?" I say.

Josh is looking out the windshield, too. "A shooting star," he says. "Yes, I saw it." He pauses and turns to me, a smile playing around his eyes. "And you know what they say you're supposed to do when you see a shooting star?"

I do. "Make a wish," I reply quickly. "You're supposed to make a wish."

"Wrong," Josh responds.

He reaches over and takes my hand, and my heart explodes like a galaxy of shooting stars. "Not make a wish," he says quietly, drawing me closer to him.

I'm nervous. I'm eager. But part of me's confused. Of course it's make a wish. I open my mouth to protest, but Josh interrupts, brushing a strand of hair from my face, his finger gentle against my cheek. I almost gasp at his touch, and I think my eyes briefly close, my body responding despite my brain.

"When you see a shooting star," he says, his voice softening, "you're supposed to kiss the person you're with."

"No, that's wrong. . . ." My brain takes hold, and I begin to argue again. Then, in an instant, as Josh pulls me even closer, my body wins. And I realize, as the stars and the car and the old latte cups and the hum of the heater somehow disappear, and our layers of coats and gloves and scarves force us to keep a tantalizing distance, you're always supposed to do what the teacher says, especially on a school night.

CHAPTER TEN

I'm taking a grateful sip of my third latte of the afternoon when Franklin appears at our office door. He's carrying a corrugated cardboard box covered with "Deliver by COB Friday" stickers. It's got to be the documents from Mack Briggs.

Usually I'd want to open it myself. After all, it's addressed to me. But I'm the tiniest bit tired from last night and I'm trying to hide it because Franklin will be relentless for details. For now, I want to keep my memories of Josh—and my hopes—to myself. Franklin can focus on the box.

As I watch him peel back the tape, though, I grow increasingly uncomfortable. We have no way of knowing what's actually inside. It comes from someone we've never seen or even talked to in person. Our only connection has been by voice mail and e-mail, and we don't know if it really was Mack Briggs on the other end. It could be someone pretending to be Mack Briggs, someone who knew we were looking for him. And the files.

Someone who wanted to stop us. I'm an idiot.

"Franklin?" I need to stop him. "What if the box isn't from Mack Briggs, and . . ."

I hear the last of the tape ripping off the box, and then the snap of the top cardboard panels being pulled apart. I wince, waiting for the explosion or the puff of white powder.

"Cool," Franklin says. "Here's a note from Mack Briggs, and a stack of papers, and it's all on top of . . . Whoa."

I uncoil myself from my terror-defense position and go see what Franklin's looking at. I knew it would be fine.

"Read this note," Franklin instructs, handing it to me along with a stack of papers, "and then look what's in the box. E-mails."

I easily recognize the e-mails Mack Briggs sent us. They're copies of the exact same Bible-looking citations I got. The note is handwritten in black fountain pen on creamy stationery, monogrammed MXB.

Ms. McNally, I read, *here are the e-mails Brad sent me. He asked: Why would Aztratech and the others be sending spam about refinancing? Before we could talk further, I learned he was killed in a car accident.*

It's signed with initials.

"I don't get it," I say. "Aztratech is a pharmaceutical company. It isn't sending out refinancing spam." I pause. I guess we don't really know that.

"It gets stranger. Look what else he sent," Franklin says.

I feel like that kid in *Home Alone,* palms pressed to my cheeks, mouth open in surprise. Inside the cardboard box I see a metal file-holding frame, and hanging from the frame are green file folders. Aztratech, then Rogers Chalmers . . . I look back at Franklin. "These are exactly the same, right?"

Franklin sits back in his chair, nodding, his hand still on the box. "This box of files is just like our box of files, his e-mails are just like our e-mails. Brad was certainly on the trail of something."

We're both quiet for a moment, remembering again what happened to Brad.

"Hang on," I interrupt our reverie. "It's about what's not in here."

"What's not . . . ?" Franklin replies.

"What's not in the stuff from Mack Briggs," I explain, the realization dawning more fully even as I say it out loud, "is one word about pharmaceutical prices, or price fixing, or Brad as a whistle-blower or anything like that. Not one word."

"You're right," he says, flipping through the paperwork. "You think this means we're on the wrong track with the 'whistle-blowing Brad' story?"

I hear a distant gurgle, as my career swirls down the drain. November, no story, no job . . . No.

"Time out," I say, making the signal with my hands. "The e-mail Brad sent me. If it wasn't about him being the whistle-blower, what was it about?"

"And what's more," Franklin replies, "why did he also send all this to Mack Briggs? Why Mack Briggs, specifically?" Franklin looks at the note again. "The monogram is MXB," he says. "What if we . . ."

He turns to his computer. "Remember when we searched his name?" Franklin asks. "I'm thinking, I never searched just M. Briggs." He hits Enter. "Did you?"

I think back while the computer whirs. "Nope," I say. "Just Mack."

The monitor flashes and a whole page of entries appears. The first one says *McKenzie Xavier Briggs.*

Franklin and I exchange looks.

"Spelling," he says dryly.

I pretend to shoot myself with a finger. "I should have thought of that." I'm so exasperated. "We stink. They should fire us."

Franklin nods in pretend acquiescence, then reads the rest of the entry out loud. "Chairman, United States Securities and Exchange Commission, 1993 to 1996."

"Chairman of the . . ." I begin.

"What would he know," Franklin asks slowly, "that no one else could know?"

"Here's a concept," I say, hitting my forehead with the heel of my hand. "I'll just call and ask him." I start to punch in the number I have in my calling log. The area code is Vermont. "We should have called Briggs as soon as we got the box."

The phone rings and this time I'm hoping it's not the answering machine.

"Hello?" I hear a quiet voice. A woman. I give Franklin a thumbs-up.

"Mack Briggs, please," I say, nodding with the good news. Any minute now, I'll be chatting with the man of the hour.

There's silence at the other end.

"Hello?" Maybe she didn't understand me. "May I speak to Mack Briggs, please?"

Another silence, then I hear the woman's voice again. "One moment, please."

This is great. This proves it was actually Mack Briggs's number, which I had secretly harbored a few nagging doubts about.

I hear the hold button click off, and a gruff voice says, "Who is this?"

"Oh, hello, Mr. Briggs," I begin.

The voice interrupts me, insistent. "I said, who is this?"

"Oh, I'm so sorry," I start again. "This is Charlie McNally, from Channel 3 TV? And—"

This voice interrupts again. "This is Officer Veloudos, State Police, miss. Why are you calling here?"

I can feel the warmth drain from my face. Why is a state trooper answering the phone? I look at Franklin, and he must recognize my confusion and bewilderment.

"What?" he asks, leaning forward. He's frowning, concerned. "What?"

"Miss?" the trooper says. "Are you a reporter? If so, you'll have to call our public relations department. We're not giving out any statements here this afternoon."

"Not giving out any statements—about what?"

"Like I told you," the trooper says. "Talk to PR."

And then he hangs up.

I'm unable to put the receiver back in the cradle. I look at it, as if somehow I could retrieve some answers.

I turn to Franklin. "It was a state trooper. He told me to call PR. And then he hung up."

The phone begins to quaver its irritating "hang up or else" signal, but I'm too flummoxed to follow instructions. "What on earth," I begin over the beeping, "could be going on?"

Franklin pushes the phone button, breaking the connection. "Time to find out," he says, flipping through his Rolodex. "I think our Mack Briggs, sender of mysterious documents, has been arrested. And we need to know why. He's the former SEC commissioner, after all. This may be a lead story."

He rips out a Rolodex card and hands me the number of the police press office.

"You could be right," I say. "Maybe Briggs is the target of some secret special prosecutor investigating SEC fraud. Or something. If that's true, it'll take hours for word to trickle down from Vermont to Boston. And we'll have an exclusive. Love it."

I hum "Ode to Joy" in my head as I punch in the number and briefly wonder—where did that tune come from? Then I remember just a few days ago, in a certain professor's office . . .

"Vermont State Police," a reedy voice answers the phone. "Detective Bogetich. Is this an emergency?"

I always hate that question. It would certainly be an emergency to me if some other reporter got this before I do.

"No," I answer. "This is Charlie McNally, TV3 in Boston." I turn on my serious investigative voice. "I'm calling for the status of the arrest of one Mack Briggs earlier today. Can you give me an update?"

Nothing.

Oh, come on. "Detective?" I prod.

"Miss McNally," the detective answers, "you're calling about McKenzie Briggs? From Cullodon Harbor? Mack Briggs is not in custody, miss."

"He's not . . . ?" I'm thinking fast and now I'm talking like myself again. "But . . . how come you guys were at his house? And how come, when I called there, your officer answered the phone? And hey, how come he wouldn't tell me anything, and told me to call you for a statement?" I take a breath. "So now, I'm calling you for a statement, okay?"

"Okay," I hear.

Finally.

"Here's the statement," the detective says. "Vermont State Police confirm the death of McKenzie Xavier Briggs, age seventy-three, of Cullodon Harbor, Vermont, at 16:30 this date. Cause of death—motor vehicle accident. As per standard practice, the accident is under investigation."

I sit back in my chair, almost dizzy. Franklin is frantically making questioning gestures, silently mouthing, "What? What happened?" but I don't answer him.

"Was there anyone else in the car?" I manage to ask, my mind now regaining equilibrium. "Was there another vehicle involved?"

"That's not in this statement, miss," the detective answers. "What I told you is all we're releasing."

Then I get an idea. A big one.

"I understand, just doing your job," I say calmly. Then I go for it, speaking slowly and confidently. "But we have information," I lie, "that this was a one-car incident, no other cars found on the scene, and also that Briggs was alone in the car. Off the record, not for attribution, can you just confirm that for me?"

Nothing.

"I'll never say it was you who confirmed it," I entreat. "I won't even say 'state police sources.' "

There's a sigh. "You're not wrong, miss," he says. And then he hangs up.

Franklin stands over me, looking as if he's ready to rip the phone from my hand. "Good Lord, Charlotte," he says. "What the hell happened?"

I look him square in the eye. "Mack Briggs is dead," I say. I can hear how surprisingly flat my voice is. "Mack Briggs is dead, and I just confirmed he died exactly the same way Brad Foreman did."

CHAPTER ELEVEN

I can't hold out another minute. I need to check my e-mail. The station's entire system had once again crashed and was still down when we left last night. If it's not back up and running, I am going to be in serious communications withdrawal.

I know I should be enjoying the hot water coursing over my hair, the scritch of Marie-Rosina's fingers on my scalp. The coconut fragrance of the lavish shampoo. But this isn't vanity, it's required maintenance, and after so many years, a salon visit is as glamorously exciting as an oil change. I'm obligated to be washed, conditioned and blown dry here once a week, and gray-preventioned every fifth Saturday. My real hair color? I have no idea.

The second M-R wraps a fluffy white towel around my head, I scramble for my phone. Maybe Franklin uncovered something about Mack Briggs.

My name is Charlie, and I'm a workaholic.

A few quick taps and I'm online. It's the weekend. But it's almost November, and we still don't have a story, and—I'm staring at an impossibility.

I've received an e-mail from a dead person.

My brain scrambles to understand this. A typo? A mistake?

I scroll down, reading as fast as I can, not grasping how I could be reading a note from someone who—according to yesterday's info from the Vermont State Police—is soon to be six feet under. But there it is: the signature line says Mack Briggs.

I slip into the salon's massage room, desperate for privacy. Perching on the sheet-draped table, I click my phone back to the top and devour the flickering words. This is . . . a joke. A trick. A scam.

Ms. McNally, I read, *by now you will have gotten the box of files Brad Foreman sent me. He was a student in my class at Wharton. I was taken aback when I received those files, because we hadn't been in contact for years.*

I scoot back against the wall, tucking a quilted pink pillow under my towel-wrapped head. I hold the phone up and keep reading, struggling to understand.

Reason for this e-mail: I should have mentioned he alluded to his search for a mortgage interest-rate reduction, and apparently had found some similarities among refinancing advertisements.

I jump to my feet. Got to call Franklin. He answers on the second ring, and before he finishes saying hello, I'm telling him about the e-mail.

"Spam." His voice crackles through his speakerphone. I can hear him clicking into his home computer as he talks. "It's about the spam. Keep reading," he demands.

Before I can continue, there's a knock on the door—then a voluptuous henna-haired woman in a black smock peers in. She's holding a pile of towels and an orange bottle of massage oil.

"Nancy at eleven-thirty?" she asks in what sounds like a French accent.

Merde. "No," I say brightly. Go away. *Go away.* "Not me."

She clicks the door closed. I figure I don't have much time left in my rosemary-scented hideout.

"Charlotte?" Franklin calls out. "You there?"

"Yup, sorry," I reply. "Let me read you the rest. 'He didn't explain, just told me he wanted me to do original research, not influenced by his ideas. He e-mailed me those citations I assume are Bible verses. I gathered he was feeling some sort of pressure, even fear, though I could be mistaken.'"

I hear Franklin typing and clicking his mouse.

"Are you listening?" I ask, exasperated. "He thought Brad was afraid of something, did you hear that?"

"I haven't missed a word," Franklin says, "but wait till you see what I just found. How fast can you get over here?"

Course they don't teach in J-School: Say So Long to Saturday—There Are No Weekends in TV.

I grab the wrought-iron railing, run up Franklin's front porch steps and give three quick buzzes on his intercom. He clicks me into the spotlessly chic foyer and into his front door. When I arrive in his study, my still-wet hair hidden under the stripey wool cap I just speed-purchased at the Gap, Franklin's hunched over the computer on his antique rolltop desk.

"Show me the rest of the letter," he instructs, without so much as a hello. "Then you've got to see what I found."

I hang my coat on the back of the door, grab my phone and click open Briggs's letter. If it is from Briggs. "Can this be—real?" I ask, holding it out to him.

Franklin almost yanks the phone from my hand. He looks as confused and concerned as I feel.

"Sit," he commands, pointing me to a leather-and-chrome chair-sculpture contraption Stephen must have chosen. "Let me read this. Love the hat, by the way. Good for your street cred."

"Okay, but read it out loud," I insist, ignoring the hat crack.

"From where I left off. Briggs must have sent it right before his car crash."

"Yeah," Franklin says, grimacing. "Anyway, it says, 'I must warn you Brad asked me to tell him if I received any unusual phone calls.'"

He sits back in his special ergonomic desk chair, swiveling slowly from side to side, and keeps reading. "'Before I could ask what was troubling him, he was killed. Perhaps you can make some headway. If I can assist you, let me know. You know where to find me. Sincerely, MX Briggs.'" Franklin looks up. "That's all."

I pause for a moment. "And I guess we do know where to find him."

"Yeah." Franklin nods his head. "Morgue."

"Two sets of identical files." I hold up my fingers. "Two car accidents. Two people dead. It all has to be connected," I say. "Doesn't it?"

Franklin gestures toward his monitor, the website he'd been reading. "Remember I had something to show you?" he replies. "Well, these," he continues, pointing to the screen, "are the specific courses Mack Briggs taught at Wharton. And look," he says. "All stock market stuff. Rules and regs, practices and procedures, securities law. So, seems like Brad suspected someone was doing something wrong, or illegal, and figured Briggs could confirm it." He pauses, still thinking. "Some stock market thing."

But I suddenly feel as if I'm seeing the other side of a coin. "Or," I say deliberately, "could it be some sort of . . . test? Brad has a get-rich-quick scheme, maybe. And who better to try it out on than his old securities professor. See if he catches on."

Franklin raises his eyebrows. "You think?"

"And that means," I continue, beginning to get worried, "Brad might not have been the whistle-blowing protector of the taxpayer's pharmaceutical dollars, but more like a money-hustling market-manipulating bad guy. And he was floating the scheme to Briggs, to see if he picked up on it. If someone with that deep level of experience and knowledge didn't catch on, of course, Brad might have figured he could get away with whatever it was."

"You could be right," Franklin agrees. "Wouldn't that be a hoot?"

I bang the back of my head against the sleek chair, deflated, defeated. "Oh yeah, a real hoot," I say. "All this research, all this e-mailing back and forth, this mysterious Mack Briggs. The poor widow Melanie. The stupid *Miranda.* Either just the random acts of an uncaring universe or the fallout from a small-time stock scheme gone wrong."

"Could be," Franklin grudgingly agrees. "Remember, Brad and Melanie were in some sort of financial straits. Maybe it was Brad, the failing businessman, trying to save the family home and his marriage."

"So his car accident was just an accident," I say slowly. "Or even truly a suicide." I pause, my realization coalescing into a lead weight in my stomach. "And at the end of it all, just one conspiracy-crazed, career-challenged reporter, desperately trying to make something out of nothing."

"Charlotte?" Franklin watches my melodrama with amusement. "Yoo-hoo, Camille. Just this once, see the glass as half-full."

I flutter my eyelashes, doing my best Garbo. "Vy?" I ask. "Ve're doomed."

"It's a reasonable theory about Brad having a stock scheme," he says earnestly, "but maybe it's wrong. Look again at the courses Mack Briggs taught." He moves the cursor arrow up and down on his computer screen. "Nothing about market trends, or predicting stock prices."

I squint to read over his shoulder. "So?"

"Look at what he did teach," Franklin says. "Securities law." He turns back to me. “It’s not about Brad, it’s about the companies in his files.”

“Thanks for trying to make me feel better,” I say, sliding away from the computer. “But I still think this is about Brad’s frantic need for money. Maybe he got inside information by hacking into Rasmussen’s e-mails, you know? And decided to parlay that into some quick stock market bucks.”

“Well, that would be insider trading,” Franklin answers. “He wouldn’t have to check with Briggs to see if he could play the market based on information from stolen e-mails indicating it was a good time to buy or sell. These days, even teenagers know you can’t do that. Martha Stewart, that whole deal.”

Suddenly Franklin’s study gets very quiet. I can hear the hum of his computer, the rumble of an electric trolley rattling through the streets of his downtown neighborhood, a hint of music from his upstairs neighbors.

I dig Brad’s spams out of my tote bag and hold the pages carefully in my lap.

“Franklin?” I say, gazing blankly at his wall of classical music CDs. “Say that again?”

He sounds confused. “Martha Stewart?”

“The other part,” I say, turning to look at him.

“Whatever.” He’s scratching his head. “I said, that would be insider trading, if Brad were using info he got from swiping Rasmussen’s e-mails.”

“Yeah,” I reply, keeping my voice even. “And then?”

Franklin is now acting as if I’ve totally lost it. “I said—he wouldn’t have to ask whether it was all right to play the market if he had inside info indicating it was a good time to buy or a good time to sell. It’s illegal. Everybody these days knows that.”

Each of the Bible verse e-mails slides slowly from my lap onto the floor, most fluttering into a scattered pile at my feet, one piece floating over toward Franklin's desk. I hardly notice—because now I think I know what may be going on. At least, I think I've figured out what these spams really are. I just don't know how to prove it.

CHAPTER TWELVE

The landscape exaggerates as I head north. The mammoth evergreens get even more lofty, and the hills grow to craggy mountains, picturesque against the intense blue sky. My directions say it's a straight shot to Vermont, and I should be there within the hour. I pull out the newspaper article I tore from today's paper and check the time. I'll make it.

I try to appreciate the brilliant New England morning, but the sun's in a losing battle against the light-sucking black hole of my disappointment.

Josh. Hasn't called me.

I don't know why I expect millions of news viewers to listen to me, trust me, when I don't listen to myself. I knew I should never have gotten involved. I wasn't looking to meet anyone, I was doing an interview. And it wasn't my fault that the interview subject was so attractive. And smart. And funny. And single.

Becoming more irate with every memory, I dig into my tote bag for gum.

I certainly didn't do anything to encourage Josh Gelston to ask me out. My tirade escalates as I pop a few sugar-free Chiclets. I wasn't the one who pulled out the shooting-star line.

A souped-up convertible, with the top down in October for God's sake, whips in front of me across two lanes and whizzes off the exit ramp. My heart races with a surge of adrenaline. If my Jeep had been going just a little faster or if I hadn't been such a good driver, I would have crashed into some midlife-crisis sports car. Or, I realize, wind up like Brad Foreman: dead on the side of Route 128. I mentally replay the video our six o'clock news showed of the accident scene: swirling blue lights, the ambulance doors swinging wide, emergency crews quiet, in postures of defeat. Brad's white sedan, upside down, charred to black, all four doors unnaturally twisted open, windows shattered. Demolished. No longer a car. Just an aftermath.

My buzzing mind goes quiet with the relief of escape. And then I remember—Mack Briggs didn't escape. His name was on Brad's e-mail. And mine, too. And, I also remember, no one knows where I am. I need to check in with Franklin.

Then I remember one thing more. Josh's name was also on that e-mail. As the traffic blurs into the background, a sinister reason for Josh's silence begins to nag, unpleasantly, at the back of my mind.

I laugh out loud. The old "he didn't call because he must be dead" excuse has never been true.

But wait. Is it possible I'm being unfair? Possible that I've been out of the dating give-and-take for so long that I'm expecting too much too soon?

Or maybe Josh is intimidated. Maybe he thinks I only attended his little school play to see if I could score more information for my story. But now he's afraid to call because someone like me, Emmy awards, TV personality, recognized in restaurants and all, must have a teemingly crowded social life.

He was all over the *Miranda* name, even had a fairly intriguing theory about it. He brought up Briggs's name, and Rasmussen's.

Which proves he must have at least been listening to me, or how else would he have remembered them?

Just. A Darn. Minute.

The road signs flash by as I play back my conversation with Josh, in fast-forward, without the romantic parts. I check the rearview and see my own expression. I look like Little Red Riding Hood when she realizes there's a wolf in Granny's bed.

I had never mentioned Wes Rasmussen to Josh.

So how did he know about him? And why?

I can't breathe. I can't drive. I have to think. I have to pull over. I look at my watch and calculate: no time. No time to stop, and no time to panic.

I read somewhere that new pilots aren't allowed to fly at night because they can't tell which way is up. They fly through the darkness, instruments useless, their horizon lost, totally confused and incapable of telling whether they're upside down.

As I head toward my destination, I know just how they feel. Could I have been completely and totally duped?

I reconstruct our evening, seeing in neon lights each moment when the diabolical Josh, suave manipulator of honest, truth-seeking reporters, pulled the pashmina over my eyes.

Didn't know Mack Briggs? Of course he did. Didn't know why Brad was asking about the e-mails? Of course he knew. Didn't know the origin of the spam? Sure he did. Didn't know what was going on at Aztratech? Didn't know Brad was ready to blow the whistle? He was probably in on the whole thing, whatever it is.

I hit the steering wheel with the heel of my hand, annoyed with myself. And Brad and Josh met at a big dinner party, I remember. Probably hosted by Wes Rasmussen.

It's so frighteningly clear he was trying to figure out how much I knew. And I was so . . . lusting . . . for romance and affection, I didn't even see through the deception.

I close my eyes in self-loathing, before I remember that I'm driving and that closing my eyes is not the best idea.

And there's my exit.

When I arrive at the cemetery, a long, slow-moving caravan of cars is snaking down a narrow, unpaved road, each car puffing up a plume of gravel dust as it curves past a stone-and-masonry sign that says Eventide. I ease my Jeep onto the end of the line, and pushing my conscience out of the way, flip the switch to turn on my headlights.

It's Mack Briggs's funeral procession, and now I'm part of it.

The cars line up to park, one after the other, on the side of a grassy rise. Beyond that, I see a dark-green canopy set up on metal poles, rows of folding chairs underneath. The first arrivals file into the seating area, men in substantial overcoats, hatless, braving the cold. Women wrapped in extra shawls and close-fitting hats against the increasing chill, their faces somber and serious, some holding flowers and small prayer books. A little boy carrying a fire truck stumbles a bit in the gravel and he grabs the hand of the man walking next to him. I can tell they've both been crying. A flock of gray birds wheels gracefully over the mourners, gliding through the sky then leaving the cemetery silent.

It's almost time for me to turn into the parking area, but now, sneaking into someone's funeral, my conscience kicks its way back in. Questioning my own motives and attempting to retrieve my moral compass, all I can think about is getting out of here. This is a hideous invasion of privacy. This is why people hate reporters. It's shocking, unacceptable, certainly a no-refund, no-exchange ticket to hell and eternal damnation.

But I can save myself. All I have to do is say I made a mistake.

I'm in the wrong place, forgive me, I thought this was someone else's service. I'm so sorry, big adios, and exit.

But, *I hafta know. . . .*

I look up, and a dark-suited attendant is waving me into the next spot. I follow his directions, lock my better judgment in the glove compartment and get out of the car.

Staking out a spot behind the rows of folding chairs, I try to stay hidden by an ancient maple tree. No one seems to notice me, but problem is, I can only see backs of heads, which is no help at all in my search for suspects.

The minister looks up from his Bible, scanning the group, squinting with stern disapproval. The mourners look at each other, concerned and upset. I suddenly hear why—someone's cell phone is trilling, muffled slightly but still a disastrous breach of etiquette for some poor—

I dive for my purse, whirling to put the tree between me and the service. It's *my* phone. I plow through my bag and smash the off button without even looking at my caller ID. Good work, I congratulate myself. Subtle.

I lean against the tree, holding my breath. A moment's pause and the minister continues. I wait, envisioning some black-suited funeral-home goons picking me up by the elbows and throwing me head over heels out of the cemetery. I see my entire life savings, including my plastic surgery fund, heading into the coffers of first amendment lawyers and going to pay huge trespassing fines.

I tentatively creep out from behind my tree, peering around the edge to see if any goons are on the hunt. But the minister's head is bowed again, and it sounds as if he's nearing the end of the service. The mourners seem to be focused on their sorrow and not some misfit with a cell phone. No goons in sight.

I echo their murmured "Amen," and then watch the group move

to pay their final respects as the casket is lowered. I'm almost in the clear. No lawsuits, no headlines. I'll just hang here until the funeral is over and pretend the whole thing never happened. I admit I still haven't seen anyone I recognize, which is a bummer, but on the bright side, no one has recognized me, either.

"Charlie McNally?"

Someone's benign-looking grandmother is headed in my direction, walking carefully in the damp leaves that have fallen on the browning grass, and she's calling my name.

"Charlie McNally, the reporter for Channel 3?" she repeats.

I knew it. Now she'll tell me how much better I look in real life than on camera, how the camera adds ten pounds and ten years, like I don't know that. I appreciate fans, but let me out of here.

"Yes?" Ten seconds. I'll give her ten seconds.

She's still smiling, but two dark-suited factotums seem to materialize at her side. Disturbingly like those funeral goons I worried about. The men hover, one on either side of her, like bulked-up robots programmed to protect and defend at any cost.

The woman loses her grandmotherly look. The swath of her black scarf barely reveals her gray hair, and that's what fooled me at first glance. But now I see her telltale over-lifted eyebrows, her too-taut skin. Her cosmetically revamped face hardens into brittle, her eyes narrow, sizing me up.

This is no fan.

"Ms. McNally," she says, her smile now icy. "I'm Andrea Grimes Brown." She doesn't introduce the robots.

Think, think, think. Andrea Grimes . . .

She continues. "I didn't know you were acquainted with Mack Briggs." She pauses, waiting for my answer.

Andrea Grimes . . . Know it. Can't place it. I edge toward my Jeep, but Brown and her wingmen edge right along with me.

Then I regroup. Who the hell is she and why is she allowed to ask me what I'm doing? I'm the reporter. I'm the one who gets to ask the questions. I have a perfect right to be here. In a way. And the best defense is a good offense.

I stop and face her down. "May I help you with something?" That doesn't really mean anything, but it's all part of my never-fail system to put her off guard and get her to tell me what she wants.

It fails.

She plants herself in my path and repeats her inquiry. "So, do you know Mack Briggs? And how do you know him?"

Two can play this game.

"I'm sorry," I reply, though I'm not, really. "Ms. . . . Brown, is it? Are you a friend of Mr. Briggs? I'm so sorry for your loss. But I'm wondering if you might like to comment for my story." I whip out my notebook and pencil, as if I'm going to take notes. "Any thoughts on his untimely death?" I figure that's how people think reporters talk.

She smiles again, like that snake in *The Jungle Book,* and taps her little prayer book against her leather-gloved palm. For some reason, this looks incredibly menacing, and I can't believe I ever thought this viper looked like someone's grandma.

"You don't want a quote from me, Ms. McNally," she replies. "In fact, I'm certain you never want to see me again. But I want to let you know there's no story for you here. No story in Mack Briggs. No story in your friend Brad Foreman."

I open my mouth to ask how she knows Brad Foreman, but her hand goes up to silence me.

"Ms. McNally, let's make this brief. I don't know what you think you know, but you know nothing. And may I remind you, I'm on very close terms with the owner of your station, and I can assure you, my relationship with Mr. Maxwell Stern Denekamp is more important to him than one reporter's job."

I try once more, ready to protest, but there's the hand again.

"We're done here, Ms. McNally," she says. With that, she and her goon squad about-face and march away.

That's pretty harsh, I decide. And kind of misguided psychology. If you're trying to threaten my job and tell me something's not a story—that only tells me it's got to be a pretty damn good story. When my ship comes in on this one, I'm going to—

Ship.

Now I see the name on Brad's documents. A. Grimes Brown. CEO of Rogers Chalmers Enterprises. And co-owner of the *Miranda*. Andrea Grimes Brown. So nice to meet you.

I do my own slow and satisfied viper smile, carefully threading my pencil though the spiral of my notebook. If I'm right about what's going on, and I think I am, there are just two little words for this situation: *Gotcha, Grandma.*

Walking back to the car, I pat myself on the back for what I now assess as my gutsy decision to attend the funeral, even though I'm left with a huge bunch of questions. Were there other *Miranda* owners at the cemetery? Scanning over my shoulder, I blink in disbelief. There—past my tree, past the folding chairs, past the back poles of the canopy—I see a face I recognize.

It's Josh.

I catch my breath and turn my back to him, hiding. Why is he at Mack Briggs's funeral? He told me he didn't know Mack Briggs. I was right. He's a scheming, conniving rat.

I whirl around, head high, ready to let him have it with both barrels—biting wit and dismissive nonchalance. I'm totally on to him.

"So," I begin, as haughty as a salesclerk at an exclusive boutique, "I see . . ."

He's gone.

I would burst into tears of frustration if it wouldn't make my eyes puffy. "Damn it, damn it, damn it," I mutter, turning back to the car. I've been threatened by a sinister grandmother, deceived by a scheming schoolteacher, I'm confused, I'm disappointed and I have to drive all the way back to Boston by myself.

And now I've gotten a ticket. A ticket? This is the last frigging straw. I yank the paper out from under my windshield wiper, ready to crumple it into a wad and toss it into the black hole of my backseat.

But then I realize. They don't issue parking tickets at funerals. I look more closely. It's not a ticket. It's a note from Josh.

Biting my lower lip, I speed-read the scrawled message.

Recognized your car. Got a moment to spare? Carno's Café? 135 Main St.? I'll wait for you. J.

Well. That settles the question of whether he saw me. Not a chance I'm going. Even though it might be interesting to hear how he tries to explain himself. I slam my Jeep's door closed and dive for the map book. Maybe I'll go just for a minute.

As the engine revs and the heat powers on, I'm flooded with memories—Josh and I sat in this very car, talking for hours, looking at the stars. I ram the gearshift into Reverse to erase the moment. Maysie's latest "inspirational" postcard—a photo of Cinderella's castle, with the scrawled *Someday your Prince will come!*—is clipped to my visor. Not likely that's gonna happen. Men. I hate them all.

CHAPTER THIRTEEN

Carno's Café is an adventure in time travel. Turquoise plastic booths, brightly labeled 45s glued to the walls, newspaper headlines of Ike Elected, Nixon and Checkers, the moon landing, J.F.K. and Jackie. Waitresses in crewneck sweaters and ponytails tote trays weighted down with milk shakes and French fries.

I see Josh in a back corner, holding up a hand to get my attention. He looks almost—contrite. A tiny sprout of hope struggles to emerge, but I stomp it before it can grow. *He misled you. He deceived you. And now he'll try to convince you he didn't.*

I hang my coat over a hook on the side of the booth and slide in across the table. "Got your note," I say. "What can I do for you?" I ooze nonchalance, telegraphing *this is just business and I'm being polite.*

Josh seems bewildered, looks at me questioningly. "Charlie, is something wrong?" he asks. "I was so happy to see you at the funeral. But I didn't want to interrupt your conversation with whoever that was, so I just left a note on your car, hoping you could meet me here. It's so great to see you again, and . . ."

There's a pathetic opening gambit. Happy to see me? I doubt

that, Prof. If you wanted to see me, you might have used that little thing called the telephone.

A waitress interrupts, asking for my order. I see Josh already has coffee, so I gesture at it, asking for the same thing.

"So anyway," Josh continues, "I was on my way to the Jordan Beach Road house—remember my place in Vermont? No classes this week, just a weekend by myself. But after the e-mails I got from Brad Foreman, and your questions about them, and then what you told me about Mack Briggs, I just thought maybe I could sniff around at his funeral and see if there was anything to be learned."

He stirs his coffee, and I notice he's left-handed. Like I am. Supposed to be a sign of intelligence and sensitivity. And he has such nice hands. I remember how they felt when . . . I yank myself back to reality. Trouble is I can't understand why Josh is acting like nothing is wrong.

"Charlie?" He reaches out to touch my hand. "You seem . . . angry, I guess. What's up?"

Very clever. He's trying to switch the focus to me. As if I'm the one with the problem.

"Nothing's 'up,' as you put it," I respond, moving my hand away. "You said you wanted to talk to me. So talk."

"Okay," Josh continues. "If you say so. Anyway, guess who I saw?"

"Why don't you just tell me?" I reply, taking my coffee from a Sandra Dee look-alike. I rip open a pack of Splenda and tap it into my cup. "But, before you do," I add slowly, "let me ask you a question."

Josh waits, eyebrows raised.

"A few days ago," I continue, putting down my spoon and staring coldly into Josh's eyes, "you told me you'd never heard of Mack

Briggs. How is it, now, suddenly, amazingly, you know he's died and you know when and where his funeral is?" Got you now.

Josh doesn't look that "gotten." He reaches into the briefcase he's tucked into the corner, pulls out a newspaper and hands it to me.

I see it's the *Vermont Independent*, according to the masthead, published in Montpelier for southern Vermont. And on the front page, a huge obit for a favorite son. The reclusive but beloved ex-SEC chief, McKenzie Briggs.

"I get the *Indy* sent to me at Bexter," Josh explains, "just to keep up on what's happening around here. So I saw the obituary." Josh takes the paper back.

That's a pretty good answer, I suppose.

"I see," I reply, as if that hadn't really been a very important question. "So you were telling me—someone you saw at the funeral?"

"Well, yes," Josh says, eyes sparkling now. "And I just knew you would be interested. I was going to call you with the news the instant the funeral was over, but then there you were!"

I can't figure out why Josh is acting like everything is still cozy between us. Shouldn't he be more defensive?

"Anyway," Josh continues. "I saw—Wes Rasmussen. Isn't that intriguing? What was Rasmussen doing at Mack Briggs's funeral? You knew Foreman and Rasmussen were connected of course, at Aztratech. And you knew Foreman and Briggs were connected because of the e-mails. But I thought you'd be interested in what seems to be clear proof Rasmussen and Briggs were connected."

I'm too stunned to answer, but Josh goes on, gesturing with his spoon. "I know, I know. Leave the research to the experienced reporter. But one more thing," he says. "Don't be upset, but I approached Rasmussen and told him we had a mutual acquaintance in Brad Foreman. Just to see what he'd do. And here's the fascinating part—he knew I was an English teacher. Who could have talked to him about me? And why?"

Oh, he's good. This Josh is really good. But I predict his elaborate cover story is just about to crumble under the weight of its own clumsiness—and now I'll just give his little house of cards the final push.

"So you went up to Wes Rasmussen," I say. "Interesting. How did you know who he was?"

Josh has a baffled look again.

"I never told you about him," I continue, crossing my arms in front of me. "So you already knew him, didn't you? That long conversation we had in my car, when you were oh-so-interested in my story. You were just trying to figure out how much I knew."

"What are you talking about?" he asks. He leans toward me, elbows on the table. "Of course you told me about Rasmussen. Don't you remember? You told me about the *Miranda,* and all of the owners."

"I . . ." I start to answer.

"What's this all about, Charlie?" Josh's eyes harden. "Why are you behaving as if I've done something wrong? How the hell would I know Wes Rasmussen if you didn't tell me about him?"

I can't possibly be wrong here. I've got it all figured out, and I've just got to be tough enough to play out my hand.

"From the dinner party he gave!" I retort. "That's how you met Brad, right? At a dinner party—Wes Rasmussen's dinner party. And you've been reporting back to him ever since you got Brad to confide in you. And when you found out I was asking around about the spam, you got me to spill the beans, too. What are you getting in return, Aztratech stock options or something?"

For some reason, Josh doesn't look dismayed that my brilliant analysis has revealed his true motives. He takes another sip of his coffee, then picks up a spoon and slowly stirs what's left in the cup.

When he finally looks up, his face is unreadable. He takes the napkin from his lap, places it on the table. "I don't know what to say to you, Charlie," he says slowly. "This is not how I hoped today would turn out."

Josh puts some change on the table, the coins clinking on the Formica.

"I had a wonderful time with you, in my office and at the play. I didn't want to crowd you—I know you're busy with your sweeps reporting and I don't really know much about the rest of your life. So frankly, I was hoping we'd somehow see each other again, and I admit part of the reason I came to the funeral was that perhaps you'd be there, too."

He gives a bleak smile. "I'm still headed up to the house on Jordan Beach Road for a few days, and had thought, maybe, that you could come up and visit. No phones, no e-mail, just rural solitude. That's part of what I wanted to talk to you about."

I know my mouth must be hanging open.

"But I guess that's not going to happen," Josh finishes, reaching over for his briefcase. "Wes Rasmussen?" he says, sliding across the plastic booth. "He certainly was not the host at the dinner party where Brad and I met."

He starts to get up, stops. "I realized it was Rasmussen because I heard someone else call his name. A lucky coincidence, I thought at the time. I thought you'd think it was—" he pauses with a wry smile "—cool."

He shakes his head ruefully. "Anyway, whatever you think I'm involved in, I'm not. I admit, I was just so taken with you . . ." Josh stands and puts both hands on the table, leaning down to face me.

I'm still staring up at him. My mouth has stopped working altogether, and my brain is struggling in emotional quicksand.

He suddenly changes gears.

"I can't imagine," he says, with a trace of bitterness in his voice, "what it is that you've concocted is going on. You seem to be implying I'm playing the nefarious villain in some complicated journalism plot. That's absurd. I would have thought you, of all people, had better instincts than that."

He pauses, tense, and I can feel his anger. Something has gone terribly wrong and I don't know how I screwed up.

"I was just trying to be part of your life," he says. "And have you be a part of mine. So much, apparently, for that idea."

And, as I watch in despair, he walks out of the restaurant. He's gone. And I'm left with cold coffee, welling tears, and utter confusion.

CHAPTER FOURTEEN

I trudge up the basement steps to the station lobby, thinking this day just couldn't get any weirder.

Wrong again.

Sitting there, in one of the lobby's puffy oyster-colored fake leather chairs, is Melanie Foreman.

She's wearing sunglasses and clutching her coat around her. Her face is so hidden in a black wool scarf I almost don't recognize her.

"Melanie?" I say. "What's . . . ?"

She leaps up, looking spooked and on edge, and clutches my arm.

"Charlie," she whispers. "I've been waiting and waiting for you. Franklin's not here and no one seemed to know where you were. They told me to come back later, but I figured you would have to be back at some point, and then the guard at the desk said it was all right for me to sit here, and . . ."

Even through her darkened lenses, I can see her eyes dart around as if she's looking for someone.

"I need to talk to you about a phone call I got this morning." She takes off the sunglasses, and I see her face is red and puffy. "I really do."

I put my arm across her shoulders and glance around the room. What is she looking for? Or whom?

"Let's go upstairs to my office," I say, trying to sound soothing. "It's private, and you can tell me all about it." I look outside at the alleyway in front of the station. It's a tow-truck trap—they'll nab you if you're parked there too long. "Did you park in the alley?"

At this Melanie bursts into tears. "No, I don't have a car. Not anymore."

Of course. Her car was destroyed when her husband was killed. In it. Charlie the idiot.

She looks up at me, her elegant face contorted in sorrow. "Can we just go upstairs?"

Melanie finishes her cup of tea, still tense as she describes the phone call she received this morning.

"And so then," she says, touching her lips with a Dunkin' Donuts napkin I had stashed away, "the lawyer person says he knows I have the documents Brad took from Aztratech. He told me they had some type of surveillance video of him carrying the boxes out and putting them in his car.

"I told them again and again, I had no idea where any such documents were—which I figured is true since I don't really know what you did with them, do I?" She manages a fleeting smile. "But he insisted it was a federal offense to have those files, and if I didn't hand them over, he was going to send the police."

"Well, he couldn't really do that," I muse. "I think there would have to be some sort of criminal charges for that, and . . ." I shake my head. "Anyway, you don't have them."

"I know. That's what I said. I don't have any documents." Melanie slumps in her chair. "But he just hung up on me."

"I can understand why you're upset," I say cautiously. "But I think it was probably a fishing expedition." I'm warming up to my own theory. "See, he's just testing to see if you'll crack. And since you didn't, no problem. He decides you're telling the truth, and he's out of the picture."

Melanie sits quietly, looking at me with those big eyes. I figure she's better now, calmed by my reassuring manner and infinite logic. But she shakes her head.

"There's more," she continues. "After the phone call I went for a long walk with the dog, and when I got home . . ." She's crying again. She sniffs and dabs at her eyes with the soggy napkin. "Well, Banjo streaked away, headed for the basement, yapping and yipping. I guess I thought a squirrel might have gotten in the house. That's happened before."

I nod at her; I understand.

"So I followed her downstairs, and, and . . ." Her voice catches, but she continues. "The basement window is smashed—glass everywhere. All the drawers open, the file cabinets. Papers all over the floor, books from the bookcase, just—chaos."

She closes her eyes briefly, apparently picturing the scene. "Banjo was under the window, teeth bared, growling and growling."

"Did you call the police? 911?"

"No." She shakes her head. "I started thinking, it's the Aztratech people, of course. And then I remembered they said they had video of Brad taking documents, and it was a federal crime. I thought if I called the police, Aztratech would just say they were trying to recover what I—Brad—we—whoever—had stolen from them, and then I would be charged with something."

"Oh, Melanie, no. You've got to call the police," I insist. "It was breaking and entering. Burglary. Call right now." I pick up the phone and hold out the receiver to her.

She shakes her head. "Nothing was taken," she says. "Not from anywhere."

"Really?" Slowly, I put back the phone. "So that pretty much proves," I continue, "it was someone connected with Aztratech, looking for the files. Those papers you gave us must really be important."

Melanie puts her face in her hands, her tiny body a portrait of fear and misery.

"Brad would never, never, have put me in danger," she says plaintively. "Why would he bring home something so valuable that people would break in to get it back? And even endanger his family?"

I sigh with frustration. How am I supposed to answer that?

"Maybe he didn't know what he had," I offer. "Maybe that's why he e-mailed me, and e-mailed Mack Briggs and Josh Gelston. Or maybe, when he found out what the documents proved, he told someone about it. And turned out, he told the wrong person."

We're both quiet for a moment.

"And then—" I break the silence "—it was too late to protect you."

Melanie's eyes tear up again. Poor thing. First her husband killed in a car accident, and now she's being threatened by corporate enforcers who send ransacking thugs to her house.

"Still," I continue, "I think you should call the police. Are you sure nothing was taken?"

While she's thinking, I allow myself a brief flash of selfish regret that Melanie came here. If whoever it was that trashed her house is smart enough to follow her, she's led them right to where the documents actually are. Here in my little office.

"Nothing was . . ." Melanie glances up toward my office door. She draws her cashmere shawl more closely around her shoulders, as if she's felt a sudden chill.

I look at my doorway. Angela.

"Excuse me," she says, bestowing Melanie with what I suppose could pass for a smile. "I apologize for interrupting your . . . chat."

She gives a tap to her obviously fake Movado. "I've been wondering when you and Franklin would return," she says. "We've beeped you both all morning, and we're—" she raises an eyebrow "—disappointed neither of you has responded."

We haven't responded to the stupid archaic beepers because we despise them, I want to tell her. We rip out their evil little batteries and hide the pernicious machines in our desk drawers.

"I'm so sorry Angela," I say, wide-eyed. "My beeper never went off. Or maybe I was out of range."

Angela is not buying this for a moment, but even she isn't boorish enough to confront me when there's a crying person sitting in my office.

"And Franklin?" she asks with one raised eyebrow. "Is he also suffering from out-of-range disease?"

"You'll have to ask Franklin." I smile, making it clear that management by sarcasm is totally ineffective. "When he gets back."

"Gets back from where?" Angela replies. "Apparently he hasn't been here all day. No one's seen him and he hasn't answered his phone, here or home."

She gives another look at her dime-store watch. "When you're finished," she says, acknowledging Melanie with a glance, "come see me in my office." In a swirl of rayon and acrylic, she turns and pudges down the hall.

"My boss, sort of," I attempt to explain to Melanie, as soon as Angela's out of earshot. "Sorry. She's socially inept."

"So it seems," Melanie agrees. "But she asked a good question—where is Franklin?"

Our office becomes very, very quiet. I look at Franklin's empty chair. The empty coatrack. There's no briefcase. No umbrella.

I look at my desk phone. Maybe he's left me a message. But the red message light isn't on. "You know, Melanie," I answer slowly, "I have no idea."

Rewinding through the day, I try to retrieve the last time I heard from him. And then, I do. Times like this I realize my quickly developing short-term memory loss can be beneficial. I'd completely forgotten about that funeral call. I rummage in my purse for my phone, relieved.

"I completely spaced," I say to Melanie without looking up. "He called me this morning, but I was at—anyway, I couldn't answer the phone." No reason to tell her about the funeral.

I find the phone and I'm already feeling better. There's a staticy silence as whatever makes it work starts to happen, then the message.

"Ricky, it's Weezer. I'm going to be late. Tell Ma. See ya."

My brain grinds to a halt, and I angrily push the replay button to hear it again. It remains the same astonishingly disappointing wrong number. I seem to have lost Franklin. And now, in a complete role reversal, Melanie is trying to console me.

"Could he have a doctor's appointment, something like that?" she asks.

"I suppose," I say, unconvinced.

"He could be out on an interview, or getting his car fixed. . . ."

I know she's trying to help, and that's admirable, of course, but she doesn't know Franklin and she doesn't know me.

"I'll get you some water," she says. "Where . . ?"

I point her to the fridge down the hall, and then try to shake off my growing panic. He overslept. He's at the dentist. The tailor. With Stephen for a stolen day of passion. To reassure myself, I decide to count up all the times I don't know where Franklin is.

And that's the clincher. I always know where Franklin is.

Melanie comes back into the room, carrying two bottles of water. In the brief time she's been away, I've figured out what's happened.

I take a sip from my water bottle, then twist the cap back on. "Melanie," I say carefully, "does anyone know where you are?"

Her eyes widen as she considers. "I called a cab," she says slowly. "So the cab company knows."

Not good. It's not Melanie's fault of course, but . . .

"Oh, Charlie," she wails. "I see what you mean. The documents are here in your office, aren't they? And since now they know I ran right to you, they'll make trouble for you . . . and Franklin."

No reason to be coy about this. "If they haven't already," I say.

Melanie collapses into sobs, elbows on her knees, face in her hands. She looks up, red-eyed. "I can't do anything right. I can't understand why Brad put me in this situation. And then I did it to you and Franklin. What's going on, Charlie?"

"He didn't mean to put you in any situation." My turn to console her now. "Things just got out of control."

"Maybe. But now," Melanie says, "won't they come here looking for the files?"

"Yes," I admit. "Definitely possible. But now at least, they're still here." I point under my desk, showing Melanie where I stashed the files she gave us. Franklin and I camouflaged the box with my backup cosmetics basket, a couple of containers of Wet Ones, a package of RyKrisp and a tote bag full of plastic silverware.

"So now we have to figure out, right away, what to do," I say. "And the copies Mack Briggs sent us. We have to hide those somewhere else, too."

We put the files Briggs overnighted to us under Franklin's desk. They're still in their cardboard carton, too, but those we camouflaged with a pile of old *Wall Street Journal*s and empty videotape boxes. I give a quick glance just to reassure myself they're still where they belong.

They're not.

I close my eyes. I'm imagining things. I leap out of my chair, then get on all fours to peer more closely under Franklin's desk.

It's ridiculous of course, a box of files is either there or it isn't. And this one—isn't.

"Charlie?" Melanie says. "What are you doing under the desk?"

I turn around and collapse with my back against the wall. From this vantage point, I can see under my desk, too. And I can also see those files—are also missing.

"I don't know what to tell you," I say, wrapping my arms around my knees. "Franklin's gone. The Mack Briggs files are gone. Brad's files are gone. And you and I may be in trouble."

My heart rushes with happiness and tears spring to my eyes. The phone on my desk is ringing, and it's got to be Franklin. Questions answered, life back to normal. He's going to be out of control over the missing files, but we'll handle that together. I jump to my feet to grab the receiver.

"McNally," I answer, plopping into my desk chair. I'm so relieved.

"Charlie," I hear. "Can you come down to my office? Now? Your guest will have to wait."

It's Angela. Not Franklin. Damn. And "come to my office"? How does "never" sound?

I explain the situation to Melanie, then remember that crime report.

"I'll be right back," I assure her. "But it's essential for you to call the police." I point. "Use Franklin's phone."

Melanie crosses her arms in front of her and chews her lower lip. "Well," she finally replies, "I suppose it can't do any harm." She picks up the receiver and starts punching in numbers.

So that's at least in the works. As for Miss News Medusa downstairs, I decide she can just cool her ratty, too-high heels. Even

Anne Boleyn got to fix herself up before she faced her executioner. I grab my faithful mirror from the wall and prop it against my computer, then pull my cosmetics bag from my top desk drawer.

I stop for a moment, mideyeliner, and sigh in resignation. I should just quit. Angela's called me down to her office, a very unsubtle power move to get me onto her territory, making me walk through the newsroom and past all the gawking reporters at their desks.

I hear Melanie getting through to the police.

"Detective? This is Melanie Foreman, of Riverside Lane? I'd like to report a break-in. . . ."

She puts a hand over the receiver. "I'm on hold," she says. "You know what? After this, I'll just call a cab and go to my mother's. Thank you so much, Charlie. I'm sorry for being so needy. I'll be fine."

Good. At least she's doing the right thing, and she'll be safe. It can only help that she's telling the police what happened. They'll be able to keep an eye on her house. I wish there were someone who could keep *me* safe.

I put the mirror back on its pushpin holder, and give it a conspiratorial wink. "Wish me luck, magic mirror on the wall," I implore. It falls and crashes to the floor, scattering jagged shards of glass all over the rug.

Ha-ha. Breaking news. The universe now has instant messaging.

Angela looks up from her no-doubt extremely important papers, gives me a weird look and closes the flap on her manila folder.

"You wanted to see me?" I say, hovering in the doorway.

"Come in and close the door, could you, Charlie?"

As I turn to shut the door, every eye in the newsroom is straining to see what comes next. I stare right back at them, defiant, but no one will meet my gaze. Cowards. Turning back to Angela, I know the bad part is over. There's really nothing more she can say to me that can make this situation worse.

"Sit down, won't you?" Angela says with one of her inevitable fake smiles, gesturing to her couch. Even she must find it a little unpleasant to fire someone. That's why she looks so uncomfortable. "Kevin wants to join us. He'll be here in just a moment."

Wrong again. That's worse. The news director is on his way?

As I perch on a corner of Angela's couch, my stomach churns and I'm faintingly hot. I realize I'd been hoarding a tiny reserve of hope that I was wrong about this summons to the boardroom. It gurgles down the drain as I come to grips with a shattering certainty: there's no reason for the big guy to be here unless . . .

The door opens and I imagine the seismic activity on the newsroom e-mail network as word spreads: *Kevin's 2 Angela's office with Charlie. This is going 2 B big.*

I watch with trepidation as Kevin unbuttons and rebuttons his tailored double-breasted jacket, looking like an agitated greyhound. He sits on the edge of Angela's desk, facing me.

"So, Charlie," he says, unbuttoning again. His entire body is telegraphing *here comes the bad news*, and I realize I've got to hold it together. I can't walk out of here crying. This could be the first day of the rest of my life. Maybe.

"Hi, Kevin," I manage to say, hoping my voice isn't shaking. I'm supposed to be the tough one, after all. I *am* the tough one. My brain is making the hurry-up signal. Get on with it. Maybe it's even the kick in the butt I need to get a new life. Maybe.

"So, Charlie," Kevin repeats. "There's no easy way to put this. Franklin's in the hospital." He hands me a piece of paper. "Here's his room number at the General. The doctors think he'll be fine when he wakes up, but . . ."

Suddenly he's not speaking English. It's just a buzzing hum of incomprehensible babble as I try to understand what's going on.

I'm not fired. That's good.

But Franklin. That's bad.

He must be—sick? Hurt? At Massachusetts General Hospital? That's really, really bad.

"Apparently," Kevin continues, "it all happened this morning, behind his condo. Police aren't sure of the circumstances yet, but they have a detective there to talk to him when he wakes up."

I find my voice. "Wakes? Police?"

"He's just sedated, not unconscious," Kevin explains. "Apparently he was hit in the head several times, but luckily the injuries aren't long-term. He's a very fortunate guy."

"Hit? Who?" I stand up, frowning, and look back and forth between Kevin and Angela. I fight crying because I don't have time for that. One word at a time is all I can manage. "Why?" I plead for answers. "When?" Another thought. "Stephen?"

Kevin shrugs, shaking his head. "Police are working on it. His . . . roommate . . . is apparently out of town, we don't know where." He gives me a fleeting smile. "Always the reporter, always asking questions. That's why we count on you," he says as he comes over and actually pats me on the back. "You all right? You can go over to the hospital now, if you like." He glances at Angela. "Why don't you call Charlie a cab?"

CHAPTER FIFTEEN

When I get to the hospital, Franklin is not alone. A uniformed police officer sits in an institutional folding chair next to the single hospital bed in room 4-1066. She's holding a clipboard, leaning intently forward.

Pausing a moment in the doorway, I take in the whole frightening picture: Franklin's gauze-wrapped head, the angry bruise under one eye, his ashen face and exhausted demeanor. I've never seen Franklin any way but spotless, polished, self-confident and healthy. Now he looks scared and vulnerable, the pale green hospital blanket pulled up under his chin, his head propped on a pile of several thin, flat pillows, only his arms and face showing.

The officer looks up and turns in her chair, acknowledging my arrival. She snaps the leather flap over her clipboard, concealing what she's written. "Are you family?"

Franklin gingerly raises the arm that's not attached to an IV tube. "She's okay," he whispers in a scratchy, very un-Franklin-like voice. "It's Char—Charlie. The one I told you about." He attempts a smile. Even battered and in a hospital bed, he remembers his manners. "Charlotte, this is Officer McCarron, Boston PD."

Officer McCarron pushes back her chair and gets to her feet.

She seems coltish and awkward in her heavily starched blue shirt, unflatteringly belted trousers and BPD-issue oxfords. "Of course," she says. "Charlie McNally."

I force a polite smile, but my heart is aching. "Oh, sweetheart, what happened to you?" I wail. "Who did this? When?" The questions come flooding out. "Are you going to be okay? How do you feel? How did you get to the hospital? Why did . . ."

Franklin smiles and glances at the cop. "That's what Officer McCarron was asking me," he whispers. "I was telling her—"

"Yeah," McCarron interrupts, gesturing with her notes. "And I'm afraid I'll have to ask you to wait outside until I'm finished, ma'am."

Two hours, one Snickers and four hideous acid-based cups of coffee later, I'm back in with Franklin. Officer What's-her-name is out of the picture. Hovering nurses have finished their pill dispensing, and a bandage-checking doctor seems satisfied with the patient's progress.

I scoot the tan metal chair closer to Franklin's bedside. I'm not leaving until I hear the whole story.

"Water?" I ask, holding out the plastic cup containing one of those bendy straws. "I could hold this for you. Or can I get you . . ."

Franklin shakes his head and closes his eyes. "I'm fine," he says. "Really. Just a little tired."

"So what did she . . ." I begin.

But Franklin's asleep. My shoulders sag in disappointment. I'm eager for some answers, of course, but no way I'll wake him up.

I attempt to get comfortable in the unyieldingly institutional chair, unable to stop staring at Franklin's green and yellowing bruises, a clear bandage covering the precise row of tiny stitches over one eyebrow. How could anyone have done this to another person? And why?

I think back to Brad's car accident, wondering for the millionth time just how accidental that really was. The break-in at Melanie's sure wasn't an accident, and Franklin's brutal beating wasn't an accident and our files are definitely missing. No accident there, either.

Melanie. At least by now she's safe, I figure, with her mother, awaiting word from the police. And Franklin is certainly safe here.

I stretch my legs out in front of me, trying to sort out the buzz of my thoughts. Another thing that's not an accident. Why do all the e-mail subject lines have that stupid misspelling: "A new re-figh deal 4-U"?

Then I hear a soft cough, and look up to see Franklin's eyes flutter open. He's awake.

He blinks a few times, stretches his eyes wide open, yawns and gives me a weary smile.

"Hey, Charlotte," he says, his voice still raspy. "You still here?"

"Of course," I reply. "For the duration. What can I get you? Water? A nurse? More pillows?" I stand up and try to fluff Franklin's pillows like the nurses do in the movies, but my patient waves me away.

"I'm okay, really," he says. "Just a huge headache." He sighs and touches his forehead. "Stitches?" he asks.

"Yup." I smile. "About a dozen, I'd say. Very hip, very *Fight Club*."

Franklin stretches out one arm, testing. "Ow." He winces. "My whole body hurts, actually, now that I can feel it again. I had a few hours of serious drugs—so I was completely out of it. Now they've worn off, I suppose." He tries to move his shoulders, and I see the pain register in his face.

"I'm calling the nurse," I say, concerned. "You need more pills." I push the green button attached to a cord on his headboard.

"Thanks," Franklin says. "I guess that would be good."

"Franklin, I—" I begin.

"Charlotte, I—" he says simultaneously.

We both laugh softly, relieved that some things never change.

His laptop, open on the nightstand, pings insistently. "Stephen's texting me nonstop from his meeting in D.C.," Franklin explains. "We're going to talk later. Anyway, I guess you want to know what happened," he continues. "And why." He pauses. "Me, too."

"So—what do you remember?" I ask, pulling my chair closer to the bed.

"Well, let's see. I was behind my condo, in the parking area, getting ready to come to work." Franklin tries to furrow his forehead, and grimaces as his stitches get in the way. He touches them gingerly as he continues. "I had just popped open the trunk with my remote when I heard crunching on the gravel behind me. That wasn't remarkable, you know. Several tenants use the lot. But it was pretty early in the morning, and something didn't feel quite right."

I lean forward, elbows on my knees, chin in my hands. I know what happens in the end, so it's even scarier to hear the story unfold.

"So I think I started to look around," Franklin says, remembering, "but then I heard some kind of noise, like a grunt or a martial-arts yell, you know?"

I nod silently, transfixed.

"So I turned back to slam the trunk closed, and just then, while I was still facing the car, I felt something hit me on the head. I saw the reflection of a person in the trunk, I think, and so I kind of dodged out of the way, didn't get the full force of the blow. I tried to run, but didn't get very far. Another person came out from behind the SUV parked next to my Passat, a little wiry guy, and he punched me in the face. I fell to my knees in the gravel, which hurt like hell, shredded my pants and started both knees bleeding." Franklin pauses. "Then the first guy started kicking me. I tried to fight back, but it wasn't working." He briefly closes his eyes. "I'm not really the fighting type, you know?"

I can't believe what I'm hearing. This kind of thing doesn't happen in broad daylight behind classy neighborhood condos. "How did you get away?"

"That's the amazing part," Franklin replies. "I must tell you I didn't think I would get away. It crossed my mind they were going to kill me. They seemed to know what they were doing and didn't say anything to me, or to each other."

"And so?"

"So," he continues, "I'm lying on the driveway behind my place, gravel stabbing me in the back, and the big guy comes over to me. I gritted my teeth and put my fists up, waiting for the worst. I knew my face was bleeding and my head was throbbing. So anyway, he comes toward me, leans down—and here's the strangest part. I'm tensed up and terrified, waiting to get nailed, but instead he simply picks up my car keys from the ground."

"Your car keys?" I say, incredulous. "They wanted your car?"

"I rolled over as best I could," Franklin goes on, "got up, and ran. I'm not sure where I was headed, just away. Next thing I heard, my car's driving out of the parking lot, and both guys are gone."

"Your car?" I repeat, still unbelieving. "That's crazy. You don't beat someone up to get a Passat."

Franklin shrugs and winces again. "Damn," he says. "Still hurts. I've got to remember not to do that." He shifts in his bed. "So I got to the street, called 911 from a pay phone, and just sort of propped myself up with the phone-booth kiosk until an ambulance arrived. I don't even remember the trip to the hospital. And I woke up in this bed, police by my side. Stitches and all."

This reminds me that the nurse with the pain pills has not yet appeared, so I punch the call button again. I'm convinced this thing is attached to nothing. It's some kind of perverse placebo experiment, to see if people feel better because they think the nurse is coming.

"So I guess the police called Channel 3," I go on. "Probably saw your press pass. So you think those guys just wanted your car?" I scratch my head, considering. "That really doesn't make any sense."

"Yeah, I agree," Franklin replies. "But why else?"

I hear the door open behind me. Still upset and jittery from Franklin's attack, I stand up and whip around to see who's coming in.

But when Betty Crocker comes through the door, I relax a little. I know this is actually her name; it says so on her name tag. Wearing a frilly white cap, pin-curled white hair and thick-soled white oxfords, Nurse Crocker is carrying a pleated paper cup of pills, and fusses over Franklin as if he's a wounded toddler and she's his doting granny.

"Here, honey," she coos protectively. "Take these and you'll feel better." She pats his pillows and turns to me. "Oh, hello, dear," she says, smiling. "Are you his . . . ?" She stops in mid-sentence, her eyes widening and her mouth making a little *o*.

"Well, bless me if it isn't Charlie McNally," she says, pointing at me. "The one on TV? I watch you every day!"

"How nice," I say, shaking her hand. "Thank you for taking such good care of Franklin. He's a good pal, and we really appreciate it."

Her fluttering intensifies as she adjusts Franklin's blanket and offers him water. "Well, don't you worry about a thing," she says. Then she looks up, a perplexed look on her face. "Oh, dear me," she says, "I completely forgot. All the excitement, I suppose."

"Completely forgot what?" I ask.

"The police, dear," she says.

We all turn as there's a knock on the doorjamb. Officer McCarron is back, accompanied by what must be a plain-clothes detective. Even out of uniform, his rumpled fisherman's sweater and brown leather jacket scream *cop*. Actually, sort of *sexy cop*, now that I look more closely.

The nurse bustles out, but I decide I'm not budging.

"How ya doing, Mr. Parrish?" the man says. "I'm Detective Cipriani. Joe Cipriani."

Franklin raises a hand. "Hey," he responds, his voice weak but friendly. "Anything new?"

Both officers glance at me, then at each other. Franklin interrupts their apparent decision-making.

"You know Charlie McNally, of course," he says. "Whatever you have to say to me, you can say to her." He gives a colossal yawn, then shakes his head. "Sorry," he says. "I guess the pills are starting to kick in."

Officer McCarron stays in the doorway, as the increasingly attractive Detective Cipriani pulls up a chair beside mine. I sit down next to him, ignoring the scent of what I think is Hugo Boss and the gold band on his left hand, figuring I've gotten the all clear to stay.

"So, Mr. Parrish," he's saying. "We found your car."

"Great." Franklin's face lights up a little, though his voice is increasingly thick, his words halting. "Where? How? My belongings?"

The detective shifts in his chair, crosses one leg over a knee. "Well, that's the thing," he answers. "We found it miles out on the turnpike, in a vacant lot in Framingham," he says. "Tires and air bags, engine, stereo, all stripped. Trunk empty."

Franklin sags in his bed as the cop continues.

"And, well, torched."

"Torched?" I interrupt, surprised. "Why would they do that?"

Detective Cipriani looks at me, up and down. I don't think I'm imagining this. He's still watching me as I cross my legs and yank my skirt down farther over my knees. He pulls a notebook from his jacket pocket and gives me a crooked smile.

"Is it McNally with *M-a-c* or just *M-c?*" he asks, clicking his pen with a flourish. "And can I get a phone number where I can reach you?"

Officer McCarron leaves her post at the doorway and comes into the room.

"That's what we don't know," she says, stepping between me and Dirty Harry. "Why they'd torch the car. Any reason you can think of?"

We all look at Franklin. He's asleep again, off in Percocet paradise.

"Ms. McNally?" Officer McCarron, whispering now, turns to me. "Anything you can think of?"

I get up and walk to the window, looking out over the hospital parking lot. It's dark outside, extra-bright spotlights illuminating the lined parking spaces, an ambulance waiting outside the emergency room door. This has been a long day. And now, I quickly have to make a big decision.

Do I tell the cops about Melanie? About Brad? About Mack Briggs? About the missing files? Then I remember, I'm the reporter here. I should be asking *them* for information. I turn back from the window, smiling innocently. "Golly, no," I say. "What are you all thinking, though? Any leads?"

Detective Cipriani looks uncertain. But it's McCarron who answers.

"Well," she says slowly, as if calculating how much to tell me. "There's been a rash of car thefts in that neighborhood. And we find the cars soon after, stripped. Just like Mr. Parrish's Passat. So this could be another—"

"But the incidents are not always the same," Cipriani interrupts.

“That’s why we need to know if there’s something you could tell us. Otherwise, we’ve got to figure it’s connected.”

“So?” McCarron again. She narrows her eyes at me. “Think one more time.”

It’s completely against my reporter nature to tell the police what I’m investigating. If they’re such hotshots, I figure they should be able to find the bad guys on their own. And if they start asking questions, everyone involved will clam up and start shredding documents and I’ll never get any answers. Or any story. But what if it could help find who hurt Franklin?

“Ms. McNally?” Cipriani asks. “We’re waiting.”

CHAPTER SIXTEEN

The glowing green numbers on my bedside clock read 2:23; the ones on my VCR say 2:29; the ones on my backup alarm clock say 2:30. Since I always set my clocks fast so I won't be late, I figure that means it's something like 2:15 in the morning.

I've been sitting in bed for an hour now, sipping a mug of chamomile, staring at the walls. Wide-awake. I'm unsettled from the funeral, distressed by my head-on discussion with Josh, paranoid about the boxes of files missing from our office, and worried as hell about Franklin. And frightened by whoever beat him up.

How am I supposed to sleep? I didn't tell Franklin about the missing files, and he is going to be beyond upset. I didn't tell the police about Brad Foreman and Mack Briggs's accidents or Melanie's break-in because I decided those things weren't necessarily connected and the cops would just interfere. What if that was the wrong decision? Have I sacrificed Franklin's safety—and possibly put others in danger—for a story?

My gaze travels wearily around the room, as if somewhere, answers are hiding. And then I see another glowing number, a flashing "three" on my answering machine.

I turn over on my side and push the button.

"Message number one," the mechanical voice says. "Received today at 8:37 p.m."

The machine beeps as I take another sip of tea. I almost choke as I recognize the voice.

"Hello, Charlie, it's Josh."

I put down my tea and hug my knees. What is he going to say?

"You know I'm up in Vermont for the week," his voice continues. "I drove out to where there's phone service, because I can't stop thinking about our conversation at Carno's yesterday. I've been trying to come up with a way to prove to you that I have nothing to do with whatever is going on."

I stare at the answering machine as if it were human, and Josh's solemn voice fills the room.

"If you don't care, you don't care," the message goes on. "If it doesn't matter to you, then I'll accept that. But do me one favor. Ask Melanie who gave the dinner party where Brad and I met. Ask her if it was Wes Rasmussen."

Josh pauses, then goes on. "Charlie, trust me, okay?"

And then he's gone.

Time is suspended as I sit, wrapped in my comforter. Could I trust him? The Bexter kids certainly adore him. He's obviously a devoted teacher. And he seemed so open about his life, his divorce. But that could be just to soften me up, get me to tell him what I know. Still, in the car, he was so tender. And interested. And romantic. And . . .

So much for the calming tea—my now-racing brain feels as if it's been hit with megadose caffeine. How long has it been since I kissed someone—since someone kissed me? How often have I imagined that shooting star, embracing the memory, yearning for his arms? That time of "together" only magnifies how often I'm just like this: alone. Even Stephen knew it. I'm alone.

But maybe things can change. Maybe I haven't demolished yet another potential relationship. Because there's no reason for Josh to call me unless he really cares about me. And the dinner-party thing must be true, because it would be so easy for me to check with Melanie and confirm it with her.

Unless Melanie's in on it, too. I feel my eyes widen as I consider this. I'm wrong. I knew I shouldn't have let my guard down. I let myself be seduced by a moment and a memory. What if she and Josh were having an affair? And maybe they conspired to get rid of Brad. Now they're trying to throw me off the trail.

Josh and Melanie. She's young. And beautiful. Could it be?

And then I remember—I have two more messages. Pushing Josh and Melanie out of my head, I hit Play.

Another beep, another time announcement, another whirr, and then, another voice.

Melanie's.

My entire body deflates. Can this be a coincidence? Yes. Damn it. It can. It's late, and my imagination is out of control. She's only calling to tell me what the police said about her break-in.

I bargain with myself. If she mentions Josh, I'll know there's something going on, and I'll have to handle that.

The message continues.

". . . hope I'm not bothering you. But I did talk to the police."

So far, so good. Nothing about Josh.

Melanie's voice continues. "They told me there have been a string of break-ins in our neighborhood, and they're thinking it may be a bunch of teenagers getting high and carousing through empty houses. They never take anything, the officers told me, and since nothing was missing from my house, they're thinking it's another of their suburban—'sprees,' I think they said."

I hear her sigh on the tape, and then she goes on.

"I suppose they're right," she says. "So, thanks so much for everything, but let's not worry about it anymore. It's late. I'm going to sleep. Talk to you tomorrow, perhaps."

Good again. And it's simple enough for me to check with the Lexington cops and see if that's true, so it would be silly of Melanie to give me that much detail, knowing it was a one-phone-call confirmation.

I open my nightstand drawer and rummage in the dark for ChapStick. Unclicking the plastic top, I try to reconcile the two calls. There's no connection, I decide, adding another waxy layer of white stuff. They just happened to call.

One right after the other. What if they were calling from the same place?

Maybe, if I listened to the messages again, I could get a clue from the background noises. Like if there was a dog barking, or the sound of (God forbid) soft music in each of them, that would prove they were together. And that could mean they were together in Josh's house on Jordan Beach Road.

The house where I should have been this weekend.

How am I supposed to sleep? I've just heard two calls from people who could be deeply involved—and maybe together—in corporate intrigue, high finance and, I admit to myself, maybe even murder.

The blinking of my answering machine distracts me. There's one more message to retrieve. For the first time in my life, I hope it's a telemarketer. I push Play.

I look at the clock on the night table again, and now it's 4:35. I guess I must have slept a little. I mentally count on my fingers—if I get up at my usual seven-thirty, that'll be about three hours of sleep. No way I can manage on that. If I get up at eight-thirty, that'll be four hours of sleep. Four hours of sleep but I'll be late for work.

I'll take four hours. I burrow down into my pillow and pull the comforter up to my ears. But my stubborn brain keeps thinking back over that last phone message. Because actually, there was no message. When I pushed Play the final time, I heard the machine spin into place, and then heard absolutely nothing.

"To hear this message again," the mechanical voice said, "push Repeat."

I pushed, straining to hear any little sound that would give me some idea of who might be calling. Silence again.

Who was calling me at home and hanging up?

I fear I know the answer. Whoever beat up Franklin. Whoever ransacked Melanie's house. Whoever killed Brad and Mack Briggs. Whoever stole the files right out of my office. And whoever it is, now they're calling me. On my unlisted phone. At home.

They know where I live.

I burst out laughing, the sound shattering the darkness.

Come on, drama queen, I taunt myself. *You've lost it*. Melanie's house was burgled by drugged-out teenagers. Franklin was assaulted by a gang of car thieves, and Brad Foreman and Mack Briggs were in similar but separate car accidents. And you, Reporter Girl, are a founding and lifetime member of the paranoia club. I hear the first car of the morning drive by under my window, and I even hear the early birds twittering in the trees.

I fall back into my pillows, exhausted and defeated, blinking into the diminishing darkness. Everything is going to be fine, I reassure myself. It always is.

Skirts. I can't find any skirts. I know I have skirts. I yank through hanger after hanger, but there are only blouses and sweaters. I have a test this morning! Why didn't I study? And now I'm going to fail and be humiliated and there's the bell for class and I'm already late and—

The teacher is going to be so disappointed in me. Why won't that bell stop ringing?

It's the phone. I bolt upright in bed, still vaguely upset about missing my test, but relieved that once again, it was just a dream. But that phone ringing—that's real. I glance at the clock, but with no glasses and the sun streaming in my windows it's difficult to see the numbers—6:46? No, 8:46.

Not a good omen. I'm late and the phone is ringing.

"Hello?" I answer. Going for the very-alert-been-up-for-hours-reading-the-newspaper tone.

"Charlie? It's Kevin O'Bannon."

Isn't that sweet. The news director's calling to find out about Franklin. That's so considerate.

"Hi, Kevin," I say. "Thanks so much for calling, so kind of you. Franklin is—"

"Charlie," he interrupts. I can't decipher the unfamiliar tone in his voice. "I have you on speakerphone, and Angela is with me."

Apprehension slithers into my sleep-deprived brain. Speakerphone? Angela? I shoo the fear away. They both want the latest on Franklin, and a speakerphone is efficient.

The news director's voice continues, crackling through the receiver. "I assume you've seen the paper."

"Seen the . . . ?" is all I can manage. My mental public-address system starts up a Klaxon wail, an all-hands danger signal. "Newspaper?"

Angela's voice now. "Yes, Charlie, the *Herald*. The front page. Surely you've seen it by now." She pauses. "It's almost nine, after all."

Like I don't know what time it is. Tension and adrenaline are overcoming my fatigue. We're in direct competition with the newspapers. If they beat us on a story, our story is dead.

"Uh, no, I stayed up very late with Franklin at the hospital, and—"

"So, Charlie," Kevin interrupts my excuses. "When you do get to the paper, you'll see the lead story headline—Feds Say No Go to Go-Go Pharma Co."

I don't understand that, but I do understand your boss is not supposed to call you in the morning to read newspaper headlines out loud.

"What again? Feds say . . ."

Angela's voice again. "Just read it, Charlie. It's a blockbuster story, all about pharmaceutical pricing fraud. Apparently some whistle-blower has ratted out this company Aztratech—it's local, it's in Boxford—and is telling the U.S. Attorney's office Aztratech has been submitting false claims to the government for medical reimbursements. Millions of dollars."

I can't breathe. I can't breathe. I have a headache and a stomachache and the walls are closing in.

"And wasn't that the story on the list you submitted for November?" Kevin asks. "Your big take-out on the fraud and corruption in the pharmaceutical industry?"

"How would the paper have gotten wind of this?" Angela asks.

"How did the *Herald* reporters get the whistle-blower to talk?" Kevin puts in.

Angela's voice. "Did you know who it was? Why didn't you get the interview?"

"I'm really disappointed," Kevin adds.

I fall back against the pillows, trying to regroup. Nothing I can do, not until I read the story. But even though I truly don't want to hear about this ever again, there's one thing I've got to know right now.

"Let me ask you," I say, heart pounding. "Does it say anything in the story about a Bradley Foreman?"

Time stops as I figure Kevin and Angela are scanning the paper. If the feds are talking about the lawsuit now, they might name the whistle-blower, and then the article would be all about Brad and his accident and I'd have to kill myself.

"Nope, nothing about anyone with a name like that," Kevin says. "Why?"

"One more question," I say, not answering him directly. "Does it say who the whistle-blower actually is?"

Another pause. I wait, still contemplating various suicide methods.

"The name is Caroline Jill Crofts," Kevin says slowly. "Says she's a former Aztratech employee, lives in Boston. Ever heard of her?"

I can't decide whether this is the good news or the bad news. Good news because we've never heard of her, so at least the paper doesn't have exactly the same story we do. Bad news because we've never heard of her. And that means our story—Brad Foreman as whistle-blower who gets mysteriously killed after he spills the beans to the government—is completely and utterly wrong.

"Tell you what," I say, trying to sound calm. "Let me check the *Herald*. See what their story is. Maybe it's different from ours." This is beyond wishful thinking. I know we're scooped bad, but I need to stall. "I'll grab the paper and call you back, okay?"

There's another pause from the Chamber of the Inquisition.

"Fine," Kevin says. "Let me know."

"And tick tick," Angela adds. I can just picture her sneery expression. "Five weeks until the rating book."

The phone goes dead. Just like I wish I was. The dial tone buzzes dismally in my ear, and I finally put down the receiver.

If I just stay in bed and never get up, I'll never have to face it. I briefly contemplate how long I could just lie here until someone notices or comes to try to find me. Or what if I just quit now, just called Kevin back and said you know, forget it. I just don't think I'm coming back to Channel 3 anymore. Then they'd be on their own for November and I could just, um . . .

I realize I'm crying. I stink at my job. My producer's in the hospital. My cat's still at the vet. My best friend's out of town. And the one man who I thought might be my Prince Charming turns out to be a toad.

I can't bring myself to get up to get the newspaper. The reality of that front page is going to be proof in black and white that I've lost it. And I can't figure out how it happened.

When "Charlie McNally, Action News" becomes just "Charlie McNally"—who will she be?

CHAPTER SEVENTEEN

I'm so miserable I can barely drag myself down the hospital hall. I feel as if I weigh twice as much as usual, carrying the double burden of having to tell Franklin about the infinitely disastrous newspaper story and also about the missing files. He rarely gets upset, but the combination of being scooped, burgled and beaten up is definitely a new emotional challenge.

When I reach his room, Franklin's sitting up in bed, propped up by pillows. His room is filled with beribboned vases of fragrant lavender and white flowers. And at least his IV thing is out. But I can't see his face because he's—reading the newspaper.

"Can you believe it?" I wail, throwing myself into the bedside chair. I yank off my coat and unwind my long plaid muffler. "How, how, how did this happen? How did the paper get this story?"

"Yeah, this is not the best outcome," Franklin admits. "I really hoped we'd break the whistle-blower story for sweeps, but while you've been moping and worrying, I've been—"

"Hoped? We'd break the—?" Then something in Franklin's face stops me. "Franklin Brooks Parrish," I say slowly. "Do you know something I don't?"

"Quite often, as a matter of fact," Franklin retorts. "And if you'd stop planning your professional demise and start listening to me, you might want to hear about it."

"Spill it," I demand. "Save my life."

"All right, quickly." Franklin ticks off the points on his fingers. "First, everything in the paper is from the lawsuit's court file. And second, since the story's written by the *Herald*'s courthouse reporter, I figure she came across it on her routine daily check of new cases."

"Right," I acquiesce. "We knew the case was in the court clerk's office, but sealed. So the *Herald* reporter must have been able to open it. But how . . ."

"Easy," Franklin says. "They unseal the files when the feds decide to get involved. Since I was laid up here, and you were sneaking into funerals, neither of us was at the courthouse when the case file was opened. The *Herald* was."

"Yeah, and they got the story," I whine.

"True," Franklin agrees. "And that's indeed the bad news. The good news is that clearly there's something more going on. The *Herald* has the story about the whistle-blower suit, but you didn't hear about any newspaper reporters getting beaten up, did you? We must be on to something bigger."

It's my turn to smile, shaking my head in admiration. "Franklin, you're truly the only person on the planet who could turn assault and battery into a positive experience."

"What's more," Franklin continues, holding up the paper, "there's nothing in here about Brad, or Mack Briggs or any of the *Miranda* owners. Or about any refinancing spam. That means there's another story—not pharmaceutical price fixing—that pulls all those things together."

"So . . ." I say. I'm exhausted and I wish my brain was working better.

"And what's more—" Franklin pauses, dramatically taking a sip from the bendable straw in his water cup, and then carefully replacing the cup on his nightstand "—our database search."

"Oh yeah," I say, leaning forward in my chair. "Is it—?"

"It's finished. And it's huge," Franklin says, looking more animated than I've seen him in a while. "Those executives own tons of stuff together. Boats, property, racehorses, office buildings, apartments, shopping malls. Seems like they're on a big-time international shopping spree. There's big bucks out there, coming from somewhere."

I'm skeptical. "How about from their salaries? Plus, wouldn't it be simple for the feds or the tax people to find? Track down if they're scamming somehow?"

Franklin waves a hand to accept the possibility. "Maybe. But the co-ownership's not instantly obvious. You'd have to specifically look for it. And on the other hand, maybe the feds do know, who's to say. We can't find out how much these guys are reporting on their taxes."

He smoothes down his blankets. "But here's the key question. All that money? I checked their pay info in the annual reports, and I don't see how they could possibly afford all this stuff."

I look behind me to make sure no one is coming, then scoot my chair closer to his bedside. "Listen, Franklin," I begin earnestly, "this is all about the spam. I'm sure of it. I was thinking—"

"Can you tell me later?" Franklin interrupts. He looks at the plastic clock next to his bed. "We've got to hurry or you're going to be late."

"Late for what?" I ask.

Franklin smiles. "I'd be patting myself on the back if my arm didn't hurt so much. Charlotte, my girl, put your coat and that extravagant scarf right back on. Got a notebook and a pen? You're going on an interview."

I run my finger down the list of apartment residents to find the buzzer marked Crofts. I've got to give Franklin credit. Tracking down whistle-blower Caroline Crofts to the new Ritz condos on Avery Street, and even more, convincing her to talk to me, was nice work from a hospital bed. I push the button for P32.

The door's locking mechanism softly clicks me in, and I enter the lobby, floor-to-ceiling art deco. Enormously high mahogany walls, embossed copper tiles glowing in the soft lighting. Elegant black-and-white scroll-worked elevator doors open into a mirror-paneled compartment and glide me upstairs.

I look around, impressed, wondering who could afford a place like this. And when the elevator stops, I see *P* means *penthouse*. Huge windows, glistening in the morning sun, surround the landing and offer maybe the most glorious view of the Public Garden and Boston Common I've ever seen. I hear the door of number 32 opening, so I put on my best reporter face and turn to meet Caroline Crofts.

But it's not Caroline at the door. I'd pictured a nerdy accountant stereotype, overpermed hair, frumpy glasses. One of those skirts with an elastic waistband and scuffed, flat-soled Mary Janes. Pencil on a cord around her neck.

"Miss McNally?" Not-Caroline says. "I'm Caro Crofts," she adds with a smile. "Come on in."

I can't take my eyes off her. She's twenty-five or so, with choppy fuchsia hair, about a thousand earrings and essentially black lipstick. She's wearing ultrapetite ripped jeans and a minuscule T-shirt that says Boys are Stupid. Throw Rocks at Them. I did get the glasses right—but hers are black with cat's-eye corners, and they're dotted with rhinestones.

"Thanks," I answer, following her into the apartment. "You spoke to my colleague Franklin Parrish on the phone—"

"Sure, gotcha, have a seat." Caroline gestures toward a gorgeous wing chair, which I recognize has the signature Napoleon bees of Scalamandré silk. I'm almost even afraid to sit down on it, until I see Caroline curl up on my chair's twin, tucking her clunky Steve Maddens under her.

"Uh, thanks." This isn't computing. Maybe she doesn't live here. Maybe it's her lawyer's apartment, and he's loaned it to her for the interview. Good theory, except her name was on the buzzer.

"Beautiful place," I begin. "Incredible."

"Yup." She waves a hand, taking in the entire room. "It sure is the real thing. That chair, and this one," she continues, pointing to mine and hers, "were in the Orsay Museum, until Dads fell in love with them. All this stuff, antique furniture, clocks, art—all stuff Dads and Mom collected. The wallpaper is from the eighteenth century. They say."

"And now your parents are—?" I pause, wondering.

"Three months in Kenya. So I told them I'd house-sit. Nice, huh? I miss my little place in the South End, but I guess I can handle it."

"Ah," I say. This is finally making some sense. "So anyway, Ms. Crofts, we read about you in the paper, of course. And as I'm sure my producer, Franklin, explained, we wondered—"

"I'll tell you all about it, short version," Caroline says, "and you can call me Caro."

I nod, and gesture for her to go on.

"Dads made all of us kids get jobs, every summer. Didn't matter what we did, we just had to work. Value of a dollar and all. So a couple of summers, I worked at Aztratech. Making copies, stamping papers, folding and stuffing envelopes. And I loved it."

She stops and smiles. "I guess you're thinking—she doesn't look like the secretary type. Yeah, well, I guess not. But no one out there seemed to care how I looked, as long as I got my stuff done. And I did."

"Anyway, I kept working there summers, and after I got my degree in computer technology, it made sense I'd go back there for a real job. So I set up websites and e-mail, as well as the billing systems. I had total access to the computers. And everything was fine. Until . . ."

Caro pauses, looking up at the ceiling. I look up, too, and notice it's completely painted with clouds and cherubs, and edged with rococo gilt carvings. Just like home.

"Until," Caro continues, "I began to notice some of the paperwork, bills and invoices just didn't reconcile. It was clear Aztratech was sending bogus invoices to a number of pharmacies, and those fake bills showed charges of far more than what the drugs really cost. Then, I found there were two sets of books. One that had the real price of the medicines—that was kept in a separate computer, hidden in another part of the office. After I finally accessed the secret system, I began to realize the charges entered in the main computer were for much more. And I know those prices were what the pharmacies were billing the government."

I think I get this. I'm in deep, deep mourning for our story. I hate the newspaper. "So you discovered the pharmacies were getting reimbursed by Medicare . . ." I begin.

"Far more than they actually paid for the stuff," Caro finishes. "And that's illegal. That's orchestrated, deliberate fraud. And so—" she looks up at me "—I told."

It took Caro almost an hour to finish her story: how her father helped her contact a lawyer, how the lawyer had explained the whistle-blower laws, how Caro would have to testify for the government against her employer. She told me how they'd waited for the U.S. Attorney's office to look over the files she'd downloaded, the hours of financial questions and explanations that finally led to the federal "false claims" case against Aztratech.

"So, let me ask you," I finally say slowly. "Who was behind all this, do you know? Whose idea?"

Caro laughs bitterly. "Who's behind it at Aztratech? That Bible-spouting weasel of a Wes Rasmussen, no doubt in my mind."

I tuck that away for later, but there's another question I have to ask.

"Do you know a Brad Foreman?"

"Yeah, I know—knew—Brad," she says quietly. "Why do you ask?"

"I promise I'll tell you everything," I say, leaning toward her. "But just tell me first, what do you know about him?"

Caro uncurls her legs. "When I first had an idea that the—evildoers—" she smiles briefly "—were at work, I had to do some financial digging. I had to get a look at the budget records. That was Brad's department. And I thought I'd have to sneak, you know, somehow."

"Yes, so . . ."

"So," Caro continues, "when I got to his office, and kinda casually asked about record keeping, I could tell he was curious. I remember he closed the door, and asked me some pretty specific questions. Like he knew."

"Interesting," I say. "And so—"

"But here's the thing," she goes on. "Brad was actually working to unravel something else. Not false pricing. I tried to get him to tell me what it was, but he wouldn't."

"Any idea what it might have been?"

"Nope." She shakes her head. "And now, he's dead."

In the silence, something pops into my mind. "Did he ever talk to you about refinancing his house?"

Caro runs a hand through her spiky hair and looks at me warily. "How would you know that?" she asks.

Do I tell her? I quickly try to size her up. Caro has got to be one of the good guys, right? She's sacrificed her job to rat out her employers, after all.

"Okay," I say, hoping I won't regret it. "Let me fill you in." And then I open my purse, pull out a stack of papers and give one sheet to Caro. "What does this look like to you?"

She looks at the paper, and back at me. "Um, Bible verse, I guess," she says, shrugging. "Is there more than that?"

I hand her a second page. "How about this?"

She takes a quick glance. "Bible verse again," she says. "Some cyber-Sunday-school assignment?"

"Here's what I think," I answer slowly. "I think these are not really spams. I think they're instructions. Instructions disguised as Bible verses. Instructions disguised as spam. Instructions that would easily pass for spam, and would be deleted, unless you knew exactly what you were looking for."

"You mean—sent out like spam, so the sender could be pretty anonymous, but actually targeted to those in the know," Caro says, nodding. "Maybe those who know to look for the misspellings." She considers for a moment. "Computerwise, that's definitely doable. But—instructions about what?"

"Yeah, that was a hard one." I sigh. "But then I started thinking about all the companies in the files. Brad seemed to be really hot on them, sent them to me and to Mack Briggs, who, remember, was a former SEC chairman. So I wondered, what about some stock thing?"

Caro's interested. "Like?"

"Like insider-trading instructions." There, I've said it. "Look at these," I say, spreading a few e-mails on the floor between us. "See how some say 'a good time to buy,' and some say 'a good time to sell'?"

"Yow." Caro looks at the papers and then back at me. "I see what you mean. 'A good time to sell' could mean . . ." She shrugs. "A good time to sell the stock."

"That's what I figured, too," I agree. "And what if the chapters refer to companies somehow, like a code, and the verses are the stock prices? Like, here, 'Numbers Chapter One' means company number one, on some list or something, and then the verses indicate the stock prices. When the 'number one' stock hits that price, that's when you're supposed to buy or sell."

"So on this one, it says, 'a good time to buy.'" Caro's sitting on the floor now, examining the papers. "And Numbers 1, Verse 56 to 57, means buy company number one, if the price is fifty-six or fifty-seven dollars."

"Yeah," I say deliberately. "Yeah."

There's a few minutes of silence as both of us page through the e-mails again.

Finally Caro says, "What companies, though? And who's getting the e-mail?"

"And there's another big question," I remind her. "Who's sending the e-mail?"

"Yeah." Caro looks up at me inquiringly. "Who?"

I shake my head. "I don't know."

We're quiet again. Both thinking hard, and both mystified. Then all at once, a high-pitched sound pierces the silence.

"Beeper," I say, shaking my head in embarrassment. It's my stupid new beeper. "Sorry."

As it continues to bleat its insistent annoying signal, I rifle through my bag for the black box, wishing I could just throw it out Caro's thirty-second-story window. I poke the message button, fearing the worst.

It arrives.

Call Angela.

"Sorry," I say. "I've got to call the office." Whatever this is, it's going to be terrible. I grab my cell phone from my purse and click the green button on.

Nothing. I click it again. Totally dead battery. "Damn it," I say, tossing the useless thing back into my bag. "I mean, rats. Could I use your . . . ?"

"Phone's in the kitchen," Caro says, pointing.

I trudge by the opulently upholstered walls of the penthouse hallway. It feels as if I'm walking through *Architectural Digest,* but I know I'm on the way to certain doom. "Call Angela," I mutter. Why on earth would I want to do that? I come to an expanse of stainless steel appliances and pick up the phone.

Newszilla answers immediately, attempting an impossible mixture of sympathy, regret and pomposity. "I'm so sorry," she says. "I know you're with Franklin . . ."

I don't tell her I'm not.

"But we need you to handle a news conference for us. Do you want to be picked up at the hospital? Or meet your crew here at the station? It's at Aztratech Pharmaceuticals," she says. "In Boxford. In two hours."

I lean back against the counter for support.

"At . . . ?"

"Reacting to that story in the paper, of course. And since we figured you know all about this anyway," she says pointedly, "you might as well go cover it. At least you won't have to play catch-up."

I can just imagine her self-satisfied expression as she throws my defeat in my face.

"Yup, sure, fine," I say. I'm in agony. I might as well just put a big *L* on my chest.

"Three o'clock, Aztratech headquarters," she repeats. "The

speaker will be somebody named Wesley Rasmussen. I assume you at least know who that is."

I drag my feet through the kitchen, back through the pantry, through the dining room, too depressed to be impressed. "Louis XV, Louis XVI, who cares," I mutter petulantly. Everything sucks.

I arrive in the living room and open my mouth to tell Caro I have to go.

She's already talking.

"Check it out," she says, eyes sparkling. "I think I have an idea."

"An idea—about what?" I ask tentatively. Please let this be something good.

"Remember I told you Wes Rasmussen is always quoting the Bible? In fact, he had one on his desk all the time, full of yellow stickies that mark his favorite passages or something."

"Yes," I say, unsure where this is going. "What about it?"

"The e-mails," she says. "They look like Bible verses, but you said they aren't always real ones. Who would know enough about the Bible to use it as a code?" She looks at me eagerly and ticks off her points on her fingers. "You'd have to be familiar with the Bible, incredibly hypocritical to use it to further some illegal insider-trading scheme and arrogant enough to think you could get away with it."

"In other words . . ."

"Mr. Wes Rasmussen." Caro nods. "Absolutely."

"You've got a point, I have to admit," I answer. I look at my watch. Still a little time to spare.

"How about this," I begin again. "He's at Aztratech. That means Aztratech is one of the companies involved. I mean, it makes sense since that's where Brad worked. And what if Aztratech, it starts with *A* after all, is number one. As in Numbers, Chapter One."

Caro sifts through the e-mails and pounces on Numbers, Chapter One. "If that's true, that would mean the stock price of Aztratech would be somewhere in the fifty-five to fifty-six range. Or would have been, around the date of the e-mail. Which was—" she checks the date line "—three weeks ago." She smiles. "Before they knew about the lawsuit, of course."

"And if there were some reason the stock price was going to go up back then—like a new drug going to be approved by the FDA or something," I add, "Rasmussen couldn't have profited from purchase or sale of his own stock. But he could have let his compadres know, by way of this secret spam system, and they could have made a ton of money. With no one the wiser."

Caro leaps up. "Got an idea," she calls over her shoulder as she leaves the room. "Be right back."

Alone in the living room, I start thinking about what you could buy with all that money. Boats, shopping malls, racehorses, property. I start thinking about all the companies in the boxes of files. It's got to be—those are the companies in the insider-trading loop.

Then I remember. The files are missing. And I still haven't told Franklin.

Caro races back into the room, waving a newspaper. "Let's just see." She opens the pages and spreads them out on the floor. "Good thing I'm saving old *Boston Globe*s for Dads while he's gone. I dug out the one for just after the date of the e-mail. It's easier than looking them up individually online." She runs her finger down the stock tables.

"Aztratech," she says slowly, "Aztratech." She flips a page and runs her finger down another list. "Fifty-six," she says, eyes twinkling behind her glasses. She picks up another paper. "Now, here's two weeks later."

I kneel on the floor beside her, eager to see what she'll find. The paper is a gray-and-black blur. I grab my purse and hunt for my reading glasses. But Caro already has her answer.

She points to the paper so emphatically it actually tears—but it's still readable. "Aztratech," Caro reads out loud. "Closed this day at seventy-one."

I'm trying to do the math. And it's easy.

"So if someone bought a chunk of it three weeks ago at fifty-six, let's say," I begin, "and sold it two weeks later at seventy-one . . ."

"They'd have made big bucks," Caro finishes my sentence. "Big, big bucks."

CHAPTER EIGHTEEN

Good thing there was a Starbucks on the way to Aztratech. I couldn't face this news conference without a little caffeine courage.

It feels as if I'm being sent to detention. Angela, grand master of mind games, certainly wants me to feel that way. Faced with my own defeat. *Scooped.* Depressing.

I dig into my purse on the seat beside me and pull out my useless lump of a dead cell phone. It beeps as I plug it into the cigarette-lighter thingy to charge it up. Wish there was a way to charge myself up.

As I pull out onto the street, I hear my phone beeping. It's the voice mail alert—One Message Waiting, it says.

A honking idiot in the car behind me gives me the Boston reminder that the light has changed to green. Instead of giving him the finger back, I hit Message Retrieve, tuck the phone under my chin and pull away as slowly as I can.

The message is from Melanie.

"Hello, Charlie," she begins. "I just got a call from your Josh Gelston."

My eyes fly wide open. "He reminded me of that dinner party

where he met Brad and me, and said you thought the party was given by Wes Rasmussen."

I hear Melanie's soft little laugh.

"I'm not sure why this is so important, Charlie," she goes on, "but that dinner was not at the Rasmussens'," she finishes. A pause.

"Oh," she adds. "The police still think it was kids who did the break-in. I'm feeling a little better about it now. Talk to you soon."

I click the phone off, and step a toe into uncharted waters, testing the possibilities. If Wes wasn't the host, then what Josh told me at the diner must have been true. Was all the rest true, too?

I plummet to the depths. It was.

And of course I, Miss Know-It-All, as much as told the most desirable man to cross my path in years that he was a lying dirtbag. I was so vile and sarcastic he actually walked out of the restaurant.

I tap one finger on the steering wheel, planning. Yes. I'll pull over and give Josh a call. Fix things. Start over. Moving into the outer lane, I scout the highway for a turnoff.

No. I can't call him. I swerve back into the center. He's at his Jordan Beach Road house, as he told me in the message, and he told me in the diner there's no phone up there. Wish I hadn't ripped up his cell-phone number.

I pound the steering wheel in disappointment. Stewing in frustration, I drive a few more miles until I reach the turnoff for Boxford. Half a mile to humiliation. Mom was right. I should have gone to law school.

Arriving at the Aztratech compound, I find a parking spot, but I stay in my Jeep, seat belt still on. Damned if I'm going in there fifteen minutes early. I scan for the Channel 3 news car and crew. Not here yet. I sigh dismally and take a sip of my finally cool-enough latte.

The blinking phone on the front seat reminds me—I should call

Franklin and tell him about Caro and the idea we came up with. Franklin's going to love it.

By the time my call gets routed from the wrong nurses' station to some other patient's room and eventually to Franklin, I only have a few minutes to spare. There's no time to explain the whole e-mail scheme, but I finally summon the courage to tell him about the files. It's better like this, anyway. Don't have to break the ultra-bad news face-to-face.

"So, Franko," I moan, "can you believe it? They're just not there. I'm so, so sorry I didn't tell you sooner, but—"

"Charlotte," Franklin interrupts, "the files were not stolen."

"Of course they were," I interrupt. "You think the trash people mistakenly threw them away or something?"

"I do not think the 'trash people' threw them away," Franklin says. His voice sounds strange. "I'm certain they didn't, as a matter of fact. Because I took the files."

I'm speechless.

"Those were the boxes I was putting into my trunk the morning I got nailed in the parking lot. I took the files home so I could compare Brad's box and Mack Briggs's box, and do some more research. That's when I looked up the CEOs' salaries."

My mind is racing. "So when they took your car . . ."

"The files were in the trunk," Franklin finishes. "So. Either the bad guys wanted my Passat for parts and then got an extra big bonfire afterward, or . . ."

"Or they really wanted the files," I finish.

"Yup," Franklin agrees. "Or they really wanted the files."

I picture the two bad guys, whoever they are, following Franklin out of the station and into his car, watching him lug the two file boxes. I picture them following him home, staking him out. I picture them coming back early the next morning, waiting for him to bring the boxes out. If he hadn't, they could just break into his condo and get them then.

Which reminds me. Melanie. And whoever ransacked her study. The "gang of teenagers" theory is becoming highly unlikely.

"Listen, Charlotte," Franklin interrupts my thoughts. "I don't like this. It's pretty clear whoever it was came after me, specifically. And someone sent them to do it. And now—"

I hear the honk of a car horn, then turn to see a Channel 3 news van pulling up beside me. "Sorry, Franko, gotta go," I say. "Talk to you later."

Head high, I approach the Waltmobile and look inquiringly at the stranger getting out of the passenger seat. She's sleek and smooth as a baby seal. Her red beret is fashionably tilted on ultra-flat blond hair that's right out of a cream-rinse commercial, and I swear I recognize the tawny designer boots I coveted at Saks. Daddy's charge must have gone platinum for those, I calculate. A thousand bucks a boot.

"I'm Charlie McNally," I begin.

"Hi," she says.

Okay, then. "Are you here with Walt?" I ask deliberately. Maybe she doesn't understand English.

"Totally." She wobbles on her stilettos as she hikes Walt's equipment bag onto her shoulder. "Oooh." She giggles.

"Hey," Walt says. "That bag is too heavy for you."

Hell is apparently freezing over—Walt takes the bag from her and slings it over his own shoulder.

"Hel-lo?" I persist. "Wa-lt?" I make his name two syllables.

"Yeah, Charlie," the photog finally growls. "This is Alissia Nevins." He cocks his head at the girl, raising a conspiratorial eyebrow. "Intern. Angela Nevins's daughter."

I don't know whether it's more interesting that the Queen of

Darkness has offspring, or that she's sent her camera-ready daughter out on a story. With me. Of course now every move I make will be reported to the inner sanctum, probably to be inscribed on some permanent record of my flaws.

That's serious tactics, I've got to give Angela credit. But I wonder, where'd this girl get the financing for that outfit? Angela doesn't make that much money.

Walt and the dauphine are already heading toward Aztratech's front door, me tagging along behind. This is a roiling disaster, I realize. No, it's a buffet. Beef jerky, cheesecake—and me, toast.

When we get to the briefing, I recognize the woman adjusting the microphones at the front of the dark-paneled conference room deep inside the Aztratech building. It's Gwen Matherton, Wes Rasmussen's fashion-plate assistant. She looks behind her, as if confirming there are enough chairs lined up for Aztratech staff, then steps to the podium.

"Mr. Rasmussen will be here in just a few minutes." Megawattage lights click on, photographers aiming them right at her. Gwen blinks a little in the sudden glare. "He'll have a brief statement, and then take questions."

She surveys the room, then, getting no reaction from the half-listening group of reporters, walks out a side door.

Alissia, who entered in a swirl of perfume and a coquettish rearranging of her scarf, doesn't need a podium to take center stage. Photographers, the men at least, ignore their video equipment and unabashedly check her out. The female TV reporters, with a nose for a new kid, look at me questioningly, concerned for their territory. I shake my head. Don't worry, I signal. She's no threat.

But to me—she might be useful.

"So, Alissia," I begin, "this your first news conference?" I guide her to the back of the room, the buzz of the media pack resuming enough to give us a little privacy.

She looks at me as if I'm her befuddled grandmother and begins a brief history of her apparently already brilliant career. It's a self-satisfied teen-queen bio punctuated by head tosses and hair flipping.

". . . and so, like, when my mom got the job at Channel 3, she told me she'd be able to get me in there, anytime. I was the anchor for my high school newscast. It's awesome."

"How nice," I reply, oh-so-sincerely. "In fact, I'm wondering if you'd like to ask the questions here today."

Anyone with any sense, of course, would never step into a news conference without having some idea of what's going on. I'm counting on her inner prima donna to lure her into the spotlight.

She pauses, then nods. "Sweet," she says. "Can't be that tough. Just tell me what to ask and that'll be so cool."

I scrawl out a list of questions, trying to keep my handwriting legible and a grin off my face.

"Here you go," I say. "Just have Walt roll on everything, that way if someone else asks a good question, we'll get that answer on tape, too. I'll stay with you until it starts, then I'll meet you back at the car."

"Sweet," she says again. "Mom is going to think you are so brilliant."

Probably not, I don't say. Alissia turns to take her place by Walt, but I stop her.

"Look. I have my own car. Your mom knows I'm headed back to the hospital, so you just take the tape to the station, and they'll tell you what to do."

"Faboo," Alissia replies incomprehensibly. "I'm so amped." With a final toss of her flat-ironed hair, she takes my list of questions and heads to the bank of cameras. I hang by the door, near the back of the room.

I have an idea. Risky, most certainly. Rewarding, very possibly.

But with Franklin in the hospital, and with what Caro and I think we've figured out—it's definitely now or never.

Wes Rasmussen enters through the side door, barely glancing at the waiting media army. No golf shirt today. He's straight out of *Forbes* magazine in a TV-perfect dark suit, pale blue shirt and yellow tie. He sits in one of the folding chairs behind the podium and whispers to some aide beside him.

I stand motionless in the back, waiting for the perfect time to make my move.

Gwen Matherton steps back to the podium and gives a brief history of Aztratech—founded eight years ago, pharmaceutical research and development, new gastrointestinal drug recently approved by the FDA.

Then Rasmussen comes to the podium, adjusting his tie and then looking down at some notes. When he looks up, every eye in the room is watching him, and every light in the room is turned to shine right on his face.

In that instant, I'm out the door. I've been in this building before and I know right where I'm going.

Plastering a confident expression on my face, I walk purposefully down the corridor and away from the conference room. I've got the trusty have-to-use-the-ladies'-room-and-oh-golly-I'm-lost excuse ready, just in case. I glance at my watch—the news conference can't be any shorter than fifteen minutes. If I can get in and get out in that time, I'm golden.

It takes just two minutes to get to Rasmussen's office. His receptionist is not at her desk, and his door is open. I can't hesitate. I close the door partway after I step into the deep pile of his extra-plush executive-suite carpeting, and once again see the glow of the *Miranda* in the showcase.

It seems like such a long time ago I first saw that.

Back to my plan. I go behind Rasmussen's desk, scanning the

stacks of paperwork and books on top of it. I don't want to move anything if I don't have to.

Bingo.

Without a second thought, I reach out and grab the prize from between the lion bookends. Just as Caro Crofts described, it's a battered leather-covered Bible, about a dozen yellow stickies marking what, I don't know. But I do know this book is key evidence to what I'm convinced is an insider-trading scheme, and now I've got it.

I imagine a darkened theater, and annoyed viewers of the Charlie-movie analyzing my every step. No way she would go into that office, someone whispers. She's definitely going to get caught. Yeah, someone snaps back. She's an idiot.

I close my ears to my persistent fears and zip the Bible into my purse. Now I just have to get out of the office and into the elevator. I take a step toward the door. That's when I hear the voices.

I gasp and my heart clenches. I am an idiot. I look wildly around the room, as if there's some magic that's going to save me from certain discovery. But I'm trapped.

The voices are coming closer to the office. How could Rasmussen be out of the news conference so quickly? I check my watch—it's been just five minutes. The news conference can't be over. I struggle to find an explanation, but I can't come up with a thing.

Maybe they'll just walk on by. Anyone could be in the hall, I've just proved that. My heart begins to slow a little. In fact, I decide, it's pretty unlikely that anyone's on the way to Rasmussen's office.

Unless it's Rasmussen himself. My heart starts up again. But he has to be in the news conference. Doesn't he?

And then I hear a louder voice. A man. "Here's the office," it says, "just ahead. Go on in. Phone's on the desk."

Everything is black. My eyes are wide open, and still everything is black. And that is such a good thing.

I clutch my purse to my chest, contraband Bible still inside, and huddle as far back against the wall as I can. I close my eyes for a moment, reeling at my own wild misjudgment. How did I get myself into this?

By pushing the right button, I answer myself. Back at that first interview, Rasmussen touched something underneath his desk that opened a hidden closet in the wall behind him. That's where he got the sport coat he put on for the camera. So, I figured, I had one chance to avoid whoever was heading for the office.

Of course if Rasmussen comes in and decides to hang up his suit jacket, there's pretty much no explanation that's going to fly. I struggle through my fear to try and get my bearings. The closet feels like it's full of scratchy jackets, and it smells like golf shoes and aftershave. Terrific. If I throw up, they're certain to find me.

What's more, at least three people are now in the office. I strain to hear them, and can pick out two men and one woman. I think. Unless, of course, there's someone else in the room who's not talking. Someone who's now moving closer to Rasmussen's desk to push the magic button and reveal the uninvited guest behind door number one. A guest who would—soon after—reside for eight to ten at the Framingham Women's Correctional Institution.

But the voices don't get closer, and some words become intermittently intelligible. Taking the quietest deep breath in history, I gingerly put my goody bag on the floor and flatten my ear to the door.

". . . something something push nine," I think I hear. It's the woman's voice.

". . . something something number?" Man's voice, and I don't think it's authoritative enough to be Rasmussen's. So. Woman and unidentified guy.

Then I hear another man. ". . . something something just relax."

That's not Rasmussen, either. Woman and two unidentified guys. In Rasmussen's office. Why?

I bite my lower lip in frustration, trying to turn my hearing up to parabolic and figure out what they're saying. Not that it matters, probably.

"It's us." The woman now. Maybe she's turned toward me because for some reason I can now hear her quite clearly. It sounds as if she's on the phone. "We got your text. What's so urgent?"

Even though my brain is stuffed with panic, a bit of room opens up, just enough to admit a tiny hint of recognition. I know that voice. I close my eyes, not that it matters in my murky hidey-hole, but somehow I think it'll make my hearing more acute. Who the hell is in the room?

I'm listening so hard I almost forget I'm trespassing in a corporate executive's hidden closet and carrying one of his possessions in my purse. When I remember that, I also remember something else. I squint and angle my wrist in every direction, but it's no use. I can't see my watch. Which means I have no idea how long I have until the news conference is over and no idea how long it'll be before Rasmussen himself is back.

And the moment he comes into the room, he'll inevitably see his Bible is gone. I hold my breath in case someone can hear me breathing. Then I decide it would be better to breathe, but softly, in case I would cough or something when I have to catch my breath.

How the heck do they hide in closets in movies, anyway? I scoot my feet farther away from the door, remembering how they always catch the closet-hider by their feet showing under the crack. *Whose idea was this?* the sane part of me demands.

I can hear the woman talking again.

"Listen," she says, and it sounds as if she's coming closer to the closet. "It'll all be fine. Stop worrying. We'll call you when it's over. Hold on one moment."

Hold on? Why is she saying hold on? Maybe she's seen my feet showing. I clench my entire body, waiting for the blast of fluorescent light that will signal my demise.

Instead, the voice seems to be addressing the others in the room. "I told you, it's fine," the voice says. "You can both meet me at the car."

Pause pause, muffle mufffle.

"Fine, just go," the woman says again. Then she continues, apparently now speaking into the phone. "Martin says, 'Chill.' Whatever he means by that."

The woman's tone goes a bit softer. "We'll see each other soon, darling, I promise. Goodbye, dear."

That voice is so damn familiar. I've heard this person before. I've talked with her. She was unpleasant then, too. My eyes fly open again, not that it would matter here in the dark. But I remember. It's Andrea Grimes Brown, the wicked witch of Corporate City who threatened me at Mack Briggs's funeral. And I bet the two other guys are her funeral-goon sidekicks. What are they all doing in Wes Rasmussen's office?

It may be wishful thinking, but it sounds as if the receiver's been put back on the hook. Leave, leave, leave, I silently chant. Leave, leave, leave. Maybe whatever higher power seemed to save Nancy Drew's ass in places like this will come through for me, too.

I count to sixty. I count to sixty again. Not a sound from the room. One more time. Sixty. Not a sound.

Okay, Charlie, question of the day. Do you open the door? Or not?

I don't care who sees me now. I'm walking as fast as I've ever walked, out the door, down the hall, steering a course for the elevator. Me, my purse and the purloined Bible. I try not to look guilty of trespassing and larceny, although clearly I am. What if, as soon as I get to the door, there's a massive clamor, like for shoplifters? What if the Aztratech rent-a-cops stationed at the security desk grab my arms and insist on looking in my purse?

I know my rights. I remember them. I don't have to let them look. They need a warrant. I'm supposed to ask for a lawyer. Then I don't say a word.

"Charlie?" A male voice comes up behind me. "What the hell are you doing?"

I feel the blood drain from my face as I slowly turn to meet my captor. "I'm—" I begin. And then I almost faint. With happiness.

Walt Petrucelli, camera in one hand, is holding out his tripod for me to carry. It's instant camouflage. As long as he and his equipment are with me, I'm transformed from "suspicious intruder lurking in the hall" to "reporter leaving a press briefing." And we're almost to the front door.

"You missed the whole damn news conference," Walt says, scowling. "That Alissia asked a load of bullshit questions. I just rolled on everything."

Walt cuts in front of me and shoulders his way out through the revolving door. As its protective glass twirls me to freedom behind him, I can still hear Walt complaining. "Bunch of bullshit," he says.

And I head into the sunlight.

CHAPTER NINETEEN

By the time I get back from the hospital cafeteria with two cups of coffee, an apple and a bag of peanut M&M's, Franklin has laid out the Bible verse e-mails across his lap. There's a *Boston Globe* folded open to the stock tables on his nightstand, the Bible's on his lap and he seems deeply engrossed in comparing them. I've already filled him in on what Caro and I think we've uncovered.

I start on the M&M's, ripping open the corner of the package and squeezing out a red and a brown.

"So? Fake spam. Amazing, huh?" I say, popping the candies into my mouth. I didn't have lunch so they don't count. Plus, the peanuts have protein. "You've got to give them credit—it's a pretty diabolical way to deliver stock-trading tips. Instant and anonymous."

Franklin nods. "And it would certainly explain where all the money came from for the *Miranda,* as well as those shopping malls and racehorses. Whoever's in on this spam operation can cash in every time they get an e-mail. And they wouldn't be caught if they were careful. If they didn't do it too often, and didn't get greedy."

I scrounge with a finger for a last piece of candy, thinking one might still be hiding. It's not. I crumple the empty bag and eye the apple. "How about that Bible, though? You think it's like—a reference book?"

"Well, yeah," Franklin says slowly. He holds up the leather volume, turning it back and forth in his hand. "I'm thinking this Bible is the way Rasmussen, or whoever, figures out which chapter and verse matches the company in play. The verse has to match the stock price of whatever company is supposed to be bought or sold."

I nod, understanding. "The Bible as decoder ring," I add. "There's a concept."

"Yeah," Franklin replies. "Might as well put the good book to good use. Plus, no one would bat an eye if someone had a Bible on their desk."

"So," I say slowly, "the companies that were in Brad's files, the same files he sent Mack Briggs, clearly those are the companies involved in the insider trading." I start on my apple, crunching happily, trying to chew and talk at the same time. "End of mystery. It's Emmy time."

Franklin, however, seems a little fidgety. "You and Caro matched Aztratech as company number one. Which does make sense. However," he continues, "even though my possession of the files was all too short-lived, I—" He pauses, an odd look on his face. "I know which company was number two."

"You do?" I say, my voice rising in delight. "You're the best." I scrape my chair around so I can sit down and still see over Franklin's shoulder. "Now all we have to do is see if the e-mail with the citation 'Numbers, Chapter Two, Verse whatever' matches its stock price. Which, of course, it will. Let's do it."

Franklin still has the funny look on his face. "Well, there's a problem," he says slowly. "A biggie. The name of the first company in the file box was 4 Corners. I remember because it starts with a number. And Aztratech was number two, not number one."

"What? You're wrong," I howl. "What are the chances Caro and I could look up the stock prices like that, and they would match? Aztratech has to be Company One, Chapter One. Has to be."

Franklin's chewing his thumb, which he never does unless he's really concerned. He stares at the ceiling, lost in thought.

I crunch the last of my apple and sip some of the vile hospital coffee. Then a knock on Franklin's door jolts both of us out of our reverie. I turn to see the world's most pregnant nurse, watermelon-size belly straining the snaps on her white uniform jacket. She's carrying a dozen or so metal-covered patient file charts, a pile so ungainly it threatens to topple at the slightest wrong move.

"Geller?" she says, moving the charts from one arm to the other. "Roger Geller?"

This means nothing to me, but Franklin says, "He's moved—gone over to E. This is D."

The nurse seems to understand. "Oh, sorry," she says, shifting her files again. "I'm new. I thought this was corridor E." She turns to leave, but with that one motion, her charts clatter to the floor.

The nurse puts her hands to her face in frustration, and stamps a white-shoed foot. "I just organized those," she mutters. "Now I have to do it all again."

She bends down to retrieve the files, and I get up to help her recover the silver folders now scattered across the floor of Franklin's room.

"I can help you do it," I offer. "Were they by room number?"

"No," she says, stacking them back onto my chair. "Alphabetical."

I stop in midmotion, one hand inches away from picking up a chart. I leave it on the floor, and turn to Franklin with a wide-eyed question.

"Brad's files," I begin. "They were in alphabetical order. But you put them like that, didn't you?" I continue. "They didn't arrive that way, did they?" I'm remembering now. "That's where we went wrong. The company names really do match the chapter numbers somehow, but not alphabetically."

Franklin runs a hand across his face, looking frustrated and despondent. "I'm so sorry," he says. "My fault. If I hadn't messed with the files, and Mack Briggs's, too, we'd have them now. Back the way they were. Before I had the genius idea to take them home."

That's so Franklin. So hyper-responsible, he's putting the blame on himself for being mugged.

"Look, Franklin," I say earnestly. "You were assaulted and robbed, your car torched. That's hardly the result of being over-organized."

"Yeah," he says, giving me a baleful look, "but—"

"As you so often say, no buts," I say, pointing a semi-stern finger to stop him. "I agree the files are just in some other order, and if we knew what order, we'd know which e-mail corresponds with each company. We just have to figure that out. I wish we had—" I stop as something nags at me.

"Had what?" he says.

"I just remembered," I answer, looking more at the wall than at Franklin, "how we can find out what order the files were in."

"Really?" he says. "How?"

"And what I also comprehend, more than ever," I continue, turning to look him straight in the eye, "is we both may still be in danger." I don't think I actually have goose bumps, but I know I'm feeling an unsettling chill.

"Well, yeah," Franklin agrees, tucking the e-mails into the Bible's pages. "Somebody thinks we know something."

"Right. And now, I have to say, it seems like the same kind of thing that happened to you, and to Brad, and to Mack Briggs, they might be planning for me." I pause a moment, give a deep sigh. "On the other hand, it seems so—"

Franklin nods. "I know. Melodramatic. But one thing more."

"You don't have to tell me," I say, shaking my head. "Josh Gelston."

Franklin solemnly agrees. "Josh. If we're in trouble, he's in trouble."

"But, listen, I think he's the key to the whole thing." I lean forward in my chair, eager to explain. "That's what just hit me. Remember when I interviewed Josh? And he told me about the e-mail from Brad? He told me, back then, Brad had sent him a box of files."

Franklin, wide-eyed, repeats my sentence. "Brad had sent him a box of files." He nods. "I completely forgot."

"Yup." I lean back in my chair, again replaying my first meeting with Josh. I'm not wrong. *Box of files* just hadn't meant anything at the time.

I sit up straight, energized. "And isn't that a good thing?" I ask. "Josh told me Brad had sent the files to his house in Vermont. Where, as we know, he's spending this weekend." I'm talking faster now, excited by my idea. "He told me where the house is," I continue. "At the end of Jordan Beach Road. I can find it. So I'll just drive up there and take a look. Josh wouldn't have rearranged anything."

I get up and start putting on my coat. "I'll call you as soon as I know what order they're in." I toss the apple core and candy bag into the wastebasket, and hoist my tote bag onto my shoulder.

"But, Charlotte." Franklin holds up a hand, stopping me. "What if Josh—"

"—is involved with multiple murders? And insider trading?" I interrupt, realizing I'll be saying this out loud for the first time. "You know, Franko, I've gotten this far by trusting myself. Josh is on our side, I'm sure of it."

Franklin scratches his jaw. "One more thought, then," he says. "How about giving old Josh a call? Maybe let him know you're coming?"

"No can do," I say, trying to sound confident. "He told me there's no phone service." I pat Franklin carefully on the shoulder. "My cell phone may not work up there, but I'll call you as soon as I can." I turn and head for the door.

"Charlotte," Franklin calls after me.

I turn back one last time. He's frowning, and briefly touches his stitches. "Be careful," he says.

I flutter a not-a-problem wave, but all the way down the hall, I'm wondering how this turned so darkly sinister. It's J-school gospel that reporters are not supposed to be part of the story. But maybe Franklin and I have changed from observer to observed. And what if I've been changed from reporter—into target?

My supersize coffee barely fits into my window-mounted cup holder, and I quickly learn The Beverage You Are About to Drink Is Hot warning printed on the side is more than accurate. This stuff is the temperature of the sun. I'll just wait a while before I take a sip from my logofied thermal mug.

Somebody's getting into the SUV next to me in the Dunkin' Donuts parking lot, so I turn on the engine and wait for the driver to back out, but then I see him making a phone call, so I pull out ahead of him and I'm on the road again.

Franklin seemed genuinely nervous about this foray north, but how could anyone know where I'm headed? Plus my excitement at seeing Josh again, and having a perfectly good excuse for doing it, has dulled some of my residual hesitation. Franklin always worries too much.

I wonder what Josh will say when I knock on the door. It's probably colder up there than it is here, so I envision him in a bulky sweater, with a fire going and music in the background. Jazz, maybe. And did he say he had a dog?

The dog barks as I pull into the driveway, and Josh sees me through the window. Josh runs out to clasp me in his arms. The rough wool of his fisherman's sweater tickles my cheek, and his aroma of wood smoke and citrusy soap makes me wobbly in the knees. Josh pushes me back to arm's length and brushes my hair away from my face.

"I knew you'd come," he says, eyes soft. "Pick a lane, lady."

Pick a? A NASCAR-wannabe in a Dodge Charger has rolled down his passenger-side window and is yelling at me at sixty-five miles an hour. I give him an adorable smile and wave as if grateful. "Thanks so much," I call out. That always drives them crazy.

The Charger guy shakes his fist and pulls away. I'm still smiling. No one can stop me, I'm going to Josh World.

"I knew you'd come," Josh murmurs, picking up right where we left off. "Silly face," he says, pulling my wool hat down over my forehead. "I've been waiting all night for you."

Inside my head the romantic scene continues to unfold, and outside, the night grows darker as I head farther up Route 93 North toward Vermont.

I hate driving at night. Every time a car heads in my direction, I'm blinded by the damn headlights.

I try to read the map to Jordan Beach Road without taking my eyes off the highway. Right in two exits. I look at the dashboard clock and add another layer of worry. This is taking a lot longer than I predicted. If Josh is sleeping when I arrive, our reunion scene is not going to be as *Affair to Remember* as I'd hoped.

Headlights behind me now. And they're too close. I squint in the rearview and give a start of recognition. Looks like the same SUV that was parked beside me at the Dunkin' Donuts. Could that be?

I shake my head, ashamed at my own paranoia. It's just another random lead foot having a testosterone attack. Why do I keep attracting these guys? I think about my coffee, but it's still too hot.

"Slow down or pass me, buddy!" I yell, though I know no one can hear me.

The car pulls up beside my window. I think I see the shadows of two men inside, hard to tell. Industrial-strength lights on each side of the highway glare on the car's rolled-up windows, blocking any good view. Plus, I have to try to keep my eyes on the road. Still, in my peripheral vision I can tell their SUV is staying exactly parallel to mine.

"Asshole!" I can't even believe I'm yelling words like this. But these drivers are scaring me. What is with this car? I accelerate to get away from them. But they stay with me.

A new set of headlights glares in my rearview, blasting a vicious halogen swath though the dark. Two cars bugging me now, and no one else on the highway. Is this just my welcome to the New England highway system? Or—

I glance out my window. In the car beside me, the guy in the passenger seat holds up an index finger—then points it at me.

And then, suddenly, I know real fear. It's instantly, shockingly, brutally, terrifyingly clear what certainly must have happened to Brad Foreman. And probably Mack Briggs. Anonymous cars, working together, manipulating their poor victim into crashing. After a couple of fast moves they speed into the night, leaving behind crumpled metal and a lone casualty. I have a nauseating flashback to that video of Brad's ugly crash. No witnesses, no evidence. And when the police arrive, it seems just like a one-car accident.

I bite my lip and vow not to fall into their disgusting trap. Brad and Mack had no idea what was coming, but I do. I can beat this. Problem is I have no idea how long I have to plan my moves. These guys could accelerate into get-Charlie mode at any second.

I long for my cell phone, but it's zipped, of course, in its damned leather pouch and buried in my tote bag a million miles away in the backseat. No way I can get it. No way I can call the police. Or anyone.

Another car pulls up beside me, this one on the passenger side.

I can feel my hands clenching on the steering wheel, so hard my shoulders hurt with the tension. The driver doesn't even glance in my direction, but now he also stays parallel with my little Jeep. "Jerk!" Saying it out loud makes me feel a little better.

We're all going about seventy miles an hour. That's speeding, but that's the least of my worries. In fact, for the first time in my life, I yearn for a speed trap, but no flashing red lights appear.

I go a little faster. The other cars do, too. I slow down. So do they. The one behind me seems to be pulling even closer now. The ones beside me don't budge.

I pass a side road—and out of it, another car speeds onto the highway, accelerating in front of me.

I glance in all directions again. Their car windows must be tinted because I can't see any faces, but there's no escaping. The cars are pasted to my front, back and both sides, boxing me in and almost carrying me along the highway.

The night speeds by, the towering highway light posts almost a blur as our eerie convoy of vehicles, the only cars on the road, races north in unison. My exit is soon. Maybe my sinister escorts don't plan to let me take it. So I might have until the next exit to come up with something. If I don't, I realize with growing dread, it's *adios,* Charlie.

A few minutes tick by, and I can't decide whether it feels like forever or an instant. But me and my shadows have just passed a big green-and-white sign that says it's a mile to Exit 17.

I can't believe how determined I am. When this is over—cross fingers, cross toes, rabbit's foot, wish on a star—I'll probably freak out. But right now, I'm ice.

Do it. I flip open the console beside me. Keeping my eyes on the road, I feel around with my right hand for what I need.

"Please be in there," I whisper. My fingers touch menus, pencils, change, mints—and then there it is. My hand curls around what I hope will be my ticket to freedom, and I place it squarely into my lap.

Never taking my eyes off the road, and driving one-handed now, I slow way down. The other cars do the same.

I make one tiny adjustment, then reach over and roll down my window. As the window hits bottom, I turn and face whoever's in the passenger seat of the menacing SUV.

"Hey, asshole," I yell out the window. I'm struggling to keep the car on a straight path, while the cold night air whips my hair and blows my voice back at me. I yell again, as loud as I can. "Hey, you incredible moron. Show your face if you're such a big man."

It probably doesn't matter what I say, I'm just trying to get him to roll down his window. Still, it can't hurt to be as unpleasant as possible.

It works. The window beside me motors down, and I get a glimpse of some snake-faced weasel, if that's possible, staring at me in shock. Perfect.

"Take this, asshole," I yell. And before he can respond, I shoot my disposable flash camera right in his face.

The guy winces, puts his hand over his eyes, as if he's blinded by the flash. My goal exactly. Thug number two, the one who's driving the car, starts to yell something about "what the hell." Mr. Weasel is bellowing, too, something about his eyes hurting.

Just a few seconds more and we'll know how this all ends.

Thug number one shifts position in the front seat and leans his head out the window toward me, his hair plastering to his head, his hands on the window frame. He's screaming at me in an indistinguishable roar and he's pushed himself out so close to me I can see his eyes narrow in anger.

Perfect. Here goes.

I reach into my handy cup holder and grab my huge untouched cup of coffee. With a single fast swoop, I throw one supersize steaming plastic container of superhot java right in the guy's face. Part of the scalding brown liquid lands exactly on target, drenching his face and hands. The rest sprays and splatters over the windshield, leaving a viscous milky coating across the glass.

I hold my breath. It's now or never.

It's now. I hear a roar of pain and a shriek of brakes. I see the car on my left swerve toward the center median, and what makes my heart leap with joy, I see the empty space that's just opened up.

With a triumphant stomp on my accelerator, I swerve to the left, plowing my trusty Jeep in front of the SUV and through to the open road, devouring the pavement and leaving my pursuers behind. Even though I'm honking the horn nonstop, I know I hear metal on metal behind me. *Serves you right, you creeps.*

I give a quick glance in the rearview, just long enough to see the car entangled in the metal median rail, and what makes me even happier, I see the car that was behind me has crashed into him. I don't see the third or fourth cars at all anymore, and figure they must have pulled over to help their partners in crime when they realized that this time, their little create-a-crash plan didn't work. And then, finally, the best sight I've ever seen—the fast-approaching green sign that says Exit 17.

I make a hard turn to the right. And I am—outta here.

CHAPTER TWENTY

The deep silence of the Vermont night surrounds me, and through the windshield I see scraps of clouds trail over the crescent moon. I finally pull up in front of Josh's house and kill the engine. My hands tremble, and I have to put them back on the steering wheel to keep them still. Overwhelmed by my narrow escape, confused by the past and terrified by the future, my spirit collapses. I put my head on my hands and shake with silent tears. I'm relieved, I'm frightened, and I don't know what to do.

The sound of a cracking branch snaps my eyes open. Glancing at my doors to make sure the locks are down, I pray for whatever made the sound to go away. I slowly move one hand to the ignition and the other to the horn. I wait.

Another crackle. Footsteps. And then a voice.

"Charlie?" it says. "Is that you?"

There's no barking dog, no bulky sweater, no soft jazz, no citrusy soap—just Josh. I open the Jeep door and collapse into his arms.

Josh uncoils his arm from my shoulders and gets up from the couch, tucking the downy plaid quilt that had covered us both back into place around me.

"Just checking the fire," he explains. "Keep talking."

I take a last sip from my mug of Darjeeling, holding the string to keep the soggy tea bag out of the way. "So then," I continue, "I just threw the coffee at him, praying it was still hot enough to make a difference. And as it turned out, I guess the driver slowed down a little, so lots of the coffee landed on his windshield. It was the only thing I could think of to do."

Josh replaces the fireplace screen as the fragrant wood snaps and pops. "Charlie," he says, "that's astonishing. I keep thinking about you, all alone in your car, chased by God knows who, and then realizing that what happened to Brad and Mack Briggs was about to happen to you." He rakes a hand through his already tousled hair. "And that move with the coffee, I'm not sure anyone else in the world would have come up with that."

I know the warmth that spreads over me is not only from the quilt and the fire. Josh had instantly taken me in, been sympathetic and comforting, as if there had never been any misunderstanding, never been that stupid argument in the diner.

"If you hadn't suspected Mack and Brad had been forced off the road," he continues, sitting down beside me, "you'd never have escaped. You had time to prepare, to think, to plan. Time they never had." He sighs, and I remember he knew Brad.

"Well, that's the next problem." I lean back against the arm of the couch. "Your name was on that e-mail, too. If they—whoever 'they' is—know I know about the insider-trading scheme, they figure you know, too. And it wouldn't be hard to find you."

A log breaks in half, crashing through the grate in a shower of sparks.

"Yeah, well . . ." Josh's voice trails off. "Makes me wonder whether I should do something, but I'm not sure what. Call the police, I suppose." He crosses his arms over his gray Bexter T-shirt. "But I'm not sure what I'd tell them."

"I'm not sure, either," I reply. "But remember, we might have a picture of someone. If my little camera worked."

Josh shifts position on the couch. Our legs are parallel under the quilted comforter, tantalizingly close. "Nothing we can do tonight, anyway." He points to the brass clock on the mantel. It says 4:10. "I mean, this morning." Josh gives a huge yawn, runs his hands over his face. "Wow, sorry," he says, blinking. "I know you need to see Brad's files, but—"

"I'm the one who's sorry." I smile at him. "I barge in here, hysterical with some tale of midnight pursuit, toting a stolen Bible and asking for files. And keeping you up to all hours." Now it's my turn to yawn. "The files will hold till tomorrow," I say through my fingers. "Then we'll figure out what to do."

"There is one thing that doesn't quite make sense," Josh says slowly. "How did he know where you were? Did anyone know you were coming here?"

"Just Franklin," I answer. I lace my hands behind my head, scooting down farther on the couch. The fire gives a hiss, and I turn to watch it sizzle into embers.

Josh, hair rumpled, glasses askew, doesn't reply. We lie on the couch, legs now touching, his patchwork quilt covering us, connecting us. I feel my last nagging tendril of doubt about him uncoil and slither away. Silent, on edge and exhausted, we stare through the dying fire and into our uncertain future.

I open my eyes slowly, groggy, still getting my bearings. On the couch. *Josh's* house. The fire is cold, and peeks of morning sun glimmer through the bay windows. I'm curled into Josh's chest, burrowed into his shoulder, though I'm not sure how I got there. I pull the comforter higher, pretending to sleep, protecting the moment. Maybe I can make this last a little longer. I should be frantic with fear. Shouldn't I? But at this moment, I feel safe.

Someone—Josh—brushes my hair back from my forehead. "Charlie?" he whispers. "You awake?"

No more pretending. I open my eyes again, smile an exhausted smile. "Mmm," I manage to murmur. "Barely." As if I've been there countless times, I burrow back down into my place on his shoulder, his worn gray T-shirt muffling my voice. "You?"

I feel a soft kiss on the top of my head, then another and another. Josh's arms tighten around me, and I'm not even thinking as I turn my face up to his.

The brown corrugated cardboard carton, tape hanging off the edges and top flaps open, takes up almost all the room on Josh's kitchen table. I pause for a moment in the arched entryway, wearing a pair of Josh's drawstring sweatpants and an oversize shirt, watching Josh flip through the files. Without taking his eyes off the paperwork, he reaches over and picks up a steaming mug of coffee perched precariously near the table's edge. He takes a sip, then sits back, still staring at the box.

How can he look this attractive after only a few hours of sleep? Sleep-crushed hair, wrinkled flannel shirt, sweatpants and thick wool socks—how can exactly what's making me look so haphazardly disheveled make him look so devastatingly sexy?

"Good morning," I say. "Or should I say 'good morning again'?" We'd finally staggered off the couch around five, bleary-eyed and creaky. Longing for sleep, longing for each other, we'd collapsed, clinging, onto Josh's cozily blanketed bed. I run my tongue along my lips, testing, remembering. My mouth still feels tender, almost bruised, from our kisses. What happens now?

Josh looks up and his smile erases my fears. "Yes, I'll admit I'm having just a bit of trouble getting my eyes to focus," he says. He comes across the room, adjusts the collar of the flannel shirt I'm wearing. His. "Some story-crazed reporter crashed in here last night demanding files," he says, kissing me gently. "And I haven't been the same since."

For a moment, we're both quiet. "What can I tempt you with now, *madame*?" he finally asks. He gestures to the mugs on the table. "Caffeine first? Then files?"

"Caffeine is one of the basic food groups," I answer, touching him lightly on the back, unwilling to lose our connection. "Thanks."

As Josh pours my coffee, I look into the box. At first glance, the files look exactly like ours. I look closer. These files aren't alphabetical.

Josh points to a small pitcher and a sugar bowl on the counter. While I stir in some milk, Josh sits back down, pulling his chair back up to the table.

"So what do you think?" I ask, taking my first sip. "Yum. Good coffee."

"Just one of my many culinary skills," Josh says. "Coffee making, sandwich stacking, ice-cream scooping. And here, peanut-butter toast. As for the files, I don't know. These look like financial and corporate information for a dozen or so companies. Thirteen, actually. I counted."

I pull a chair up to the table. Our knees are almost touching underneath. I struggle to keep my mind on our search for answers. And my hands off Josh.

I take another sip, and a crunch of toast, organizing my thoughts.

"Okay," I say. "We think every Bible chapter corresponds to a company name. We're assuming the companies are the ones in this box. That could be wrong, of course."

"But you don't think so."

"Right." I run my hand over the tops of the files. "So, remembering what Caro Crofts and I figured out—if Aztratech was number one, I mean, chapter one, the code system worked."

"I just opened these this morning," Josh interrupts. "Whatever order they're in hasn't been changed. And—Aztratech is number one."

I get up and come behind Josh's chair. I lean down, relieved he can't see what must be the swoony expression on my face. Though my body is on another mission altogether, I make my voice all business. "Really?" I say, squinting at the file's labels. "That's great."

I stare at the file box, confirming. "That means we could be on the right track. So all we have to do now," I continue, "is get—"

"The other e-mails," Josh interrupts. "Find the chapter number, count into the files to see what company name matches that number—"

"And then see if the numbers of the verses listed are anywhere near the stock price," I finish, nodding in agreement. "It's pretty ingenious, isn't it? Communicating stock prices by fake spam? Who'd ever catch on?"

"I'll get today's newspaper from the porch," Josh says. "We can match chapters and companies, then try to check the prices in the stock tables." Josh gets up and heads out of the kitchen. I hear him take a step or two, then stop.

I look up from the files, concerned. "Is something wrong?" I ask.

Josh folds his arms in front of him, and the way he looks at me makes me happy that I'm sitting down—otherwise, I'm not quite sure I could count on my equilibrium.

"Nothing's wrong," he says, still smiling. "Everything's right, in fact. A beautiful woman in my kitchen, drinking coffee and looking pretty hot in my old plaid shirt. You're quite a picture, Charlie McNally."

He heads out to get the paper, the warmth of his compliment enveloping me like expensive perfume. I check my reflection in the shiny surface of the toaster, attempting to make sure my hair hasn't gone haywire, when a radical thought presents itself out of nowhere. What if he likes me, just the way I am? Even just sitting in his kitchen, hair funky and face makeup-free, reading glasses on my head? The possibility stops me in my tracks—and then I hear Josh's footsteps and the crackle of a newspaper.

"Let's do it," he says. With a swift motion he unfolds the business section, refolds it to the stock listings, then places it on the kitchen table. "Aztratech, we know. Let's start with Chapter Two."

I select the file, hair forgotten.

"Rogers Chalmers," I announce. Then my shoulders sag. "Rats. What's the stock symbol for that?"

Josh scratches his head, thinking. "Well, says here, Verse 42 through 44. Look for something that begins with *RO*, or maybe *RC*." Josh reaches for the paper.

"I'll find it." I grab the paper, and Josh follows my finger down the row of agate-typed symbols. We both pounce on RCHA. Stock price today—thirty-four.

"So check it," I instruct Josh eagerly. "Does the e-mail from then say 'good time to sell'?"

Josh finds the e-mail and gives me a thumbs-up. "Yup," he says. "It does."

"What's next?" I ask. I can't wait to look up another one. "Is there a Chapter Three?"

"Chapter Three . . ." Josh sorts through the files ". . . is Electrometrics. *E-L-E* . . ."

"Got it," I say, already searching the list under *E*. "ELEC yesterday closed at seventy-two and three-eighths. What's the e-mail say?"

"It's dated last week," Josh replies. "And it says, Verse 60 to 62. And it also says, 'a good time to buy.'"

"Wow," I say, staring at Josh. "We're right, aren't we?"

Josh has a little twist of a smile on his face. "Well, doesn't seem likely it's a coincidence, I'll give you that."

My mind is racing with the certainty that we're on to something. Someone—or a group of someones—is running a nationwide big-bucks insider-trading scheme. And Josh and I have cracked the code they're using. With Franklin's help, of course. And Caro's. Seems as if we've got it nailed now.

We check Chapter Four—Fisher Industries. The prices match the verse numbers.

Chapter Five. Again, the prices match.

Josh looks up from the file box. "I have a question," he says. "How would the people involved in this deal know which spams to answer? I mean, people get hundreds a day."

"See the heading? 'A re-figh deal 4-U.'" I point to one of the spams. "See? They're all the same. All misspelled, and with that hip-hop *4-U*. And remember, then they all say either 'a good time to buy' or 'a good time to sell.'"

"So you're thinking—whoever received the e-mails with that heading would know to search Google for the next line of whatever random snippet the fake spam contained. And then, they have to send that back as a reply. Like some sort of a coded message? Because only people involved would know to do that?"

"That's my guess," I answer.

"So it's almost like a password system," Josh replies. "Answer two e-mails properly, and whoever's running the show would know you're legit."

"Yeah, that's what I figure. Most people would ignore it, and hit Delete. Remember, I sent back answers on impulse, on a whim, because I thought the e-mails were so strange. The third time is when I got the Bible verse thing. I didn't understand it, but of course the 'Bible verse' is just what the traders would be waiting for."

Josh looks at me with worry in his eyes. "I keep thinking about what happened to you last night. The stakes could be so high. And you could be in so much danger."

I come up beside him. "You, too," I say, gently putting one hand on his arm. "And I got you into this, I know," I add quietly. "I was following the trail of a story, and you just happened to be part of the trail."

Josh puts one arm around me and we gaze into the October morning.

"So, looks like we're both on the trail now," he says.

I feel him kiss my hair once, softly; I let myself relax into his shoulder. I close my eyes, savoring the moment, smell soap, and peanut butter and coffee. I hear Josh sigh.

"And," he says, "I guess we'll see where the trail goes."

CHAPTER TWENTY-ONE

"So, I tossed my entire supersize coffee at them, and peeled away as fast as I could." I'm on my cell phone to Franklin, waiting for Josh to come out of the drugstore. Franklin is sputtering out question after question, but I can't answer everything at once. "Listen, I'll tell you the whole thing when we get to the hospital. Josh had the files. We figured out the code. You'll love it."

We had driven halfway to Boston in case the bad guys were still lurking in Vermont, then dropped the film off at a drugstore with one-hour photo developing. "What's more, the picture I took should be ready now. Josh just went in to pick it up."

Franklin is still trying to get a word in, but I see the revolving doors of the drugstore start to turn, and I peer through the windshield. It's Josh.

"Here he comes," I say into the receiver. "I'll call you when—"

Franklin interrupts, almost shouting. "Charlotte! Do not hang up!" he commands. "I'll hold on while you open the photos. I'm not being left out of this."

I shrug my shoulders, even though Franklin can't see my dismissive gesture. "But you're on the phone. It'll be tough for you to see, you know? But hey, whatever you say. Hold on."

Josh opens his Volvo's door and gets into the driver's seat. We've hidden my Jeep in Josh's garage and taken his car, just in case any highway muggers are still on the lookout.

"Do the honors?" he offers, handing me the package of developed prints.

I attempt to tuck the tiny cell phone between my cheek and my shoulder, but it pops out onto the floor. "Hang on," I tell Franklin, retrieving it. "Dropped the phone."

I hand it to Josh. "Here," I direct him. "Talk to Franklin while I open the pics."

He gives my phone a dubious look, and I remember he's never met Franklin. *Men.* "Never mind," I say taking the phone back. "You hang on," I tell Franklin. "I can't open the pictures and talk to you at the same time."

I hear a faint, tinny "Okay" as I plunk the phone in my lap. I look out the window for the millionth time, eyeballing the traffic to see if anyone is following us. I don't think so, but with thousands of cars on the road from Vermont to Boston this afternoon, I admit I'm not sure if I could really tell.

I take a deep breath and rip the pull tab on the top of the photo package. I hurry through snapshots of the clothing I donated to charity, Botox in the snow, the person I thought was Mick Jagger walking outside of Bloomingdale's and a shot of a broken parking meter I plan to use fighting a ticket at City Hall. It's the final photo that stops me.

"Look at this," I say softly, staring at the picture. I turn to Josh, my eyes widening, and say it louder. "Look at this."

From my lap I hear a faint buzz, and I know it's Franklin yelling, eager to hear what's going on.

"Just a sec," I call down to my lap. "I'll be right there."

Josh takes the photo, and together we stare at the image. An amazingly in-focus shot of the weasely man in the passenger seat, and in the background, a partially visible profile of the driver. He's somewhat blurry, but if someone knew the guys, they could recognize them both.

And I do.

I prop the photo on the dashboard in front of me and slowly pick up the cell phone. Looking at Josh, I begin to talk to Franklin.

"The picture of the guys in the car came out," I report in a quiet voice. "Both of them are definitely recognizable."

"Hey, that's great," Franklin replies. "Now we can go to the police and . . ."

Josh is talking at the same time. "Perfect," he says. "All we have to do now is . . ."

But I'm not listening to either of the men in my life. Instead, I'm looking at the two guys who tried to end it. And I know who they are.

Weasel and friend are still there—caught on camera, one face contorted in angry surprise, one focused on driving the car that was supposed to run me off the road. And I've seen both of them before. At Mack Briggs's funeral. They're the goons, the thugs, the dark-suited robots who accompanied Andrea Grimes Brown.

Andrea Grimes Brown. Viper-faced CEO of Rogers Chalmers. Part owner of the *Miranda*. Certainly in on the insider-trading plot. And now, it seems clear the woman's trying to kill me.

"Charlie?" Josh's voice sounds as if it's somewhere in the distance even though he's right next to me.

"Charlotte?" Franklin's voice buzzes into my ear.

"Yeah," I answer both of them at the same time. I know my voice must sound flat, as if all the wind's been knocked out of me. And that's exactly how I feel. But I have to tell them. "Listen to this."

We're halfway home. Josh pilots the Volvo, a grim expression on his face, as I watch the dashboard's digital readout count down the miles. I wonder if we're heading away from trouble or right into it.

I sneak a look at Josh. He's got one elbow resting on the car's window ledge, his other wrist draped over the steering wheel, and he's wearing a chunky black turtleneck and a black down vest. He's the perfect picture of "cool guy headed out for a ski weekend." Problem is he's actually an innocent schoolteacher dragged by a pushy TV reporter into a murder-and-insider-trading conspiracy.

Josh flicks his eyes to the rearview mirror, then turns as he sees me watching. He looks guilty, as if I'm the one who's caught *him*.

"You got me." He gives the mirror a little tilting adjustment. "I was hoping you wouldn't notice me scouting for your highway buddies."

"I'm doing a little highway scouting myself," I admit. "I'm so sorry," I say, briefly touching Josh's shoulder. "I know it's my fault and . . ."

Josh switches hands on the steering wheel, puts one of his over mine before I can take it off of his shoulder. "It's not your fault, Charlie," he says, giving my hand a squeeze. "Remember, it was Brad who first asked me to look into those e-mails, and Brad who sent me that box of files that are now locked in the trunk."

"I never thought about it that way," I say. He's right.

At that moment, a shiny black Lincoln sweeps down the entrance ramp at top speed and slides in front of us. I involuntarily grab my armrest, my heart racing, and I can see Josh's knuckles turn white on the steering wheel.

Josh never takes his eyes off the road. "Well, now," he says softly. "Let's just put him to the test here, see if our Mr. Lincoln has any friends."

The highway signs flash by as Josh moves into the right lane. The Lincoln stays where he is, just ahead of us. We speed up, he speeds up. We slow down, he slows down. I'm trying to see the driver, but I can't even tell how many people are in the car.

My eyes are widening with fear, and I can see the muscles in Josh's jaw clenching.

"That's not one of the . . ." Josh begins.

"No," I reply. "I've never seen this car before."

We drive in ominous silence for a few moments, hearing only the hum from the car's heater and the drum of our tires on the highway.

Josh hits the accelerator again. This time the Lincoln stays behind us. He's on our tail, falling back a few car lengths, staying in a parallel lane. Or maybe he's not on our tail at all. Maybe he's just some well-heeled owner of a sleek gas-guzzler, heading home to the city, completely unaware of the freaked-out couple in the Volvo in front of him.

I turn in my seat to look back. Still there. Not getting any closer, not getting any farther away.

"He could just be a bad driver," I offer, trying out my hypothesis. "Just because someone pulls out in front of you doesn't make 'em a homicidal maniac." I go for a little humor. "It just makes 'em a Boston driver, you know?"

"He still back there?" Josh asks, ignoring my theory. "He's exactly in my blind spot now."

"Yeah," I answer dully. "He's there."

Road signs are whizzing by now, offering burgers and ice cream, chicken and pizza. Billboards for Canobie Lake, Mohegan Sun, Walden Pond. Mileage to Concord, then Lexington. And that gives me an idea.

"Josh," I say, calculating. "The next exit coming up will take us to Lexington. To Melanie's. Let's get off, see if the guy follows us. If he does, we'll head straight for the police station. If he doesn't . . ."

"If he doesn't, we're just two middle-aged paranoids who have seen too many spy movies," Josh replies. His jaw is set, and he's not smiling.

Thirty seconds go by, the exit to Lexington looming ahead. At the last possible moment, Josh yanks the wheel to the right and peels off the highway. I hear the horn from some car behind us blare in outrage, and our tires squeal their complaints as Josh, ignoring the speed limit, expertly steers us though the curve of the exit. I grab the passenger strap to keep my balance. There's a stop sign at the upcoming intersection. As we slow down, I take one last prayerful glance in our rearview.

We're alone.

I can see the blur of an eye come close to the peephole. There's a pause, and then a click as Melanie unlocks and opens the door.

The reactions race across her face—surprise, calculation, even what looks like fear. She brushes a strand of hair back from her forehead, and it looks as though she's struggling for composure.

"Cha—?" she begins. She's looking at Josh, then back at me.

I interrupt her, embarrassed we've intruded on what must certainly still be her time of deep grief.

"Oh, Melanie, I'm so sorry. We should have called in advance."

Melanie backs into the entryway, gesturing us through the door. "Forgive me," she says, seeming to shake off whatever confusion our arrival had engendered. "I was just a little shocked to see you." She looks at Josh. "And you. But of course—" she's smiling now "—come in."

We follow her down a hall to what must be the library, a room I've never seen before. She turns, offering us a seat, and I notice she doesn't have the weary, worn-out demeanor I'd expect in a new widow. And no flowers. No cards.

Give her a break, I say to myself. We all handle sorrow in different ways. Maybe she went to a spa. Maybe she doesn't want reminders of grief. More power to her.

Josh and I perch on the edge of what looks like a brand-new suede couch, luggage-tan with brass studded trim. Melanie sits down opposite us in a curvy chintz club chair, hands in her lap, waiting for us to make a first move.

I slide my tote bag under the coffee table in front of us. Inside are the e-mails, Wes Rasmussen's Bible and the chart we made of the stock symbols and Bible verses.

"I don't know exactly where to begin," I say, "but I think we may have some clues about what happened to your husband. Would you want to hear about it?"

Melanie tilts her head a little, an inquisitive expression on her face. She says nothing, holds out a hand to indicate I should continue.

I bend down to my bag and zip open a side pocket to retrieve the Bible. Pulling it out, I hold it up for Melanie to see. "This may be the key to a conspiracy." I hold it between us for a moment, but she makes no move to take it. She looks guarded, nervous, one foot softly tapping.

I guess I'd be a little apprehensive, too, if someone was about to tell me why my husband died.

I put the Bible on the coffee table, then tell her the whole story. Caro Crofts, Wes Rasmussen's office, the Bible, Josh's copy of the files, our discovery of the chapter-and-verse code, what Brad must have also discovered.

"And so," I finish, "that's how we think whoever is in this insider-trading scheme passes information. If we get the SEC filings of the stock trades these guys made, we'll be able to prove who's sold what, and when, and connect it to the spams."

I wonder whether Melanie understands what I've described. I have no idea of the extent of her financial knowledge, whether she's stock market savvy or clueless. Maybe this whole thing is too complicated, way over her head.

Should I start at the beginning, make it easier? I wait, watching her process what I've just told her. She's staring over my shoulder, hands still clasped in her lap, silent.

Am I imagining she's gone a little pale beneath that flawless makeup? And now I can see she's breathing harder, her chest rising and falling. This was a terrible idea.

Melanie puts one manicured hand over her mouth and stands up, eyes reddening and glistening with tears. "Can you give me a few moments?" she says through her fingers. "I'll be right back." Melanie turns and almost runs out of the room.

"Wonderful," I whisper to Josh. "Now we've upset her." I screw up my face in regret. "I should have thought this through. Poor thing, she's—"

"And you didn't even tell her about the guys who tried to run you off the road," Josh whispers back. "And the photo you have of them. And how you know they're Andrea Grimes Brown's sidemen. How come?"

"Well, that's a relief, at least." I'm still whispering, worrying Melanie will come back and hear us. "Can you imagine if I'd had time to spring that whole thing on her? Um, excuse me, Melanie? Thought you might want to know we also figured out who killed your husband, and here's their picture. What do you say after that? Have a nice day?"

Josh shakes his head. "We have to tell her," he says quietly. "But let's just see what happens when she comes back."

I look around the room, uncomfortable in the silence. This despondent woman, trying to keep herself together in a time of unimaginable sadness, and here comes the crusading reporter with her cute new boyfriend, reminding her of everything she must feel is gone from her life forever. I bow my head in personal despair, wondering if I'll ever learn to keep my nose out of other people's business.

Apparently not. On the coffee table, I see a thick black photo album, leather bound and brass cornered. On the front, embossed in gold, it says Our Wedding. I hafta look.

I reach out a hand to open the album. Josh instantly grabs my wrist, stopping me.

"Do not look at that," he orders. "Come on, Charlie, give her some privacy." He holds on to my wrist, and breaks into a bemused smile. "You are too much, Murphy Brown," he says, letting go. "You can't paw through people's photo albums without permission."

"It's out on the coffee table, in plain view. That's permission," I say, wheedling. I lean forward again, about to open the cover, but then, out of the corner of my eye, I see Melanie in the doorway.

I quickly rearrange myself. "Are you all right?" I ask. "Do you want us to come back? Talk about this later?"

Melanie doesn't answer. She stands in the arched doorway, framed by its elaborate white woodwork, hands behind her back. Slowly, she brings her arms in front of her, and in one hand, she's carrying a book.

She takes a few steps toward us, holding the book out as she walks. "I got this from Brad's nightstand drawer," she says, gesturing at it with her head. Her face turns grim. "Here," she says defiantly, tossing the book toward me. "Look familiar?"

Surprised, I almost don't make the catch, but the leather volume lands in my hands with a soft smack.

I look down, and do a double take. I look at the book, and then at its exact double in front of me. Two brown leather-bound Bibles. The code book for the spam conspiracy. One I swiped from Wes Rasmussen. And the other apparently belonged to Brad Foreman.

"This is—" I begin. "How did—? When did—?" There's almost

nothing Melanie could have done that would have surprised me more.

I examine the Bible cautiously. It looks exactly like Rasmussen's Bible, the one we're so familiar with by now. The print, the paper, the binding, all the same.

"Melanie?" I begin again. "You said this was Brad's? Do you know where he got it? When?"

"It looks exactly like Rasmussen's Bible," Josh adds. "Question is, did Rasmussen give him this copy? Or did he give one to Rasmussen?"

"Or did someone else hand out Bibles to both of them?" I wonder, thinking out loud. "And if so, who else has them?"

Melanie begins to pace, almost as if Josh and I were not in the room. She goes toward the built-in bookshelves lining one side of the room, then turns, heading to the chintz-draped bay windows. And then back again, ignoring us.

Josh and I look at each other. He asks a silent question. What now? I briefly hold up a hand. Wait.

"So," Melanie says suddenly, her voice cutting through the silence. "It just gets worse and worse, doesn't it? What am I supposed to do now? Call the police and tell them my husband was actually the mastermind of some illegal Internet stock market scam?" She begins her pacing again, talking to the floor. "That'll be enchanting," she mutters. "Police investigations, federal inquiries, search warrants or whatever they do." She stops, looks directly at Josh and me.

"Because here's the rest of the story." Melanie leans against the bookcase. "That spam scheme? Sending coded trading tips via Internet junk mail? I'd already heard about it."

"Already—?" I can't seem to finish a sentence around here.

Melanie continues, almost talking to herself, remembering. "That was Brad's big moneymaking idea. Brad's! He was always coming up with far-fetched plans to strike it rich." She brushes her hair back again, looking almost angry. "Guess he thought it was easier than earning real money."

"But, Melanie—?" Why didn't she tell me this back when I first interviewed her? Hadn't we talked about whether Brad was into the stock market?

"And now of course," she ignores me and continues, her face clouding with raw emotion, "that could mean Brad wasn't actually murdered. Maybe it was an accident. Or—" Melanie is having a difficult time getting the words out "—maybe he did kill himself, like the police think."

A million questions crowd into my brain, but I can't figure out what to say and how to say it. What's the proper way to interrupt a widow who's imagining the reasons for her husband's death?

Melanie continues her narrative, picking up steam. "He killed himself, knowing the feds were on to his system. Had somehow learned of it." She shakes her head again, looking bitter. "Killed himself. And left me to deal with the whole thing. Of course."

I can't stand it. "Mack Briggs?" I say tentatively. "Also died the same way? So maybe it—?"

Melanie whirls toward me, laser-eyed. "Mack Briggs?" she says, her voice rising. "Mack Briggs? Maybe it was Mr. Former SEC Commissioner Mack Briggs who alerted law enforcement to what Brad was doing. That's what I think. His death? Just an accident. And now, because of your little discovery, I'm going to have to keep Brad's secret, or lose everything." She pauses, then lifts her chin imperiously. "And don't even think of putting this on TV. I'll deny every syllable."

Melanie turns her back on us—I can see her shoulders shaking as if she's deeply upset, maybe even crying. I sneak a quick look at Josh. He's staring at Melanie, looking confused and concerned.

I probably look exactly the same. Melanie's reaction is beyond bizarre.

I shove Rasmussen's Bible back into my purse, and then, while Melanie's still not looking, I sneak in Brad's twin copy, too. I figure she actually gave it to me, didn't she? And however this turns out, it's clear having these two Bibles will prove there's some kind of conspiracy underway. I shift on the couch to get Josh's attention, gesturing with my head. *Let's get out of here.*

Josh and I both stand up, edging toward the door. "Um," I begin, floundering for words again.

Melanie turns to us, eyes flashing and wet with tears. "Just go," she says. And she runs out of the room.

CHAPTER TWENTY-TWO

"Man," Franklin says. A gauze bandage now covers his forehead, but he's looking significantly healthier. "She had a Bible, too? Brad's? I'm missing everything."

Josh and I sit in the hospital's folding metal visitor's chairs, drawn up close to Franklin's bedside, sipping rancid hospital coffee and sharing Milk Duds. Josh has one arm thrown casually across the back of my chair, the international man-signal for *taken*. Not that Franklin would care, but I sure do.

"I'm trapped here, and you're . . ." Franklin shifts in his bed, continuing to complain. He struggles to find the words, waving his good arm back and forth in front of us. "You're Nick and Nora frickin' Charles."

Josh laughs. "Well, from what Charlie's told me, she's used to working as a team. So I'm only subbing while you're out of commission."

"Yeah, yeah," I interrupt the male bonding experience, eager to get back to business. "Listen you two, I'm having a brainstorm. After Melanie's performance today, I'm seeing a whole new picture." I hold up my hands like a film director bracketing his shots. "Andrea Grimes Brown—not a murderer, just doing some insider trading.

Wes Rasmussen—not a mastermind, just a player. Mack Briggs—not killed in a mysterious car crash, just a coincidental casualty. Melanie—not the poor widow, but queen of the cover-up. And as for Bradley Foreman—he's not the victim, he's the bad guy."

Franklin and Josh are staring at me, listening.

I tick off the points on my fingers. "Spam scheme. Brad's idea. He tells Melanie. She loves money—look at all her expensive clothing and jewelry. Plus, she thinks he'll never get caught. So Brad sets it all up for his boss Wes Rasmussen and the other CEOs of the companies he's documented in the files. He knows he and Melanie can cash in, too, because he's the only one who knows the system.

"So. Brad concocts the Bible code," I continue, "and gives everyone a Bible just like his. He sends the spam from his own computer. Then, he gets cocky. He decides to send the spam to Josh and Mack Briggs, to see if either of you will crack the code. You, Josh, ever-trusting nice guy, just do as you're asked, look up the quotes. No problems from your end. Mack Briggs dies before his suspicions are confirmed."

Silence from my boys. This just proves how right I am.

"So," I continue, "all we have to do is get the records of those CEOs' trades, compare them to the spam, trace the spam to one of Brad's computers . . . and oh, I just thought of something else." I point to Franklin. "That's probably why the Aztratech lawyers were telephoning Melanie that first day. They were probably on to Brad's scam, and were already investigating."

Franklin looks back at me, scratches the stubble on his cheek. "You're saying, then, when Melanie did the interview with you, and when you and I went back to look at the files, it was all part of a cover-up?"

I nod enthusiastically. "Pretty good, too, huh? We'd never have suspected her, right? She's the 'grieving widow.' Baffled by all those files. We thought we were so clever to get her to let us take them. She was actually luring us to sneak them out of her house, so the Aztratech lawyers couldn't subpoena them or something."

Josh raises his hand, like a kid who wants to be called on. "But here's what I'm wondering," he puts in. "Caro Crofts said Brad helped her with the whistle-blowing investigation. Why would he do that?"

"That's easy," Franklin puts in. "Distraction. Misdirection. The more the focus was on the price fixing at Aztratech, the more the focus was off the stock trading. And remember, when you're playing the insider-trading game, the market doesn't matter. Stocks go up, stocks go down, you can make money either way."

Josh nods. "So maybe that's why Brad sent you the e-mail, Charlie. He was going to tell you about Caro and the lawsuit. Misdirection again."

"Now we just have to prove it," I say. "Imagine the impact on the whole market," I continue enthusiastically. "It'll be much bigger than Martha. Even bigger than Enron. And we'll have it first—and just in time for the November ratings."

Franklin chews his thumb, his thinking pose.

"Just a second, Charlotte," he says. "There's still one thing I have to ask."

I drop my hands into my lap, rolling my eyes in impatience. "Okay, killjoy. What's the big question?"

Franklin ignores my annoyance, looks at Josh, then back at me. "Question is," he says deliberately, "if what you think happened is true, who killed Brad Foreman? And why?"

I deflate more quickly than yesterday's birthday balloon. My mind squeals into reverse, returning, in defeat, all the way back to square one.

"Yeah, yeah." I shake my head, unhappily comprehending my

mistake. "And who came after you in the parking lot? And me on the highway? I'm wrong."

"So who is the big cheese, then?" Franklin asks.

I dig into my purse and get out the sheaf of spam e-mails. They're now ratty and crumpled from being in my bag.

"Okay, listen," I say, smoothing them out. "The files are still in the Volvo's trunk, but we wrote the corresponding company names on each of these e-mails. Let's just go through these and see if anything pops out. Reminds us of someone we forgot."

Franklin opens his nightstand drawer and takes out a notepad and pencil. That guy is always ready to work. "Here's some paper," he says, handing it over. "Give me the e-mails, and I'll read you what's on each page. It's still a little difficult for me to write."

Josh stands up, stretches and holds up his empty coffee cup. "While you journos do your stuff, I'll run down to the caf for more of this delicious hospital coffee—anyone else interested?" He pauses. "No? Okay, back in a flash."

As Josh leaves, Franklin begins to read the company names.

"First, Aztratech." He looks up at me. "Got it? Okay, second, Rogers Chalmers. Realm of the delightful Andrea Brown."

"Okay," I say, writing. "Go on."

"Third, Electrometrics. Then, Fisher Industries." He pauses, waiting for me to catch up. "Islington Partners. Gyro Engineering. HGP, Inc."

"Wait a minute," I interrupt. "Hang on."

"Sorry," he says. "Going too fast?"

I stare at the notebook, holding the pencil between my teeth. I take out the pencil, absently wipe it on my coat, and look at Franklin, who's ready with the next e-mail.

"Franko," I say deliberately. "Does the next company name begin with *D*?"

"Begin with . . . ?"

"Go with me here," I say, tapping the pencil on the pad. "Does the next company name begin with a *D*?"

He looks down at the next page. "Well, yeah," he answers. "It does. Dioneutraceutics. How did you know that?"

"And the next one—begins with *E*?"

He turns the page again. "Exotel," he answers. "What's—how do you know what letter comes next?"

I lean against the back of the chair, holding the notebook to my chest. "You've got to give them credit, whoever it is," I tell Franklin. "This is one clever operation."

"What, what, what?" he says. "What?"

"I always wondered," I begin, "how the people in on this insider-trading group figured out which so-called Bible verses went with which companies. Not to mention, with all the spams on everyone's e-mail, how they knew which spams they were supposed to answer. You know?"

"Yeah," he says. He looks perplexed. "But didn't we decide it was the ones that said 'a good time to buy' or 'a good time to sell'?"

"Yes," I answer, nodding. "And that did make sense. But how about knowing which companies you're supposed to buy or sell? This is so blazingly illegal—I kept thinking it would be dangerous to keep a list of the company names anywhere. So I wondered, did the traders just memorize all of them in the proper order?"

"They could have, I guess."

I sit up and wave the notebook at him. "They could have indeed," I say. "But they didn't."

The door clicks open and Josh arrives, balancing a tray with steaming foam cups of coffee and granola bars. "Room service," he announces brightly. "May I offer either of you a . . . What?" He stops, looks back and forth at us, apparently picking up on the tension in the air. "What's going on?"

"Hang on," Franklin says. "Charlotte has some theory."

Josh puts the tray on a side table and leans against the wall, listening.

"What I was saying," I begin again, "is that the traders needed some way to keep track of the order of the companies, to know which one coincided with which Bible verse. Did they memorize a list in order? I say, nope, they didn't have to."

I pause. "They didn't have to memorize the names in order because the order was right there in every e-mail."

"Huh? No, it wasn't," Franklin interrupts, holding up the e-mails. "Look again. There are no company names here. What are you talking about?"

"You lost me, too," Josh adds.

I pick up the notepad, turn it to face them. "Look at the order of names, you guys," I say, pointing to what I've written. "Aztratech is first. Then Rogers Chalmers," I continue.

Then I read the first letters of each company. Out loud. Pointing to each one. "*A. R. E. F. I. G. H. D. E. . . .*"

"Holy shit," Franklin says.

Josh takes the notebook from me, looks at it again. "Pretty damn ingenious."

Franklin scrambles through the final pages of e-mails he's holding. "Put the rest together," he mutters, "and—it spells out the whole thing."

I look at Josh and Franklin, and say it out loud. "'A refigh deal 4-U.' Just like it said on the subject line of every e-mail. The last companies are 4Corners Real Estate and United Optical."

"That's why they used that spelling we could never understand," Franklin says. "They had to include every company's name in the anagram."

I peer at the list. "And Aztratech is alphabetically before the other *A*, Azzores Partnership. And Electrometrics comes before Exotel."

"It would be easy to just remember the names, once you knew which companies were in on it," Josh says. "Using an anagram means no lists, no files, no proof."

"You've got to hand it to them," Franklin puts in. "We only figured it out because you wrote down the names from the e-mails. Without that, without the files, we never could have figured it out. Nor could the cops or securities investigators."

"But someone knew someone figured out something," I remind them.

"English, Charlotte," Franklin demands. "Proper nouns."

"That's what's driving me crazy," I reply. "I don't know. But that 'someone' killed Brad, and maybe Mack Briggs, and tried to run me off the road, too. And most likely that same 'someone' ordered those two goons to snag the files from you in the parking lot before we could discover their secret."

Josh picks up his coffee, goes over to look out the window. "Speaking of which. Have the police come back to check on you? Show you mug shots, or whatever?" He turns to ask Franklin, "Do they say they have any leads?"

"No and no," Franklin says. "They haven't been here at all."

"That stinks," I put in. "You'd think they'd be all over it—big-time TV producer mugged, car torched, files stolen. Wonder what's up with that?"

No answer from Josh or Franklin, so I just keep going.

"But remember, they were pushing the theory that it was part of a string of muggings, so maybe it turned out that was true." I pause, considering. "You think?"

"No way," Josh replies. "They probably don't have lead one."

"And I'll be home in a day or two," Franklin says morosely. "So I'll feel nice and safe. Knowing those guys are still out there."

Franklin's got a point. And I realize that could put Stephen in danger, too. I decide not to mention that.

"But—hey," I say, brightening. I've just remembered we haven't told Franklin our biggest news. "I can't believe we forgot. But when Josh mentioned mug shots—"

"Hell, yes," Franklin interrupts. "The picture of the slimes who tried to run our Charlotte off the road." Franklin holds out his hands, gesturing for me to hurry. "Bring 'em out, Miss Nikon."

"There's just one you need to see," I say, digging in my tote bag. "Here."

Franklin stares at the photograph I've just handed him. The look of disbelief I read on his face is enough to keep me quiet. Josh comes around behind my chair, resting both his hands on my shoulders. Together, we wait for Franklin to speak.

He drops the picture into his lap and lowers his head to look at it again. When he looks up, expressions cross his face more quickly than I can interpret them.

I can't stand it any longer.

"What? Who?" I realize I'm whispering, though I can't remember consciously deciding to do that. "Come on, Franko. Who's in the picture?"

A sheen of perspiration appears on Franklin's forehead, and he turns the photo around so Josh and I can see it.

"Those police officers who were here about the mugging, McCarron and Cipriani?" Franklin begins.

"That's not who's in the picture," I interrupt. "They—"

He continues, resolute. "We need to call them. Right now."

There's silence again for a moment, as what he's suggesting sinks in. "You're—kidding me," I say hesitantly.

Franklin slowly shakes his head, looking at the picture again. "Not kidding at all. Your two highway goons are the same two I encountered so unceremoniously in the parking lot behind my condo. The same two who arranged for my little stay here at Mass General Hospital."

"Okay, team," I say. "Time to bring in the police. Franko, I've already put you in enough danger. Josh, you're clearly next on the hit list. I know it's a hell of a story. But . . ." I look down at the floor. When was the last time I gave up a story? Never. But now, I don't feel like I'm giving up. I feel like I'm . . . getting. "But I can't risk . . . losing you. Either of you."

I get up and head for the phone. Then I stop, turning back to Josh and Franklin. "You know, though," I say slowly, "I just thought of another mystery the photo might solve." I pick up the snapshot from the nightstand and point to the two men. "I'll bet these are the same creeps who broke into Melanie's house. She said nothing was taken," I continue. "And she was afraid they were looking for the files, remember?"

"She called the police from your office to report it." Franklin says, considering. "Man. I'll bet you're right."

A sharp knock on Franklin's door turns our attention to the hallway, where a frowning white-coat is giving us the evil eye. "It's far beyond visiting hours," she says sternly. She flips up a silver watch hanging from her belt loop. "One minute," she intones. "And then I'm calling security." She turns on her heel and strides away.

"Okay, look," Franklin says. "What if I call Melanie and give her the scoop on the photo? She knows what happened yesterday—I told her—and I'll see if she wants you guys to stop by with the picture. Maybe she'll be less upset by now."

"So we hold off on the police until then," I say. "Till we see if Melanie recognizes anyone. If they're from Aztratech or something. We can also see if the Lexington police know who they are."

"Right. It's a plan," Franklin says.

I lean over and give him a quick kiss on his bandaged forehead. "We've got this nailed now, but you be careful," I say as I stand up. "And this time tomorrow—"

A gravely voice from the hallway interrupts. "Ten seconds."

Josh puts one hand on my shoulder and salutes Franklin with the other. "Come on, Brenda Starr," he says, turning me toward the door. "Let's get you somewhere safe."

CHAPTER TWENTY-THREE

It's late, I'm frazzled and I'm yearning to go upstairs to my own little bed. Question is: with Josh? Or without him? I give him a surreptitious glance across the Volvo's front seat. Good thing he can't read my mind. Or Maysie's latest postcard admonition from Disney World that "every Beauty needs a Beast."

"So here we are," I say. I hear myself sound awkward. Nervous. Maybe it's just fatigue. "Thanks so much for chauffeuring me. And—for everything else."

Josh swivels toward me, propping one arm across the back of the front seat, making no move to leave. The engine's still humming, but he's put the car in Park. How do we always wind up like this?

I gesture toward my apartment building. "I . . . should go inside."

"I suppose," he says softly. He stops, midsentence, and gives a quick gesture of disbelief. "You sure? You don't think I should take you to—say—a hotel or something?" He puts a gentle hand on my knee. "You're certain you feel safe enough?"

"I suppose," I reply, although I'm not a hundred percent. "I won't let anyone in, of course. And . . ." I frown, and give another anxious look around tiny Mt. Vernon Square, the peeling white bark of the river birches eerie in the dim streetlights. Most windows are dark. "I mean, I guess they are still out there, you know?" And it feels as if they have me in their sights. Josh, too. But I'm not going to let them frighten me out of my own home. Plus, the voice mail from the vet says Botox is home now, and she can't be left alone. "No," I say. "This is fine."

I curl my hand over his and we sit in silence, staring through the windshield. Not another car on the streets, not another soul walking by. I'm emotionally exhausted—the fear, the tension, the uncertainty—but sharing this tiny midnight moment with Josh makes me want so many more.

"Would you like, uh, coffee?" I ask. Then I'm suddenly—shy. It's pretty obvious my invitation is not really for coffee, and I'm surprised at myself for being so bold. Too late now.

Josh squeezes my hand. "I'd love, 'uh, coffee,'" he says, smiling. "Anytime. But you know—how about I call you first thing in the morning? Get some sleep, get your own clothes. Lock your doors. Then tomorrow I'll come get you, and we'll see what happens with Melanie."

The old Charlie would have felt rejected. But I feel . . . relieved. I need a shower, my hair is somehow lank and frizzy at the same time, my face is probably breaking out and I really need some sleep. But somehow I'm certain there'll be more moments like this. Josh and me. Together.

"Deal," I say, gathering up my stuff. I turn back to Josh one last time, concerned. "You'll be safe at Bexter, right? You'll watch out, too? Don't talk to strangers, all that?"

Josh leans over and kisses my forehead. A tender, soft kiss. Lingering. I can feel his longing—or is it my own? Then he pulls me to him, this time kissing me hungrily, again and again. "I don't want any more goodbyes," he whispers. He sits back, his eyes locking onto mine. "You be careful, Ms. McNally. I'll watch until you're inside, and tomorrow I'll call you, first thing."

The entranceway door snaps closed behind me with a solid comforting click as I begin the three-flight trudge to my apartment. I'm happily weak in the knees as I round the landing to the second floor, clinging to our moments in the car, forgetting my fear. The last of my energy disappears as I drag myself up the steps by the banister.

And then something streaks by me, flattening me against the wall. I drop my purse and tote bag, terrified, and try to figure out if it's a person, or a rat or God knows what.

Meow.

My little calico pal pads up the stairs and curls her tail around my legs. I scoop Botox up onto my shoulder, and she burrows her head into my neck.

"Hey, sweetheart," I coo. She revs up her highest-level purr. "How are you, little one?" She nuzzles deeper, then touches my face with a paw. "I'm glad you're okay, baby cat," I tell her.

I stop in midpat. What the hell is Botox doing in the hall? I always leave a secret key under the cactus plant by my front door, and the vet's assistant knew to look for it there. But she'd never leave without making sure Botox is inside with food and water. The cat moves like quicksilver, but something seems very wrong here.

Still carrying Toxie, I softly make my way up the final steps to my door. It's closed. I stand outside, ear to the walnut wood, listening intently. Nothing. I slowly try the old-fashioned brass knob. It's locked.

"Do not move," I whisper to the cat as I put her on the floor. I tilt the cactus pot to see if the key is still there. It is.

I frown, confused. The door's locked. The key is in its proper place. But the cat is out. Someone was inside, no question. The vet's assistant? Well, yes, but . . . what if someone else is inside right now? Waiting for me to come home? And what if the cat got out when they got in? I feel a clammy wave of apprehension.

I consider running back downstairs. To where? Knocking on a neighbor's door. Saying what? Calling 911 on my cell phone. What's the emergency? Call Josh to come back?

I try to get my weary brain focused on reality. The easiest answer is always the correct one. And, since the door is locked and the key is where it's supposed to be, that means the cat got out when the vet's assistant left.

Slinging my tote and purse over one shoulder, scooping up Toxie and fighting off an intensifying foreboding, I stick my key in the lock and turn it.

Charlotte Ann Gelston. Charlie Gelston. Charlotte McNally Gelston. Mrs. Josh Gelston. Mrs. Joshua Something Gelston. I can't believe I almost Googled James last week. Long ago, far away, history.

I roll over, rearranging my pillow and trying to get comfortable. Botox, jolted out of a deep slumber, scrambles to stake out a new sleeping spot on my back. That cat can sleep through anything. I'm not having as much success.

Something is wrong with my pillow, there must be. I try to punch it back to its proper shape. Everything was fine when I walked into my apartment. Of course. No sign of anyone coming in, or anything being taken. But even here in my nest, safe, I stare at the ceiling. My body is exhausted, but my brain is churning along full-speed ahead. The green glowing lights from my alarm clock taunt me—it's already past 4:00 a.m.

I close my eyes, trying to distract myself. Wonder if Josh and I will have a wedding album. On our coffee table. Like Brad and Melanie. Wonder if our announcement will be in the paper. Maybe in the *New York Times.* Maybe even in "Vows," as the featured wedding of the week.

I sit straight up, sending Botox skittering across the bed, mewing in protest.

Melanie said she sent a wedding announcement to the paper. Time for me to look that up.

Padding to my desk in my thick wool socks, I can't believe I'm doing this. I could just as easily wait until morning. But then, it technically is morning. I click on my computer, and check the *Boston Globe*'s pay-per-bride section. Nothing. Then the *New York Times.* It takes me just a few moments to find "Vows" online. Those articles contain every bit of wedding-announcement minutiae anyone could ever want—gowns, ceremonies, relatives, education, occupations, pictures. I wonder if this one might also contain some answers.

Botox jumps onto my lap as I continue my search.

In seconds, up pops the same picture Melanie showed me that first day I interviewed her. The arty, soft-focus photograph, the floaty Vera Wangish dress, Brad's affectionate gaze. But here, underneath, is the whole story of their wedding.

Botox sits up, positioning her furry body exactly where it'll block my view of the computer monitor. I bat her back down onto my lap and lean across the keyboard as if sitting closer will allow me to read faster.

I see Brad got his MBA from Wharton, where, I remember, Mack Briggs taught. And then I read: Melanie, too. That's where they met, the article says. And she was valedictorian. So much for my theory she wouldn't understand the insider-trading scheme.

I pause, my brain struggling to extricate a memory. Didn't she tell me *Brad* was head of the class?

Ceremony at some church, reception at Tavern on the Green, very nice. Bridesmaids, many, but no one's name I recognize. Best man, Melanie's brother Martin.

A little bell goes off in my head. Martin. I flip my mental Rolodex. Martin.

Honeymoon in St. Bart's, I read on. Expensive. Couple will live in Lexington. I know that.

All perfectly interesting, but nothing earthshaking that I can see.

And then, finally, at the end of the article, there's a quote from the mother of the bride. It's not what she says that shocks me—it's who she is.

Andrea Grimes Brown.

Coffee. I need coffee. My gray-flannel clogs clunk down the hallway as I head toward the kitchen, yawning uncontrollably. Four hours of sleep again. I struggle to get my brain into gear.

Franklin is going to go bananas when I tell him what I found out last night. Josh, too. And the police. The enormity of my discovery perks me up—who needs sleep when you've got a good story?

I squint toward the living room, confused. It looks as if there's a funny shadow on the couch. Maybe I left my coat there last night. It's too early for contacts, and I wish I had my glasses. I squint harder as I get closer to the room.

It's not a coat. It's a person. Sitting on my couch.

I take a few more steps—then stop. Now I can see.

Flawless posture, tailored suit, matching patent pumps and

pocketbook. White gloves. Melanie Foreman, watching me calmly, looks more like a guest at afternoon tea than someone who could be arrested for breaking and entering.

"Melanie?" I can't think of anything else to say. Maybe she's discovered something about the Bibles. She doesn't know what I found, so maybe she's just lonely. Or wants to apologize. But why didn't she call? How did she get in? "Did we," I begin out loud, trying for my calmest voice, "have an appointment?"

She smiles, holds up the key to my apartment between two manicured fingers. "Under the plant," she says, not answering my question. She drops my key. I flinch as it clatters onto the glass coffee table.

"You weren't here yesterday when I came to visit," she continues, still with that brittle smile, "so I decided to come back this morning. We need—to talk."

Who would dig out someone's key and just come in? That's creepy. And clearly how Botox got out. I cinch my terry-cloth bathrobe tighter around my waist, then stuff my hands into the pockets. The back of my neck is suddenly clammy, and my throat gets tight.

"Melanie?" I say again. I hear the tension in my own voice and realize I'm clenching my fists. *Relax*. "Talk about what?"

"I know you have the files," she says. "The ones Brad sent to Josh. And now, I'm here to get them back." She picks up the shiny purse next to her, puts it in her lap. She snaps the clasp. Open. Closed. Open. Closed. "I couldn't find them yesterday. But I'm sure you can retrieve them for me."

Not a chance. I take a faltering step backward, away from her, thrown off balance physically and emotionally. Logic says Melanie cannot be sitting in my living room.

I fleetingly hope—maybe it's a dream? I smell Melanie's perfume, fragrant and floral. Hear a dull hum as the furnace kicks in. I try to lick my lips, but my mouth is dry. I'm awake. And this ain't no friendly visit.

"Or don't," Melanie says. I hear the click again as she unsnaps the metal clasp on her purse. I see the morning sun glint on the gleaming silver pistol she extracts from inside.

A .22, my mind registers. As if that matters.

She doesn't point it at me, just holds it carefully in her gloved hand.

Her gloved hand. I feel a trickle slide down my back. I'm in trouble.

I need a—what? My eyes dart around the room, looking for some kind of weapon. With escalating dismay I realize there's not much deadly force available in my living room. I could throw a pile of old *New Yorker*s at her. Clonk her with my TV remote. That's the extent of my firepower. I'm screwed.

"Suit yourself," Melanie continues. "Although it's hard to believe you'd think some box of papers is worth—well, you see the consequences."

Stall, my brain commands. Stall. Josh is going to call, any minute I hope, and if I don't answer the phone, he'll be here instantly. Or as instantly as he can, driving in from Bexter. Maybe he'll call the police. I've got to stall.

"I do," I say, pretending fear isn't making me feel as if I'm about to faint. I need to take up as much time as I can. The files aren't here, of course, but she doesn't know that. The good news and the bad news. "Though you know, I did read an interesting article in the *New York Times* last night."

"Oh?" Melanie questions. She puts the gun beside her on the couch and adjusts her Chanel-looking skirt. "And I care about that because . . . ?"

"Because the article was about you," I say pleasantly. I take a step or two toward the couch. "About you and Brad. Your wedding, in fact. In 'Vows.'"

"I see," Melanie replies, eyeing my progress and picking up the gun again. "And what—"

"Quite the write-up," I continue. "Nice dress. Nice ceremony. I was surprised to learn both you and Brad went to Princeton. And so you knew Mack Briggs, too, even though you told me you didn't. But what surprised me the most," I say slowly, willing the phone to ring, "was learning about your relatives. Your mother, most specifically. Your mother—Andrea Grimes Brown."

"Ah." Melanie nods. "So you know."

"Do I?" I ask. "I mean, most mothers and daughters shop, have lunch at a nice restaurant and share stories about their kids. Gossip about the neighbors. Give advice about husbands. Swap recipes. But you two, apparently, cooked up an insider-trading scheme. Very twenty-first century." I pause to see if Melanie will admit it. "Let me ask you, Melanie. Did you come up with this? Or your mother? You told me . . ."

Melanie gives an airy little laugh. "It was Brad's idea? Hardly," she says. "No harm in you knowing it now, I suppose," she adds, glancing at her gun. "It was actually an old boyfriend's idea. The spam, the quotation response system, the Bible-verse code. He's long gone, and anyway, would have been too much of a—" She pauses, as if selecting the exact word. "Wimp. To make it happen." She makes a gesture of dismissal. "Mother and I aren't wimps."

"And since your mother already had a high-level position at Rogers Chalmers," I say, encouraging her, "it must have been easy for Andrea to convince her bigwig colleagues to come in on the deal. Wes Rasmussen and the rest."

"It worked perfectly," Melanie says with a smile. "We all had Bibles. We all had big money. And not a whiff of trouble." Abruptly, she shifts from serene to staccato, her face darkening, her voice clipped. "Until Brad started piecing it together. Finding my Bible. Accumulating those files. Always searching. Always checking. Hacking into my computer."

"Your—?"

"Of course. My computer. You think that study at my house was Brad's? Of course I meant you to think so. I couldn't have you snooping reporters suspecting I was involved."

"And that's why you did the interview?" I'm getting this now. "To convince us you were simply the despairing widow?"

She sighs. "He had to send that damn e-mail. To Mack Briggs, and your little Josh Gelston, and to you, of course. I was so thrilled when you didn't answer it. Imagine, if you had just left well enough alone, we wouldn't be here now, would we?"

I frown, thinking back over that first day at Melanie's. "But you were upset I didn't answer him," I say. "You were so concerned that he was trying to tell me something."

Melanie laughs. "Was I? That's what you decided, perhaps. But I was actually wondering if you had contacted him, whether he had told you anything I wasn't aware of. I was delighted you hadn't answered."

"But your house was ransacked," I persist.

"Was it?"

I still don't understand this. "You reported it to the Lexington police."

Melanie laughs again. "Did I?"

I remember that morning in my office. Was it just days ago? I had assumed she was on the phone to police. But of course I'd never heard anyone on the other end. Had she only pretended to call? I was so worried about being summoned to Angela's office, I hadn't given her phone call another thought.

"But you gave Franklin and me the files—"

"Meaningless, unless you had the key. Besides," she says quietly, "I knew you wouldn't have them long."

Something in my heart sinks so deeply, it takes my breath away. Knees weak, I lower myself onto the chair across from Melanie, and my eyes well with tears.

"You sent those men after Franklin," I gasp. "And after me."

Melanie unsnaps her purse again, draws out a package of Newports and a silver lighter. "May I?" she asks. Tapping out a cigarette, she flicks open the top of her lighter, the flame mirrored in her eyes. "Although I guess your house rules won't be in effect much longer, anyway," she says, lighting up with an exaggeratedly elaborate gesture. "Will they?"

I have an idea. I stand up and look around the room, acting nervous and upset, which isn't actually that difficult. "Could I have a cigarette?" I ask.

Melanie briefly looks surprised, but offers me the pack and the lighter. "Knock yourself out."

I reach for the two items, but Melanie is faster. "I see," she says grimly, snatching back the lighter. "I'll do it for you."

Damn. I can't use the lighter as a weapon. I need a plan B. Meanwhile, my reporter brain, apparently more fearless than the rest of me, continues to insist on answers. *I hafta know what happened.*

"You sent those men after Franklin," I say again.

Melanie raises her eyebrows, doesn't answer.

"But—why did you give us the files in the first place?" I persist. "What if someone had asked us about them?"

"Come on, you're the reporter," she replies sarcastically.

"I'm the . . ." I think about this for a moment, all the while eyeing the glinty little gun. Then I understand. "Ah. Right. I'm the reporter. We promised you we wouldn't tell anyone about the files. And even if a lawyer subpoenaed them, you figured we'd never give them up. We'd go to jail rather than give up confidential documents. So you get them out of your house and out of your life."

"It has a certain . . . symmetry . . . doesn't it?" Melanie smiles. "Your pitiful journalism-school ethics became my key to freedom."

"And without the files, no investigators could crack your little code." I shake my head, understanding her malevolently twisted thought process. "Wow."

Melanie recrosses her legs, smoothes her chic cropped hair. She looks more like a post-deb blue blood than a cold-blooded mercenary. But I know she's killed for money and to cover up her crimes. She shepherded me to Josh and Mack Briggs, using me to find out what they knew. And obviously I'm not the only one in her sights. Josh will be next.

I take a puff of my disgusting Newport, trying not to cough, and step closer to the hallway, exhaling carefully. Plan B has just presented itself.

Melanie, watching me, curls her fingers around the gun.

I can see she's tensing, wired, about to crack. I have about as long as this cigarette lasts or I'm going to be as snuffed as this Newport. And Josh will be next. My brain thrums as I try to battle my escalating panic.

"You sent those men to run your own husband off the road," I continue, struggling to keep my voice even. "Your own husband. You were in 'Vows.'" *Till death do us part,* she'd promised. No kidding.

Melanie gives a dismissive wave, smoke trailing from her gesture. "Brad," she says coldly. "He had a choice. Could have kept quiet and cashed in. No outsiders had the vaguest inkling of our deal. That's why I need those files."

"But—Mack Briggs." I shake my head, remembering the solemnly sad mourners at his funeral. "You sent them after poor old

Mack Briggs." I take one more step toward the hallway, now almost angry, glaring at her. "And you sent them after me, too."

"Before I left Mack Briggs's funeral, I told Mother to warn you to stay out of this." Smoke from Melanie's cigarette is spiraling up toward the ceiling. "But you wouldn't listen."

This sucks. Here I am, uncovering the biggest story of my life, and someone else is going to write it. I've got no notebook, no tape recorder, no camera, and it's looking more and more like the only eyewitness to what's apparently planned to be a fatal shooting, one Charlotte Ann McNally, is not going to be around for the big interview. Because Charlotte Ann McNally is also going to be the victim. And dead.

I guess this is what my sixth-grade English teacher meant by irony.

But Mr. Thornburg also taught us about the surprise ending. Plan B.

I take an enormous drag on my cigarette, and then exhale a huge puff right into the smoke detector. In a heartbeat, it begins to shriek and wail. And less than a second later, so does every smoke alarm in my apartment, and then every one in the building.

Melanie's face pales, then twists into fury. She leaps to her feet. "You bitch," she seethes. She comes toward me, pointing the gun.

"Who, me?" I reply. I'm so not the bitch here.

Outside, I hear doors opening and slamming shut, footsteps running down the stairways, voices yelling, "Smoke alarm! Get out! Everyone get out!"

I can tell Melanie is assessing her options. I decide to help her.

"I wouldn't fire that gun at me now, if I were you," I say, raising my voice to be heard over the increasing commotion. "There's no way out for you . . . except right into the arms of every firefighter in Boston. That alarm is wired to the fire station," I tell her. "I'm afraid you're trapped in a nonburning building."

Now, as more people tramp through the halls, I can hear multiple sirens in the distance. My heart fills with triumph, but somehow Melanie has regained her composure despite the chaos I've set in motion.

She sits back on the couch, crossing her legs and taking another drag on her cigarette. "You're right," she says.

I can't understand why she's so calm.

"The building is not burning. All those firefighters will find that out soon enough." She settles into the upholstery, still holding that gun in one hand, her cigarette in the other. "So we'll just wait for everyone to go away. Then later I can say you invited me over, told me where the key was, I arrived and found you—well, you know."

"That'll never work," I say. The shriek of the smoke alarm pauses, then picks up again.

"Won't it?" she answers. "All those unpleasant characters you sent to prison in your little stories? I'm sure the authorities will wonder which one returned to take his revenge. But me? Why would I be suspected of killing you?"

"Listen, Melanie—"

Then, finally, finally, finally, the phone rings. I make a move toward the kitchen, but Melanie sneers and points the gun at me. I stop short.

"Don't. Even. Think about it," she says.

"If I don't answer the phone, they'll know something is wrong." It's a long shot, I know, but maybe this will work.

"And they'll be right, won't they?" Melanie replies. She looks at her cigarette. "I just have one more—"

Suddenly, there's pounding on my door. People are right outside, waiting to see if I answer. I could yell, but just then Melanie stands, gun in hand. She looks at me maliciously and holds one finger to her mouth, signaling me to be silent.

I remember with dismay my car is in Josh's garage, not in my assigned space in the parking lot behind the building. There's no reason for anyone to think I'm home. This may be my last chance. Just three steps to my front door. I'd have to get there, unclick two locks and yank it open. Could I do it before Melanie shoots me in the back?

CHAPTER TWENTY-FOUR

Commotion continues in the hallway. The smoke alarm wails. A cacophony of police and fire sirens are converging outside my window. Melanie, calmly seated again on the couch, ignores what must be hordes of arriving rescue crews.

"Charlie?" someone yells. "Miss McNally?" More pounding on my door, and my doorbell buzzes insistently. "Are you in there? Smoke alarm!"

I look at Melanie, trying to gauge my options. She's impassive, unfazed. And absolutely crazy. She's just decided to wait it out, figuring whoever's outside will go away.

And suddenly, they do.

The smoke alarm stops. The voices cease. Footsteps fade away down the hall. The place is silent. The quiet is so profound, it's almost a noise in itself.

Melanie smiles again, that arrogant and self-satisfied smile.

"Gone," she whispers. "They're all gone."

We stare at each other. Her eyes are narrowed and calculating. Mine are filling with angry tears.

Botox peeks her head around the corner, her eyes tentative and wide. I wonder if she's the last friendly face I'll ever see.

At that moment, all at once, my world spins into fast-forward. Someone bangs on my front door again, then rattles the lock—but I know no one has a key. A clamor of voices shouts my name. One even sounds like Franklin's voice. But that can't be true. I know Franklin is still in the hospital.

I'm still trying to comprehend the chaos when Melanie crosses the room in a few quick steps and grabs me by the arm, holding me close to her. She hisses in my ear, "Not a sound. And do not move."

She presses that stupid gun against my neck. I feel a chilling metallic circle on my skin, gag on her perfume, and for an instant I'm so woozy and panicked I think I see stars. Melanie's grip tightens and I almost despair. But then, my adrenaline soars. She's much smaller than I am. What the hell.

With a yell, I duck away from the gun, simultaneously stomping one clog-heavy foot as hard as I can onto her pretty little patent-leather pump. She screams and twists away from me. There's an earsplitting crack—her gun? Am I shot? No. It sounds like—a tree falling, my brain insists, but I know it can't be a tree falling. There's a deafening thud, a whoosh of air, and voices yelling insistently. Who? Melanie—where is she? A fraction of a second later, I see Melanie wailing in pain, holding her shoulder, her gun spiraling across the floor.

I can't figure this out. Why is she holding her shoulder when I stamped on her foot? Doesn't matter—I'm free. I run toward the front door, but the door isn't there anymore. The police are.

Two uniformed police officers crash through the newly created opening, both bellowing just like they do on TV—demanding, commanding, taking up all the space in the room with noise and brandished weapons.

"On the floor! Now!" one yells, pointing her gun at Melanie. "Right now, Mrs. Foreman."

I watch Melanie assess her problem, realize her defeat and hit the floor. Actually she hits my Pottery Barn sisal, probably the closest her designer suit has ever been to dirt.

Gun still aimed at the now-prone Melanie, one cop circles around behind her, clicking a set of handcuffs from her belt loop.

Another officer, gold badge on his navy winter coat, arrives from downstairs, puts his arm protectively around me and shepherds me out toward the stairway landing. "You're all right now, Charlie," he says reassuringly. "We'll take care of her."

He glances back into my wreck of an apartment. "Door must have just missed her head," he says, evaluating clinically. "Good thing you were out of the way."

"How—?" I begin. "What—why?"

"But you should have called us, Charlie," he says, scratching his head. "Catching the bad guys is our job, not yours."

"I should have—?" I look at him again, baffled. Then I realize why he looked familiar. The navy coat fooled me, but now I recognize Cipriani, the leather-jacketed sexy detective from the hospital.

"But how—?" I can't figure this out. How did they know to show up?

"We need a medic," the first officer yells, as Melanie, now handcuffed, continues to wail. "Looks like some of that front door landed on our Melanie here. Her shoulder." She looks again at her prisoner. "Sorry about the suit, ma'am," the officer adds dryly. Her apology doesn't sound very sincere.

I look more closely and realize it's Officer McCarron, Cipriani's mousy little partner. With that big Glock, and holding Melanie in custody, she doesn't look that mousy anymore. As for Melanie, I guess it wasn't my intrepid clog maneuver that got her, but pieces of the door hitting her as Boston's finest crashed through.

Cipriani turns to look at me again and gives a thumbs-up.

"She'll live," he says sarcastically. "Though with what we know now, probably most of it will be in the state pen in Framingham. By the way," he adds. "Smoke alarm? That your doing?"

I manage a weak smile. "I don't smoke," I say. "But when she lit up, it gave me the idea."

He nods approvingly. "Very resourceful," he says. "But she still would have killed you."

And in that instant, I'm overwhelmed. Two minutes ago a money-crazed suburban socialite was holding a gun at my neck. My past hadn't flashed before my eyes then, the way they say it does when you're facing disaster, but now my future rolls by in Technicolor. Everything I would have missed. Josh, Franklin, Maysie, my kitty, my career, days of success and failure and new experiences. I feel the shock set in, and I can't hold back my tears any longer.

I put both hands over my face as my fear and tension dissolve into watery relief. This all happened so fast, and I thought I knew what I was doing, but in the end, I was almost a casualty of my own curiosity.

Course they don't teach in J-school: When the Sword Is Mightier than the Pen, the Bad Guys Might Win.

Then, through my sobs, I hear footsteps and a voice on the stairs.

"Charlie, you okay?" It's Josh, who's running up the stairway two steps at a time. He arrives at my landing and puts his hands on my shoulders. "I never should have left you alone," he says, gently kissing my forehead. "And I never . . ."

I'm eager to hear what he's going to say next, but then another voice interrupts.

"Charlotte," I hear. The most familiar voice of all is coming from around the second-floor landing. Franklin clambers slowly up the stairs, hanging on to the railing and pulling himself up, step by careful step. He stops and eyes me from below, his face the definition of relief.

"I was so worried we wouldn't get here in time," he says, getting a second wind and puffing up the last few steps. "It is Melanie, isn't it?"

I wave them toward the scene in my entryway, where a handcuffed Melanie, face now smeared with tears and leftover makeup, is being read her rights by Officer McCarron.

Franklin uses his good arm to high-five Josh. "Score one for the good guys," he says.

"You can't know how glad I am to see you," I say, still teary, "What if—?" For a moment, I can't continue.

Josh takes my hand and tucks it through the crook of his elbow, pulling me closer to him. I lean into his body, grateful for his strength and support, but apparently my potentially deadly curiosity has nine lives. I still need answers.

"Just to make sure I'm not nuts," I begin. "Didn't I hear you on the landing a few minutes ago? Before—" I gesture through my newly destroyed doorway "—all this?"

"They made us go downstairs when they decided to break down your door," Franklin explains. He's still wearing a bandage over one eye, and one arm is in a fabric sling. "They figured if Melanie was in there with you, she probably had a gun."

One more thing I need to know. "I'm incredibly, unfailingly, unceasingly grateful that you superheroes came to rescue me," I say. "But how—how did you know I needed rescuing?"

A crisscross of yellow crime-scene tape blocks off my front doorway. Botox, apparently thinking this is some fabulous new cat toy, incessantly bats the crackly plastic with her paw. The police have promised a carpenter will replace my shattered door by the end of the day. Meanwhile, Josh, Franklin and I are sitting in my living room, drinking hot tea and guarding the place.

And I'm finally getting the scoop.

"The picture you took of the guys in the car?" Franklin begins, getting comfortable in his armchair. "You figured they were the two who broke into Melanie's study?"

"Yeah, so?"

"So I had this great idea," Franklin continues. "Call the Lexington police, and see if they'd recognize the snapshot guys as the ones who'd been doing the break-ins in Melanie's neighborhood. Well—" Franklin leans forward "—turns out Melanie never called the police to report any break-in."

"I know," I reply. "She admitted that. Right before she put the gun to my head."

Josh puts his arm across my shoulders, squeezing reassuringly.

"Anyway," Franklin goes on, "when I heard she'd never reported a burglary, I figured there probably wasn't one. She just made it up so she could come to Channel 3 and find out if you were on to her."

"Then what?"

"Still, we did know your photo boys were the ones who beat me up. So I called Detective Cipriani and McCarron. They were on duty, and came right over. I told them your whole highway escapade, including the coffee and the snapshot," Franklin says. "They were very impressed, by the way. And then I showed them the photo."

Franklin pauses. He does this on purpose, I know, to heighten the suspense. He's in TV news, after all.

"Come on," I whine. "Just tell me what they said."

"Well," Franklin says dramatically. "They each looked at the picture, then looked at each other. Then Cipriani says, 'Martin Brown.'"

This is worth the wait. "Whoa," I say softly, as the puzzle piece clicks into place.

"Right," Josh puts in. "And you know who that turns out to be? Melanie's—"

"Brother," I finish.

Now it's Franklin's turn to look confused. "How did you know Martin Brown was Melanie's brother?" he asks. "We didn't even know Melanie's maiden name was Brown."

"I was going to tell you the whole thing this morning, but as you remember, I was so rudely interrupted," I explain. "Hang on a sec."

I retrieve the "Vows" story from my printer, and hold it out to Josh and Franklin. "I found this last night."

I wait while they both read it.

"So when Melanie showed up this morning, it wasn't a surprise." I rethink this. "Well, it was a surprise that she was sitting on my couch with a gun, but it wasn't a surprise that she was behind it all."

Franklin laughs, waving the printout. "Got to give you credit," he says. "Only you, Charlotte, could solve an insider trading and murder conspiracy using clues from the wedding section of the *New York Times*."

"Well, as we always say, journalism is all about the research. Got to keep digging." I give a modest bow. "Anyway. So the police knew Martin Brown?"

"And his brother, Luke, too," Franklin says. "He was the other one in the photo."

"The cops told us the Brown brothers have ugly criminal pasts. Both have records, jail time," Josh adds.

I think about this for a moment.

"But Brown is such a common name." This doesn't add up to me. "How would the police know they're related to Melanie, whose name isn't even Brown anymore? And to Andrea? She's Brown, but there must be a zillion Browns."

"That's the cool part," Franklin explains. "The cops pulled out their records, dates of birth, criminal history, all that. And the files also included their last known address—2519 Riverside Lane. Lexington. And I knew that was—"

"Melanie's house," I finish. I digest this for a moment. "Oh, I get the rest," I say, making the final connection. "Melanie said her parents gave them the house after they moved to a condo. So it was also Andrea's former address."

"Just a little family affair," Josh puts in. "Melanie must have been the older sister from hell."

"Sunday brunch at the Browns'," I imagine out loud, "must have been quite a scene. By the way, where are the Brown brothers now?" I ask. "And Andrea? In custody?" I glance up where my nice lockable door used to be. "I hope?"

"Oh yeah," Franklin assures me. "After McCarron and Cipriani saw the snapshot, they sent SWAT guys to pick up Martin and Luke. They're both behind bars now, charged with all kinds of murder and conspiracy. Andrea, too."

Botox, tired of battling the crime-scene tapes, trots in and jumps on my lap, stretching out one paw and resting it delicately on Josh's thigh. "She's very forward," I explain. "Give her tuna fish, she's yours for life."

"Very cozy," Franklin smiles, then wrinkles his nose. "Hope you're not allergic." He sneezes twice. Botox gives him a sinister look, which he shoots right back at her.

I take a sip of tea, warmed by the fragrant jasmine, and by the company of those I love. But I still have questions.

"I still don't understand," I begin, "how you knew I needed rescuing."

"Well, as soon as the cops nailed Martin and Luke's IDs,"

Franklin begins, "I knew you were in danger. I called, but you didn't answer the phone."

"Melanie was already here," I say. "Wouldn't let me answer."

"So then I called Josh to see if you were with him, but he told me he'd dropped you here."

"So I came over right away," Josh says.

"Meanwhile, the police had scooped up the boys, and Andrea, but Melanie wasn't home." Franklin shakes his head. "It did not look good for you at that point, kiddo," he says. "I said to hell with the hospital, threw on my jeans and raced over here with my new cop friends. And I'll tell you," he adds, "your neighbors had decided you weren't inside, since your car wasn't parked in the spot."

I curl up more closely in Josh's arms, suddenly self-conscious. I begin to play back the morning in my head, remembering my first fuzzy glimpse of Melanie on the couch, my misguided sympathy, my realization of her past, my understanding of her deadly goal. She fooled everyone. Including me.

"It's hard to explain," I say quietly, "how it feels to be that close to . . ."

The phone jangles, clamoring through our silence. Botox leaps up and bolts down the hall, but she's the only one who moves. I look at Josh. Josh looks at Franklin. Franklin looks at me.

"It's *your* phone," Franklin says dryly. "Probably the newspaper, ha-ha."

We look at each other, realizing it's potentially not so funny. It probably *is* the newspaper.

The phone rings again.

"Can you imagine? Scooped on our own story? Again?" I say. I can't bear it. "Franklin." I point to him. "You answer. Tell them I'm—"

At that moment, we hear the answering machine pick up. It's not the newspaper. It's Channel 3.

"Charlie, hey, yo. It's Ron at the assignment desk. What the hell is up? Someone got arrested in your building? You know about this? Is there a fire there, or what? Call me. ASAP. I hope to hell you're out of town or something. Kevin won't be happy if you've screwed us."

Ron may have said more, but the sound of our laughter obliterates the rest of the message.

"Yeah, we know about it," Franklin calls out to the machine. "We got this one covered, News Boy."

I reluctantly disengage from Josh's arm and point to Franklin. "You—call our pal Ron and tell him we're on the way in. Make them give us a photographer. I don't care if they have to pay OT. Me—I'll get dressed fast as I can. Then, you and I are headed to the station."

"I can drive you," Josh offers eagerly. "I can help."

I give him a kiss on the cheek; brief, but full of promise. "Thanks, Prince Charming," I say. "And you know I'll miss you. But you'd better stay here and wait for the door."

EPILOGUE

Seven Months Later

Franklin and Stephen, both wearing tuxes and big smiles, are the first to join Josh and me at Channel 3's table at the Emmy awards ceremony.

"Give us a twirl, Miss Charlotte," Franklin commands. "Let's see a 360."

I pretend to be reluctant, though I know my new black sheath is simple and perfect. I also know the star of pavé diamonds twinkling around my neck is even more perfect. Earlier this evening, Josh explained it was our private reminder of that first time together, the night we watched the shooting star. I give the necklace a secret touch for luck as I return to my seat.

"Very nice," Franklin confirms. "I just hope you get to show that off up onstage."

"Don't even talk about it," I say, cutting off any jinxing discussion of winning. "We'll wait and see."

I scan the Copley Plaza Hotel ballroom as it fills with every TV reporter, producer, director, writer, photographer and editor in New England. Glittering gold helium-filled balloons float from silver ribbons; crystal bowls overflow with white roses; tiny white candles twinkle in sterling silver votives. Newbies strut in recycled prom dresses and overlacquered updos, veteran anchors cruise for attention in couture and borrowed jewelry. It's a crowd so full of ego and ambition, it's amazing they could even find room for the tables.

But tonight, I'm feeling satisfied with what I already have.

"You know, I've decided I really don't care if we win," I say to Josh. "At least four people are already in jail because of our story, and more on the way. We cleaned up in the November ratings, won big. So who needs a statue, right?"

Josh, looking more Gregory Peck than ever in black tie, puts down his scotch on the rocks, lifts my chin with a finger. "Bull," he says.

A peal of familiar laughter cuts through the babble of the crowd.

"Whoo hoo, the winner's circle," Maysie calls out. She's just off the team plane after a Red Sox road trip, and I haven't seen her in weeks. "We are here to kick some big-time TV butt." She's thrown a tangerine pashmina over a black silk camisole, and tonight, her black jeans are satin. She waves at the table as she and her husband take their seats. "Everyone knows Matthew, right? He refused to wear a bow tie with his tux, you'll notice."

"Made me look like Mr. Peanut," Matthew says, indicating his round glasses. "The cummerbund was bad enough."

"Okay, kiddo, give me the scoop," Maysie demands. She takes her seat, flapping open her napkin and turning toward me. "So Melanie's brothers have ratted her out?"

I take a sip of wine, nodding. "Yup. And since the boys gave prosecutors the whole story," I say, "Melanie and her mother are sunk."

"I've seen a lot of slimes come through my own law office, but those two take the prize," Matthew adds.

"It was probably the only way they could avoid the death penalty," Franklin says.

"So now, Melanie and her mother will have to plead guilty," Matthew predicts. "Like Charlie says, they're sunk."

"That Melanie, though, she's tough," I reply. "Maybe she and Mommie Dearest have some genius lawyer who says he—or she—can get them acquitted. And it could happen."

Maysie dismisses me with a wave of her fork. "I don't think so." She grins. "Greetings, Brown family," she intones, in a dead-on imitation of her AOL system. "You've got jail."

The ceremony is ten minutes away. Maysie's table-hopping, Josh and Matthew have gone to get drinks, but there are still two unoccupied seats at our table. I know they're reserved for Kevin O'Bannon and Angela Nevins. I touch my star necklace. Maybe she won't come.

Stephen interrupts my reverie.

"One more thing?" he says. "What was the deal about the Bibles? I missed that part."

I slip off one satin slingback and tuck my leg under me, leaning forward toward Stephen. "Well, that's pretty interesting," I begin. "We thought they were some sort of decoder book, you know? And that's why all the people in the spam scheme had to have one."

"And they did," Franklin adds. "All of the CEOs the feds arrested had an identical Bible. Melanie had even circled the Book of Numbers in each one's table of contents. Get it? 'Numbers.'"

Stephen nods. "And were they code books like you thought?"

"Well, no," I continue. "Turns out you didn't really need a

Bible to figure out the spam, you just needed the 're-figh deal 4-U' mnemonic device. The Bibles were more like . . ." I pause, searching for the perfect description.

"A membership card," Franklin offers.

Exactly. "Melanie gave them to all the players," I explain. "But here's the heavy irony. Once the Brown brothers told the cops about the special Bibles, how Melanie had handed them out, they became key evidence to the conspiracy. The police got search warrants to look for 'em, and once they found 'em, case closed."

"Twelve more major-player CEOs," Franklin says quietly. "Soon to be in the license plate–making biz."

"We did good, Franko," I finish, pantomiming applause. "And I don't care if we win tonight or not. I really don't."

I feel a whisper in my ear. "Bull," Josh murmurs again. He's holding a glass of champagne and lifts it for a toast. "Before they announce the awards, let me just say how happy I am to have met you all, and how . . ." he pauses, and then gives me a look I hope I never forget ". . . how my life has changed so wonderfully since Miss McNally walked through my door."

My eyes well with happy tears as my tablemates and I clink glasses. I've lived for so long on emotional speed-dial, on professional fast-forward. Rushing to find answers, pushing, hurrying, always looking for what's coming next—the next problem, the next story, the next award. Now, for a moment, the universe hits the slo-mo button, and with astonishing clarity I see what I almost allowed myself to miss. To embrace what I already have—not focus on what I need to get. Loyal and honest Franklin, who revealed he just turned down a job in New York. Said no to the big time—to stay with me.

And there's Josh. How does it happen that you open a random door and a whole new world is behind it? I'm comfortable with temporary, sure. But permanent has its pluses. And I'm ready to take a chance.

Besides, I allow myself a moment to smile, we've changed some lives. Stopped some bad guys. Did what we're supposed to do. Not by luck, not by chance, but by using our heads, taking risks and working hard. We're good at this. I'm good at this.

Married to my job? Maybe it doesn't have to be like that. Maybe television and I can just be—good friends. No vows, no promises. We'll stay together—as long as we're both happy.

That said, I mention quietly to the journalism gods, don't get me wrong. I'm not ready to go totally Hallmark. Winning would still be just fine.

"Hey, Charlie, good luck," someone behind me says, putting a hand on my shoulder.

I turn to see Kevin O'Bannon, suavely tuxed and carrying a glass of champagne. He raises it briefly. "You deserve to win," he says, smiling. "And whatever happens, let's chat about your contract Monday. And let's make it long-term—I don't want to lose you."

I open my mouth to say something, something witty and confident and gracious. But nothing comes out.

"I'd better go get to my seat," he continues softly. He starts to turn away, then turns back. "Angela," he says. "Just so you know. She's not coming tonight. She's no longer with the station."

I try again to talk, but my brain has flipped into overload. "She's—?"

"Pursuing other opportunities," Kevin says dryly. "We wish her the best." He gives an inscrutable smile and heads to his chair.

I turn to Franklin. "Did you hear that?" I gasp. I flutter my fingers and make a snarky face. "Ciao, newsie."

"The devil you know," Franklin replies. "Let's see who's in her office on Monday."

I don't have time to worry about this as the lights dim, the rumble of conversation quiets and a spotlight hits center stage. All eyes turn to the front of the room as the awards begin.

In what seems like hours, but also seems like seconds, we hear our category.

"For Investigative Reporting, the nominees are . . ." a blonde in a last year's Versace begins reading a list of names.

I feel Josh's arm go across the back of my chair, and I see Stephen's go around Franklin's. I hold on to the edge of the table with both hands.

Blondie opens the envelope. "And for Investigative Reporting, the Emmy goes to . . ."

There's a roomful of applause, a whoop from Maysie, a thumbs-up from Kevin and a hug from Josh. I feel all the energy instantly drain from my body and then rush back in again. The giant onstage video screen blares the Channel 3 theme music and animated logo, and Franklin and I wind our way through the maze of tables and toward the stage.

The journey is brief—but my brain takes a short trip of its own. Smiling my way past tables of well-wishers, I remember that first spam I read, how Franklin and I thought Melanie was a poor, silly widow, how we were baffled by the boxes of files. I remember how Angela tried to kill the story—I also remember how Franklin could have been killed getting it. And me, too.

Our video clip rolls on the big screen, as vivid as Technicolor in the darkened ballroom. It's my closing stand-up, taped on a chilly November afternoon in front of the gold-domed Massachusetts State House. My black cashmere coat pops in front of the redbrick building, and, thanks to a sapphire sky and some elaborate off-camera lighting, I look pretty great for fortysomething. Okay, fine. Forty-six. My voice booms through the loudspeaker.

"As for ringleader Melanie Brown Foreman, the U.S. Attorney's office says her criminal enterprise included murders, attempted murders, burglary, assault and car theft. With Wall Streeters in shock, Securities and Exchange Commission officials also say they are now targeting more than a dozen CEOs in what one investigator called the most insidious and widespread case of insider trading they have ever seen."

My taped voice fades away, and Franklin and I are center stage, side by side at the podium, each of us holding a glistening statue.

The rules say only one of us can make a victory speech. I step back and wave Franklin to the podium. Producers are usually behind the scenes, but tonight it's his turn to be in the spotlight.

"This is a team effort," he says, holding his Emmy aloft, "and I'm proud to be on Charlie McNally's team." He turns and toasts me, then finishes. "And just wait till you see our next story! Thank you so much."

The audience cheers as we carry our statues off the stage and into the logo-draped room designated for winners' photographs.

I lean toward Franklin so he can hear me over the applause. "What story?"

"Ah, who knows." Franklin laughs. "We always think of something."

"But what if we don't?" I wail. I don't think Franklin's that funny. And next year, I'll be forty-seven.

"Charlie, Franklin, look this way," I hear. Flashbulbs pop and sizzle as photographers clamor for the best angle. "Smile and hold up your Emmy!"

We face the bank of cameras, arms across each other's shoulders. My vision swims with blue dots as the flashes pop. Then, just as quickly as they arrived, the paparazzi swarm to the next target, and I can see again.

I see Stephen, eyes shining with pride, heading for Franklin.

And behind him, I see Josh, holding two crystal flutes of champagne. You know, I tell myself, we always do come up with a story. No reason to think next time will be any different. And if we don't win next year, well . . .

I touch the little diamond star around my neck. And I make a wish.

ACKNOWLEDGMENTS

2016:
Thank you, beyond description and imagination, to Kristin Sevick and everyone at Tor/Forge. And thank you to agent Lisa Gallagher, who knows we should reach for the stars.

2007:
You might think writing is a solitary endeavor. It isn't.

To Ann Leslie Tuttle, my gracious, wise and brilliant editor.

To the remarkable team at Harlequin and MIRA Books, Tara Gavin, Charles Griemsman, Margaret O'Neill Marbury, Valerie Gray and Donna Hayes. Your unerring judgment and unfailing support make this an extraordinary experience.

To Marianne Mancusi, without whom *Prime Time* would simply never have existed.

To my producer and early reader Mary Schwager, who is not fictionalized as Franklin, but who is no less a genuine journalist, genuine friend and genuine partner in crime.

To Francesca Coltrera, for whom no detail was too small, the skilled and ruthless editor who shepherded me with humor and respect, and who allowed me to believe all the changes were my ideas.

To those who unselfishly and generously advised me and wished me well: Jan Brogan, Jenny Crusie, Tracy Dunham, Roberta Isleib, P. Amy MacKinnon, Jennifer O'Connell and Susannah Taylor.

To Elisabeth Weed, the first to believe. Her mentor Ike Williams. The paragon Hope Denekamp.

To Thomas Thornburg and Alice Blitch, who taught me to love Shakespeare.

To devoted reader Amy Saltonstall Isaac.

To Kristin Nelson, my agent. I'm convinced she's Superwoman in disguise.

To my darling Jonathan, who read every word. Twice maybe. Who never complained, except when he had to read the mushy parts about Josh.

A special thanks to every news photographer I've worked with. You took a hit in this one, but without your skill and talent, I know I'd have a career in radio.

Turn the page for a preview of
the first Jane Ryland novel

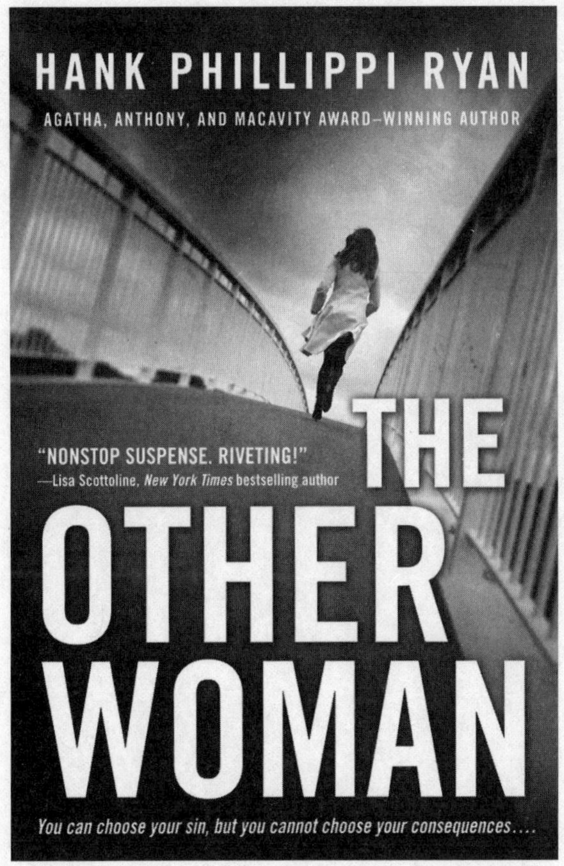

AVAILABLE NOW
FROM TOM DOHERTY ASSOCIATES

CHAPTER ONE

"Get that light out of my face! And get behind the tape. All of you. *Now.*" Detective Jake Brogan pointed his own flashlight at the pack of reporters, its cold glow highlighting one news-greedy face after another in the October darkness. He recognized television. Radio. That kid from the paper. *How the hell did they get here so fast?* The whiffle of a chopper, one of theirs, hovered over the riverbank, its spotlights illuminating the unmistakable—another long night on the job. And a Monday-morning visit to a grieving family. If they could figure out who this victim was.

A body by the river. This time, the Charles, down by the old dock. Her legs, black tights striped with mud, leather boots, one zipper down, splayed on the fallen leaves and slimy underbrush on the bank. Her head, chestnut hair floating like a punk Ophelia, bobbing and grotesque in the tangled weeds.

Too bad I can't call Jane. She'd love this.

Jake's yellow beam of light landed on that Tucker kid, notebook out and edging toward the body. Rubber boots squished in the muck of the riverbank, still soft from Boston's run of bad-luck weather. "Hey, you, newspaper kid. *Out.* This means you. You don't wanna have to call your new editor to *bail* you out."

"Is it a serial killer?" A reporter's voice thin and reedy, carried in the chill wind. The neon green from the Boston Garden billboards, the purple beacons decorating the white-cabled Zakim Bridge, the glaring yellow of the chopper's spots colored the crime scene into a B-movie carnival. "Are you calling it a serial killing? You think it's one person? Was she killed the same way as the other?"

"Yeah, tell us, Jake," another voice demanded. "Is two murders serial?"

"One a couple weeks ago, one today, that's two." A different reporter's voice. "Both women. Both by water. By bridges. Both weekend nights. Both dead. That's serial. We're going with that. Maybe . . . 'the River Killer.' "

"We are, too. The Bridge Killer."

"Have you figured out who the first victim is?"

"Outta here, all of you!" Jake tucked his flashlight under one arm, zipped his Boston Police–issue brown leather jacket. Reporters scrambling to nickname a murderer. Crazy. *What does Jane always say? It bleeds, it leads? At least her stories aren't like that.* A siren screamed across Causeway Street; then the red-striped ambulance careened down the rutted side street. Every camera turned to the EMTs scrambling out the opening ambulance doors.

No need for them to hurry, Jake thought. His watch showed 2:15 A.M. She'd been dead for at least three hours.

Just like the other woman.

Jane Ryland had thrown up after the verdict.

She'd twisted her damp hair away from her face, avoided the mirror, and contemplated how long she could hide in the Suffolk County Courthouse ladies' room. *Forever would be good.* Instead, she'd gritted out a smile for the scrum of cameras as Channel 11's defense attorney promised her television colleagues an immediate appeal of the jury's decision. The two then marched down the granite steps of the courthouse, the lawyer's pin-striped arm protectively across Jane's shoulder, as if a million-dollar damage verdict were the honorable cost of doing journalism business.

But soon after, Jane could read the counterfeit smiles, rescheduled meetings, abysmal story assignments. Her TV reporting career was over. She'd protected a source, but nobody was protecting her.

MILLION-DOLLAR MISTAKE, the headlines screamed. RYLAND NAMES WRONG MAN AS JOHN IN SEX-FOR-HIRE CASE. Indy rag *Boston Weekly* called her "Wrong-Guy Ryland."

Jane knew she hadn't been wrong. There'd been no mistake, but it didn't matter. Days later she was fired.

"And most incredibly bogus of all, they pretended it wasn't about the verdict." Jane had banged out a bitter and bewildered e-mail to her pal Amy. Once newbie co-anchors together in Iowa, Amy had landed a high-profile reporter gig in Washington, D.C., then Jane got a similar deal in Boston. Amy's star was still rising. Plus, as she never let Jane forget, *she* was married.

"After three years of promos, all those promises," Jane typed, "they said they wanted to 'go another direction' with their political coverage. Are you kidding me? There's an election coming. It's the biggest story since the Kennedy thing. What the hell other direction can they go?"

"I'm so sorry, Janey honey," Amy typed back. "They had to blame somebody. Everyone hates TV reporters. And everybody hates TV. I'm probably next, you know? We should have gotten real jobs, kiddo."

Now Alex Wyatt—*Register* city editor Alex Wyatt, of all people!—was about to offer Jane a real job. Such as it was. At least the *Register*'s headlines had been objective. GROCERY MAGNATE WINS SLANDER SUIT.

Jane closed her eyes briefly at the memory. Dad would take care of her, if it came to that, even urge her to come home to Oak Park. Then he'd probably urge her to go to law school, like younger sister, engaged sister, good sister Lissa. Dad would be supportive, at least try to be, but Dr. Ryland never approved of failure. She was on her own. And she'd be fine.

Perched on the couch in Alex's new and already file-strewn office at the *Boston Register,* surrounded by the clutter of his half-unpacked boxes, Jane was working hard at being fine.

She wished she could just say no. Leave town. Change her name. Forget the jurors, forget the verdict. Talk to her mom just one more time.

But reality included a hefty mortgage on her condo, payments on her suddenly extravagant Audi TT, looming utility bills, and evaporating severance pay. She'd once reported heartbreakingly headlined stories about the terrors of unemployment. Now she was unemployed. Jane knew she'd tell Alex yes.

"I vouched for you with the bigs on the fifth floor." Alex positioned a framed Columbia J-school diploma against one beige wall, raised his wire-rimmed glasses to his forehead, then marked the wall with a pencil, turning his back to her. "Told 'em you were nails on the street. Tough and fair. Beat me on a couple stories, that's for sure. The hospital thing last year, remember?"

I sure do. "The hospital thing" was an overnight stakeout of a politician injured in a suspicious hit and run. Alex and Jane, each refusing to leave while the other kept watch, shared the last of the murky coffee. Jane had secretly contemplated sharing a lot more than coffee. Luckily, as she later admitted to Amy, she'd checked Alex's third finger, left hand. *Taken.* At least she'd eventually gotten an exclusive interview with the victim.

Alex was still talking. "But here at the paper, we respect reporters who protect their sources. We don't fire them. Told 'em I figured your source threw you under the bus."

He turned to her, glasses back in place and pencil now behind his ear. "Speaking of which. About the case. Sellica Darden told you, didn't she? She had to be your source. Want to talk about it? Off the record?"

Not now, not ever. "Lawyers, you know? The appeal?" Jane smoothed her black wool skirt over her knees, carefully pulling the hem over her best black leather boots. Looking anywhere but at Alex. Why didn't life have an "Undo" button? She hadn't realized she was risking her career for Sellica. She tried to keep the sorrow out of her voice. "I can't. I really can't."

Alex narrowed his eyes. "There's nothing that'll hurt the paper, though, right? Nothing'll come back to bite us? All any of us has is our reputation, you know?"

"Right," Jane said.

Mortgage. Heat. Health insurance. Food. Mom would have said, "Jane Elizabeth, you should remember every closed door means another door opens."

"You can trust me, Alex. I know times are tough for newspapers. I'm grateful Jake—Detective Brogan—called you about me. I'm grateful, really, for the opportunity."

The room went silent.

Maybe Alex was getting cold feet, no matter what Jake had told him. Maybe no one would trust her again. The jury was wrong, not her. But how can you battle perception? Jane gathered her black leather tote bag, ready to be dismissed. Maybe it was too soon. Or too late.

Leaving his framed diploma propped on top of a peeling radiator, Alex leaned against the side of his battered wooden desk. He smiled, running a hand across its pitted wood. "They told me

T. R. Baylor himself, founder of the *Register,* used this very desk back in the day. Brinks job, Mayor Curley, the Boston Strangler. All the Kennedys. They offered me a new desk, you know? But keeping this one seemed right."

Jane smiled back. "Wonder what T.R. would think about your Internet edition? And maybe there's a new Boston Strangler now, the one they're calling the Bridge Killer."

"Times change; news doesn't," Alex replied. "People sure don't. The *Register*'s covering it, but we're not calling anyone the Bridge Killer yet, that's for sure. Who knows if those killings are connected? But yeah, you can't understand the future if you don't understand the past. I'm hoping this desk reminds me of that."

He pulled a yellow pad from a pile beside him, flipped through the top pages, then held up a hand-drawn calendar. In several of the pencil-line boxes was written JANE.

"Anyway," Alex continued, pointing to the schedule. "You're dayside. We're all about teamwork, and saving bucks, so I have you sharing a desk with Tuck. Tuck's covering the 'bridge killings'—whatever you want to call them—always out, so you'll probably never see each other."

She was in. She felt a reassuring flutter of the real Jane. *I'll scoop the hell out of those jerks at Channel 11.* "Sounds absolutely—," she began.

"I have to give you a six-month tryout," Alex interrupted, gesturing "upstairs" with his notepad. "Fifth floor says that's the deal. Are you with us?"

Jane managed a network-quality smile. Even if "network" was no longer in her future.

"You got yourself a newspaper reporter," Jane said. She looked square into the city editor's eyes, telegraphing she was not only the right choice to cover the election and share a desk with Tuck, whoever that was, but a valuable addition to his staff as well. One who did not make mistakes.

His eyes, however, were trained on the screen of his iPhone.

"Alex?" she said. If he dissed her on day one, she had low hopes for the teamwork he promised. But, facts be faced, her hopes were fairly low to begin with. She was still navigating the raw stages of grief over her dismissal from Channel 11.

It had been a while since her heart was broken.

Jane had avoided all the good-byes. She'd gone to the station one last time, after midnight. Packed her videotapes, Rolodex, fan mail, and three gilt-shiny award statues; stashed the cartons in the musty basement of her Brookline brownstone. The next two weeks she'd wrapped herself in one of Mom's afghans, parked herself in a corner of her curvy leather couch, and stared at her television. A screen no longer her domain.

She hadn't gone outside the apartment. Hadn't answered e-mail or the phone. A couple of times, drank a little too much wine.

Dad had been brusque when she called to tell him. "You must have done *something* wrong," he'd said. It was okay. Even after all these years, Jane knew he was still missing Mom. She was, too.

Mrs. Washburn from downstairs had appeared with the mail, bearing her famous mac and cheese, Jane's favorite. Little Eli, the super's starstruck eight-year-old, tried to lure her, as always, into an Xbox marathon. Steve and Margery, once her producer and photographer, sent white tulips, with a note saying, "Television sucks," and suggesting beer.

"Television sucks" made her laugh. For about one second.

Week three of unemployment, she'd had enough. She had clicked off the television, cleared out the stack of empty pizza boxes, and popped open the résumé on her laptop. The next day she rolled up the blinds in her living room, dragged the unread newspapers to the curb, and had her TV-length hair—the stylist called it walnut brown—cut spiky-short. She savagely organized all four closets in her apartment and dumped her on-air blazers in a charity bin. She'd listened to every one of her voice mail messages, and one was Jake. With a lead on a job at the *Register*.

And now she had an offer. Such as it was.

"Sorry, Jane, had to answer that text. So? Can you start tomorrow?" Clicking off his blinking screen, Alex tucked the iPhone into a pocket of his tweedy jacket. He'd been promoted from senior political reporter to city editor in time for the *Register*'s geared-up election coverage. Once Jane's toughest competition, Alex Wyatt—"Hot Alex," as Amy persisted in calling him—was about to become her superior.

Jane couldn't ignore the irony. The up-and-coming Jane Ryland, award-winning investigative reporter. Crashed on the fast track and blew it at age thirty-two. Possibly a new land speed record for failure. Her smile still in place, she pretended she hadn't noticed her potential new boss had ignored her.

"You got yourself a reporter," Jane said again. Now she just had to prove it.

Turn the page for a preview of
the next thrilling Charlotte McNally mystery

AVAILABLE APRIL 2016
FROM TOM DOHERTY ASSOCIATES

CHAPTER ONE

It's statistically impossible that my mother is always right. So why doesn't she seem to know it?

Besides, it's demonstrably true that I'm not always wrong. I have twenty-one Emmys for investigative reporting—won number twenty-one after I was stalked by murderous thugs, threatened by insider-trading CEOs and held at gunpoint by a money-hungry sociopath who I proved was mastermind of a nationwide insider-trading scandal. Every one of them is in prison now. So I must have been right about a lot of things.

But at this moment, struggling for balance on a cushily upholstered chair at Mom's bedside in New England's most exclusive cosmetic surgery center, somehow I no longer feel like the toast of Boston television. I feel more like toast. Once again, I'm a gawky, awkward, nearsighted adolescent, squirming under the assessing eye of Lorraine Carpenter McNally. Two months from now, provided her face heals in time for the wedding, she'll be Lorraine Carpenter McNally Margolis.

"Charlotte," Mother says. "Stop frowning. You're making lines."

Millions of viewers know me as Charlie McNally. I'm not Charlie to my mother, though. As she's repeatedly told me, my news director, my producer Franklin Parrish, my ex-husband Sweet Baby James, admirers who hail me on the street, and certainly Josh Gelston when she meets him: "Nicknames are for stuffed animals and men who have to play sports." After that pronouncement, she always adds: "If I'd wanted a child named Charlie, I would have had a boy and named him that."

Mom and I do better by long distance. Most of our conversations begin with me telling her about something I've done. Then she tells me what I should have done. Then I ask why nothing I do is ever good enough. Then she insists she's not "criticizing," she's "observing." As long as she stays in her skyscraping lakeview condo in Chicago, we do a good job pretending we're a close-knit pair.

But here she is in my hometown, swaddled in a frothy peach hospital gown, surrounded by crystal vases of fragrant June peonies, reclining against down pillows. She insists that I shouldn't come visit her every day, saying she's certain I have better things to do. Patients "of a certain age" who have "extensive surgery" stay here through recovery, minimum fourteen days. So this is going to be an interesting couple of weeks. And by interesting I mean impossible.

At least Mom doesn't look as bad as I expected for a few hours after surgery. No bruises yet, no puffy eyes. She's got bags of what look like frozen peas Ace bandaged to each side of her face to keep down the swelling, and I can still see the little needle marks where her precious Dr. Garth injected Restylane to erase the lines in her forehead.

"All the pretty girls are doing it," she says. She would have given me her trademark raised eyebrow for emphasis, I'm sure, if she could move her eyebrows. "And if you don't make an appointment with the plastic surgeon at your age . . ." Her voice trails off, apparently rendered speechless by my continuing refusal to face reality.

She settles into her plump nest of pillows, adjusts her peas and pushes harder. "Charlotte, you know I'm right, and . . ."

Keeping my face appropriately attentive, I begin a mental list of all the things I should be doing at nine-thirty on a Monday night instead of babysitting with my mother. Thinking about a blockbuster story for the July ratings. Calling Franklin to see if he's come up with another Emmy winner. Making sure I have a bathing suit that won't freak out my darling Josh, who has only known me since last October and has not yet encountered my 46-year-old self in anything but sleek reporter suits or jeans and chunky sweaters or strategically lacy lingerie. Under dim lights.

"And local TV is so—*local*. . . ." Lorraine is reprising one of her favorite themes. Why is it, she wonders, that I've never wanted to move to New York and hit the networks? Or at least move home to Chicago, where she could set me up with a handpicked tycoon husband who would convince me to abandon my television career and become a tycoon wife? For the past twenty years I've told her I'm fulfilled by my career and am comfortable being single again. Mother makes it clear I'm wrong about this.

I look dutifully contemplative, nod a couple of times and continue my mental should-be-doing list. Feed Botox, who's probably already ripped the mail to shreds and tipped over her litter box to prove who's boss. E-mail best friend Maysie, who's at Fenway Park covering the Red Sox, and see what I'm supposed to bring to her annual Fourth of July cookout. Call Nora and make sure my younger sister will take her turn at mom-sitting when Mother finally goes home. Dig up a book about adolescent girls and see how experts suggest I deal with Josh's daughter Penny.

Penny. Right.

I've been to war zones, chased politicians through parking lots, wired myself with hidden cameras, even battled through the annual bridal gown extravaganza in Filene's Basement, but spending my summer vacation days with a surly eight-year-old and her blazingly attractive father? This may be my toughest assignment ever. Not counting the bathing suit.

"Look in the mirror," Mother urges. She starts to point, but then, after a quick scan, apparently realizes the flatteringly lit pink walls of her posh little room—which looks more like plush grand hotel than sterile hospital—don't have any mirrors.

She forges ahead, undaunted by reality. "Well, find a mirror, and look in it," she says. "Charlotte, this isn't a criticism, it's an observation. I'm your mother. If I don't tell you, who will? Your neck is, well, worrisome, and you'll instantly see how your cheeks are drooping."

Happily for our relationship, there's a soft knock on the door. As it opens, Mother's expression softens from imperious to flirtatious. Talk about worrisome. Still, I've got to give her credit for believing she's alluring in that frozen pea and Ace bandage getup. Wisps of her newly reblonded hair escape in a way she'd never allow if there were mirrors, but she's still got the McNally brown eyes and Gramma Nell's good posture. If it's true we become our mothers, I guess I'm not going to be so bad at sixty-eight. Plus, the nursing staff at the New England Center for Cosmetic Surgery is certainly used to women in the awkward stages of transformation.

"Miz McNally?" A romance novel cover-model wannabe in a white oxford button-down and even whiter pants consults the chart clamped to the foot of Mom's bed. His smile is snowier still. "I'm Nurse Justin. How are we feeling?" He clicks some switches on a bedside contraption, checking the heart and respiration monitors the center requires for every patient. Mom coos at him as he muscles a rolling bed table across her lap, pretending she doesn't want to take her latest round of pills because the painkillers make her "silly."

Nurse Justin is just one of the pill-dispensing glamour boys I've seen in the center's modishly fashionable nursing whites. Some are older and gray-templed, some younger with panache-y little ponytails, but they all look like they've just come from shooting the latest Ralph Lauren catalog, and only do this nursing thing in their spare time. I don't know how the center gets away with this obviously discriminatory hiring practice. Plus, who'd want a hunky guy seeing you as a *before?* Mother, apparently, is all for it.

I tune back in to her chitchat. It's about me.

"On Channel 3," I hear Mother explaining. "Charlotte, dear," she says. "I hope you're going to be on the news tonight. We'd love to watch you."

Not a chance, of course. It's now almost ten o'clock, and the news goes on the air at eleven. But Mother has never understood how television works.

"Nope," I say, smiling as if this isn't a ridiculous question. And, I grudgingly realize, she's just being a proud mom, which is actually very sweet. "I do long-term investigative stories," I explain to the nurse, just an amiable daughter joining the conversation. "I'm only on the air when we've uncovered something big. So, nothing tonight." I shrug, smiling. "Sorry."

Nurse Justin's face suddenly changes to a scowl, which is baffling until I see he's pointing at my tote bag. Which is ringing. "No cell phones allowed in guest's rooms," he says, still scowling. "Strict rules. We're all about patient privacy. And quiet. Cell phones are allowed only in the outer lobby."

I cringe. "Forgot to turn it off when I left the station," I say, which is true. I whap it to Off without even checking the number, figuring Justin will forgive me my first transgression, and whoever is calling will call back. His face begins to soften—and then my purse starts beeping.

I dive for the beeper they still make me carry, knowing full well I forgot to turn that off, too. I push the kill button, but the illuminated green letters that pop up are inescapable. CALL DESK, it demands. RIGHT NOW. And if that weren't attention-getting enough, a second screen flashes up at me. NEED U LIVE FOR ELEVEN PM NEWS.

Mom was right again.

ABOUT THE AUTHOR

HANK PHILLIPPI RYAN is the investigative reporter for Boston's NBC affiliate. She has won thirty Emmys and ten Edward R. Murrow Awards for her groundbreaking journalism. The bestselling author of four mystery novels as well as *The Other Woman,* the first book to feature reporter Jane Ryland and Detective Jake Brogan, Ryan has won two Agatha Awards, as well as the Anthony, Macavity, and Mary Higgins Clark Awards.